About the author

Mark Malcolm is a twenty-something long-term book lover, enjoying reading many different genres and thoroughly enjoying each individual book for its own unique story. Moving on from being just a reader, Mark Malcolm is now embarking on the first steps of his writing journey, exploring the new world of book publishing from the side of the author and not the reader.

ANGELS HIDE BEHIND THEIR MASKS - MEETING MY ANGEL

Mark Malcolm

ANGELS HIDE BEHIND THEIR MASKS -
MEETING MY ANGEL

Vanguard Press

VANGUARD PAPERBACK

© Copyright 2021
Mark Malcolm

A CIP catalogue record for this title is
available from the British Library.

ISBN 978-1-80016-028-6

*Vanguard Press is an imprint of
Pegasus Elliot MacKenzie Publishers Ltd.*
www.pegasuspublishers.com

First Published in 2021

**Vanguard Press
Sheraton House Castle Park
Cambridge England**

Printed & Bound in Great Britain

Chapter One
Escape to a new world

"Mother, how did you and Father meet?" a young boy asked.

"That's an easier question than normal, little one." The mother smiled as she spoke. "We met at an academy on the ground below." Responding to her child was a woman wearing a white summer dress who was sitting in her favourite garden chair.

The garden was always a place of comfort for her throughout her time up in the clouds. It started as a cold place but she had eventually made this garden her own, most noticeably by adding her favourite flowers, white lilies.

"Will I ever get to visit the ground below?" the child asked eagerly.

"Maybe, when you're older."

"I really want to see it. I want to find someone I can be close to that isn't Mother. Someone my own age who will want to talk to me. There is no one here like that." The child spoke with hope, trying to hide his unhappiness caused by his present situation.

The mother's face saddened, her child was surrounded by family, the living complexes housed almost five hundred blood relatives not including their non-blood spouses. The fact that her child felt lonely in this place was something that caused heartache.

"When you're older, I'll take you," the mother replied with a smile.

"Do you promise?" the boy responded with joy and hope in his eyes.

"I promise. Now let's talk about something else, do you have any other questions?" The mother meant her promise with all her heart but also didn't want her only son to be chasing it blindly his whole life.

Years passed and when the child was fifteen, he walked full of purpose as he walked along the corridors; looking straight ahead and full of conviction, he passed a garden. A garden that looked like it had not been attended to for several years, the flowers had all withered and not even weeds were able to grow in the now dead soil.

Ignoring the garden and gripping tightly a piece of paper in his hand, the boy continued on his journey; this journey he had the intention of using to change his world.

The boy passed many others, people similar in age and those much older, all when they saw him, shifted their gaze and most did it with an expression of disgust. The boy had an idea why, many had ingrained it into him with their past comments, comments that had led to him knowing better than to interact with anyone he could consider family.

Again, ignoring his surroundings, the boy grew closer to his destination. He arrived at two large decorated wooden doors. The doors were decorated in many beautiful patterns, every pattern was related to his family's history. It was his family's history, but it was a history that he was ready to reject for what he would consider freedom.

Full of conviction, he opened the doors and stepped through into a large open space. This space was filled with columns and many other decorations, the most notable of which were the pictures of all the past patriarchs and matriarchs of his family, the last picture being a picture of his father.

On one side of the large open room was a small spiral staircase which ascended directly to the upper floor and was connected to a single door. This staircase and door were the last two steps to reach his destination. Behind that door was the person he was seeking.

Without hesitation but full of nerves, the boy once again ignored his surroundings and was focused only on his task. The boy walked up the stairs and without knocking opened the door.

The room was well furnished and was designed in a very efficient way, nothing was out of place and everything served a purpose. At the end of the room was a man sitting at a desk. He did not look up when his son entered and continued his work despite the distraction.

When the boy saw the sight of his father, he was filled with nerves, his conviction started to waiver. He knew he had to act fast and now or forever be unable to do so. He gripped the piece of paper in his hand tightly and thought of nothing else apart from how he would act from this moment. He marched directly up to his father and placed the piece of paper onto his father's desk.

"Father, please read this letter I received." The boy spoke confidently despite his nerves.

His father ignored him.

"Thud!" The boy picked up the paper and this time he slammed the piece of paper directly on top of his father's work.

"Hmph." The father sighed, annoyed by this action. He would have to give some of his attention to this matter, despite it being obviously unimportant.

"What is it, son? Why have you come to visit me?" The father spoke without looking up or reading the letter.

"Read it, Father," the boy ordered forcefully.

"Just tell me what it is, son, I'm very busy with important work. As you are well aware." The father spoke coldly and acted distant, his normal attitude towards his son.

"Fine!" the boy exclaimed and turned around, moving to leave.

"Hmm!" The father sighed angrily. His attention was now definitely being dragged away from his work. He picked up the letter and read it, skimming through it, only reading the essential parts. "No," the father said as he threw the letter now crumpled at his son.

The boy turned around immediately when his father spoke and panicked. The boy picked up the letter and stood motionless and he tried to hold on to his conviction. "I didn't come for permission, Father; I came to say goodbye. I have made all the necessary arrangements. I'm fifteen now so I'm allowed passage away from the island. And I've used an alternative name so no one will know who I am or be able to connect me to the family. Everything is already arranged; I didn't come for, nor do I need your permission. I'm leaving today and that's final. So that's that. Goodbye." He spoke quickly and flustered. After speaking he was almost out of breath.

"Are you finished? You can't go, you can learn everything you need to know here. Are you upset with your tutors? I can have them easily replaced. Why do you want to go down to the surface, anyway?"

With resistance from his father, the boy had no other choice but to use his trump card, something he was reluctant to do.

"Mother promised I could go to the surface."

"Tch!" The father grinded his teeth angrily.

"You might think I'm using her memory to fulfil my own desires but it's true she did say that."

Unbeknownst to the son, his father had heard about that conversation and his wife had made him promise that he would keep the promise she made to their child. This fact didn't mean that he had to be happy with the situation, ideally his son would have had given up on such a fantastical idea years ago, letting it die along with his mother.

"Fine, you win. Get out," the father said coldly.

The son allowed happy emotions to wash over him, but as he went to thank his father something unexpected happened. "Thank yo... urgh!" The son struggled to speak as he was struck by an attack from his father.

The son flew across the room and landed by the door that he had used to enter the room. The pain pulsed throughout his entire body. He felt complete shock from the attack and he started to panic.

"Father, why? Urk!" The son was struck again as he tried to speak. This time his body flew out of the room and missed the stairway, his body being propelled into the air and smashing into the floor below.

The father stood in the doorway, looking down at his now bloodied son. Blood ran down from his son's nose and he was covered in bruises.

"I said get out. Don't talk back to me! And don't come back here for that matter! I don't want to see or talk to you; you're acting like a brat!" The father yelled in anger; his son was only causing him frustration and he was busy enough with his own work as it was. The father disliked unnecessary interruptions.

The son was unsure of what was happening, it sounded like he had got what he wanted. So, why did he have to endure so much pain? He wanted to ask his father, but the pain throughout his body told him to do otherwise. He struggled to his feet and wiped the blood from his nose. He struggled and staggered as he walked away. He exited from the large open room and headed towards his bedroom. This was a bittersweet victory.

Walking much slower than he did before, the boy headed towards his room, walking back through the corridors he had walked through before. Again, he passed many members of his family who showed the same indifference as before, all except for those who had expressions of joy at the boy's injured state. And once again he endured and ignored their vicious stares. He had been naive when he was younger, but he had learnt the hard and harsh way that he should keep his distance from the rest of them.

As he finally reached his room, he was able to regain some of his movement, all of the swelling from the bruises had gone down, and the colour of them had already started to change. It would only take another ten minutes or so for his wounds to heal completely. The speed of his recovery did little to numb the pain and discomfort.

With mixed emotions but an unwavering conviction, he grabbed the bag he had already prepared for his new world and exited his bedroom. He gave his old room no second thought and was happy that he could leave without any regrets. Not having to spend another day here was the ultimate freedom.

The boy headed towards the outskirts of the floating island, travelling through the dense forests and plentiful plant life through the only pathway that cut through them. The boy ran along this path. His excitement had finally kicked in and he entered the transport he had already arranged and sat down. After a few seconds, the transport powered up and started moving, it's destination the ground below.

The transport landed softly. Leaving the island in the sky goodbye, the boy exited into what he could now call his new world.

Chapter Two
The academy and rank 21

Academy 1 was located on the outskirts of city 1, the city in which the academy got its name from. The academy was home to a thousand and one pupils and offered on-site accommodation to each one. The ages of the students ranged from fifteen to twenty-one, age twenty-one being the mandatory draft age regardless of a lack of academic success. Despite it being a well-known academy, the boy was unable to gather much else about its inner workings. The academy was comparable to his family's island in that it had almost full autonomy over itself.

He had made all the arrangements beforehand and therefore was able to land in an area governed by the academy. As soon as he took his first step out of the transport he had entered the academy, the place that would become his new home. Just like nearly all the other pupils he had planned and made arrangements to live in one of the allocated dorm rooms. Unlike the other pupils, the boy was forced to make these arrangements himself and not have it done by an adult who was responsible for him.

He looked around at his new surroundings; tall and

large stone buildings surrounded the entire area all except for the building in the centre. The building in the centre was by far the largest building and in contrast was uniquely covered in metal and looked as if metal was the only material it was made from. Such a strong and sturdy structure almost looked out of place, when the rest of this world was made from stone.

Looking around taking in all the new sounds, sights and smells, the boy quickly made himself acquainted with his new surroundings. After finally seeing a sign pointing out the direction of the main reception building, he headed straight for it.

Many students were wandering around the academy grounds; this was the first day of the boy but to the rest it was the start of the second term. Just like he had acted in the sky island he ignored those he passed by, secretly wanting to talk to everyone he met, his nerves made him do otherwise. He was hopeful his dream of making a friend would come true in this place, but a lifetime of isolation was hard to forget and so was the behaviour he was used to.

He arrived at the reception building and entered through the double wooden doors that blocked the entrance to it. Unlike his family grounds, the doors were plain and devoid of decoration. Despite their lack of features, the boy found their appearance to be quite comforting.

He entered and walked into the building noticing a desk and what he believed to be a receptionist. As he went to make his way towards the desk, his path was blocked by an unfamiliar person.

The person standing in front of him was an honest looking person whose age appeared similar to his own. This person was full of confidence and wore a smile as he looked the boy up and down. The unknown person stared at the boy and nodded to himself as he took his measurements. The boy felt that he was undergoing a very serious exam and immediately worried about what might happen if he failed.

"Hmm." The unknown person mumbled happily to himself and extended his hand towards the boy seeking a handshake. "Hi, I'm rank 21 it's a pleasure to make your acquaintance. I have to say I'm really happy to be guiding our new rank 3 around our great and prestigious school. Please, if you would, shake my hand." The unknown person started speaking. His voice was soft and sounded kind, however there was a looming sense of insincerity about the way this boy acted.

The boy, now revealed to be the new rank 3, which by itself was enough to cause a shock, was certain he would be given the lowest rank being the newest addition to the academy.

The new rank 3 extended his hand towards rank 21 and shook it. Immediately he noticed a strong pressure; it seemed as if rank 21 was trying to crush his hand. That's what it seemed, but it had no effect and when rank 3 tightened his grip, rank 21 winced in pain.

"Oooh, very good," rank 21 exclaimed. "It seems

you might be worthy of your rank after all. At the very least I'd wager your physical level is definitely higher than mine. Hehe, let me give you the tour." He kept hold of rank 3's hand and proceeded to drag rank 3 along with him.

Unable to not be sucked into this person's flow, rank 3 had no choice but to follow him. If rank 3 wanted answers to the questions he had, he would have to get them while they were moving.

"Wait a second, where are you taking me? Don't I need to register before I go anywhere else?" Rank 3 spoke while trying to maintain his composure. This was a very confusing situation for him, in the letters he had exchanged with the academy, not a single one mentioned a guide or anything about a predetermined rank.

"Huh? Register?" rank 21 said puzzled. "Of course not. All of your paperwork has already been taken care of, surely you don't think it's an accident you ended up rank 3. Because if that's true, you're not going to like what comes next?"

"What would come next?" rank 3 asked nervously.

"Oh, man, you really don't know anything. I'm talking about the rank matches silly. No, wait." Rank 21 stopped moving and put his hand on rank 3's shoulder and sighed. "You were too strong at your old academy that you never got to fight anyone. That's sad, that saddens me." Rank 21 let out another sigh. This one sounded much sadder than the other. "You've had a tough life so far, but don't worry, from today you're going to find out that this place is a lot of fun. Come on, let's get going already."

Rank 3 found rank 21's words too confusing to refute anything he said and instead was sucked back into rank 21's flow.

Rank 21 increased his pace as the excitement on his face grew and in the corner of his mind, he planned on how his and rank 3's relationship would develop. But firstly he had to at least perform the basics of his job. The rank 21 tour was now underway.

Rank 3 followed silently and in awe as he discovered more and more of this new place. This new world was truly nothing like the one he used to know. The buildings were much larger and lacked any form of decoration save for the few flags and etched emblems of the academy. The buildings gave off a sense of total efficiency, each building gave off an aura that it was in its most perfect form.

They didn't enter any of the buildings they had come across. After a brief description rank 21 quickly moved them on until they reached one of the largest buildings. This building was unique by the fact it was the only one that was almost completely covered in windows, demonstrating the startling amount of rooms it housed.

"This building, the building north of the arena, the central building, is our dorm house. Containing a thousand and one rooms each containing a bedroom, bathroom, kitchen and two other spaces that students can make their own designations for. One could easily live comfortably here for the rest of their life. This building is simply one of the reflections of our academy's glory. No other academy boasts such impressive accommodations. Any questions?"

Rank 3 was awestruck. His family's island was many times the size of the academy and yet due to its architecture and layout it wouldn't be an exaggeration to say more than a few thousand would lead to housing problems. But with a building the size of some of the gardens, a thousand and one students could be housed easily.

"So, you're saying all thousand and one students live here, and I'll be living here as well?"

"Yes, that's correct. Well, technically a thousand students live here including you but that's a whole other story. So, shall I take you to your room?"

"Yes!" rank 3 shouted happily. He already felt like he belonged more to this place than his old home and was more vocal than he had been in years. "I mean, please take me," rank 3 said quieter.

Rank 21 dragged rank 3 into the building revealing a reception area leading on the several sets of stairs. Surprisingly, it was completely empty.

"Where is everyone?" rank 3 asked nervously.

"They're at the return to the lessons assembly, you don't need to go to that, principal's orders."

"Oh, OK. Will you show me my room now?" His

nerves and surprise were completely suppressed by his excitement.

"Sure, I've got your key here, you're on the top floor obviously, all the top ranks are on the top floor. In fact, you can think of me and you as neighbours. Well, no time to waste."

Travelling up all the flights of stairs, rank 3 didn't have time to notice the difference in the quality of appearance between the floors. In this building the bottom and the top floor were two completely different places. Arriving at the top of the stairs, they found their path blocked by a golden door.

"Why is something like this here?" rank 3 asked, confused to see something so decorative in a world of cold stone.

"You'll find appearances can be deceiving; the inside of the academy is nothing like the outside." Rank three put his hand in a small hole in the door. "And even on the inside, some places are much nicer than the others. Tch!" Rank 21 retracted his hand, and he had a tiny cut on his finger.

"Are you all right?" rank 3 asked as the door opened in front of them.

"I'm fine, as you can guess this is the only way to get in. I'll let you do it next time. You don't need to do it now. Once it opens, it will stay open until someone closes it."

"Er? OK, I guess I understand why."

Rank 21 walked through the door followed by rank

3 and rank 21 closed the door to rank 3's surprise.

"Why are you closing the door now, aren't we the only ones here?"

"It's a habit. You should develop it too. The last thing we top rankers need is the lower ranks snooping around, they're already annoying enough outside the dorm. Follow me down this corridor to the right and I'll take you to your room."

"Thanks, you've been really helpful," rank 3 said honestly and full of gratitude.

"All in a day's work, friend. Although normally I'm a bit of an air head, so I guess today's your lucky day, haha. Well, here we are, I'll wait outside while you get everything sorted. You have roughly an hour now, so get settled and get changed into your uniform, after we'll head to our first lesson. It's the boring one though, it's the one where you have to think about stuff haha. Oh, and you might get to see something special." As rank 21 pushed rank 3 into rank 3's room, he gave him a quick wink as he finished speaking. Afterwards he closed the door separating the two of them.

With the door closing behind him, rank 3 was once again alone in the academy and this time he was standing on the edge of his own home in this new world. He slowly took the steps he wanted to take and entered his new home: his dorm room and once again he was taken aback.

The dorm was indeed not as he had imagined it, the facilities were indeed all that you would require to live very comfortably. Surprisingly all the cupboards were fully stocked with food and his wardrobes were full of clothes. He had expected a uniform, but this was much more than that, especially the two 'free rooms' both of which he expected to be empty.

In the first 'free room' rank 3 found it filled with exercise and physical combat training equipment along with a series of books all containing various training programmes. This was something out of a dream, back in his old home he was only allowed to play with his ability not actively train it. Also, physical training was seen as something that would only make the boy act aggressively towards others.

And the second 'free room' taking advantage of the almost limitless capabilities of the room was a garden in close to the exact same condition the garden his mother used to tend to. A single tear shed from his eye when he saw the room and was immediately followed by him closing the door. He did not want to see this sight nor would he be able to get rid of it. This door would stay closed.

Dismissing the sight and deciding that that door would never be opened by him again, he entered his bedroom and opened the wardrobe to reveal his uniform. To his surprise a number 3 emblem was embroidered into the blazer. This was especially surprising as it now meant that it was most likely that he was the last person, especially the last person who needed to know, to discover that he was rank 3.

Feeling slightly embarrassed to be wearing a uniform he felt that he didn't deserve, he grabbed the bag that had already been prepared for him and headed towards the door to leave. As he went to turn the handle, nerves struck his entire body and a fearful feeling struck him. It was in this moment that he realised, he had almost left his most precious belonging behind. Grabbing it, he finally turned the handle and exited his room greeted by an anxious rank 21 whose mood was immediately elevated by rank 3's appearance.

"Look at you! Looking like you're one of us now. So, you were happy with your room? From previous experience some students have found the rooms to be lacking the luxury they're used to."

Puzzled, rank 3 responded, "I don't know what you could be talking about, everything I could ever need is in there. I was surprised by how thoughtful the academy is."

"Right," rank 21 said warily, he respected power but was cautious of those who were just as naive as they were powerful especially if they had no distinguished background. A powerful individual who knows nothing of how the world works and is easily appeased would undoubtedly become the pawn of someone weaker but someone who had many connections.

'It's my responsibility to show him what the world really looks like.'

"That's great to hear you like your room, I'll guide you to our first lesson."

"We're in the same class?" rank 3 asked excitedly, the more time they spent together the higher chance they could cement a friendship.

"Yes, we share all the same classes, it's the main reason I was selected to be your guide. The academy has to look after its top ranked students after all. Now come on, don't just stand there."

The two of them exited their top floor accommodation level and left the residential block through the same way they had entered. This time however, when they left the building there were students all rushing around trying to get to their first class of the term.

"Hey don't look so nervous, everyone acts like this on the first few days, but once routine sinks in you'll be fine. Besides, we have the same lessons every day, it's only on special occasions that you'll have to watch out for. Don't want you missing out so come on we don't want to be late. Teacher won't be very happy and he can get, well let's call it antsy."

"Errm, OK?" Rank 3 responded in the only way he could.

"Follow my lead," rank 21 said with a huge smile. He was about to give an important demonstration.

With steps full of confidence and pride rank 21 followed by rank 3 marched into the crowd. Instead of being consumed by the crowd as rank 3 expected, he found that students immediately moved out of their way, each student giving off expressions of fear.

"Why is everyone acting afraid of you?" Rank 3 asked curiously.

"Huh? Isn't it obvious? I'm stronger than them so it's only natural for them to avoid me, besides right now they are more afraid of you. They have no idea what your temperament is like. Of course I know better, but to them one wrong look at you could cause them a broken bone, hahaha," Rank 21 said full of joy. He always found enjoyment seeing other students squirm.

Even though rank 3 was opposed to promoting such behaviour, he felt he had no choice but to ignore it for now and just continue on to his first class. He wanted to make a good first impression with his classmates, befriending every other student would come later.

The pair quickly and very easily made their way across the academy entering one of the many other buildings. This building like the two next to it had no unique features and their sole purposes were purely academic. These buildings contained the classrooms for teaching and the libraries which stored an almost immeasurable number of books.

Each class had twenty students with the exception of the top and bottom classes, with them having eleven and thirty students, respectively. And with another reason to feel surprise rank 21 revealed to rank 3 that they were both in the top class.

Walking down a corridor with many classrooms and doors they suddenly stopped outside one particular door. This door's only discernible feature was the number displayed above it. It was a relatively small number 1 considering you would only be able to properly identify it if you had already known where to look.

"So this is us. For the rest of the term we will be coming to this room for our academic lessons. Make sure you don't forget which one it is, it can be a real pain to find."

"Oh, don't worry I already memorised the route we took."

"Ooh that's impressive. Shall we go in?"

"Yes, let's I'm excited see what's insid… ack!" Rank 3 let out a strange noise.

"Whoa are you all right?" rank 21 asked while getting slightly flustered.

"Yes, I'm fine, something just bumped into me. Haha, that tickles stop it."

"Hey! What's happening to you?"

Chapter Three
The masked student

A few moments before rank 3 started bursting into laughter, another student was making their way to the same class. Unlike rank 21 and rank 3, this student didn't warrant special behaviour based on other students' fear of them. Nevertheless, this student was also actively avoided.

This student looked slightly different to all the other students. No other student had anything other than their bag carried around with them, but this student had much more than normal.

This student boasted no notable background but had still been granted special permissions, all due to various reasons, all of which were unknown to the other students.

The student was not recognised and accepted like the other students; they were ranked, but they had never been involved in a single ranked match during their time at the academy. A rare and infuriating feat, thus determining that this student would forever possess rank 1001.

The lowest-ranked student would be identified to be the weakest and least deserving of their place in the academy. This was more than enough reason for the other students including rank 1000 to express outright animosity even if they expressed it from afar. Even though rank matches were encouraged and promoted, all combat and violence outside of them was regulated. Broken bones and lost limbs were reserved purely for the rank matches. However, there were loopholes to this rule; accidents happen.

Being rank 1001 would be in itself enough to make a student's time at the academy a hardship and the past rank 1001s understood that fact very well. However, this rank 1001 wasn't just rank 1001. The current rank 1001 was also regarded as very strange and in not so nice terms a freak. All the other students considered him weird, albeit for somewhat obvious reasons and rank 1001 did nothing to refute or remedy this.

Every student was required to wear the school uniform displaying their current rank; rank 1001 was no exception to this and wearing the school uniform brought forth no particular problems. It was the other items of clothing that the student wore; these items were gloves, slippers instead of shoes and a silk mask covering his entire head concealing bandages. These bandages also covered the rest of his body. All the items worn made it so that not a single millimetre of flesh would be exposed.

Rank 1001 had poor vision, along with his attire he also carried around a red and white walking stick, the item known as his signature. It was with this item that he navigated his way around the academy and it was this which was why other students made sure to avoid him. Causing an unwarranted and unnecessary accident would land them in trouble. In the academy everything was decided by power, but only the one who started a fight has to abide by that fact. Bullying those much weaker than yourself would not be tolerated.

Rank 1001 had begun his day the same way as always, always abiding by routine, getting washed then bandaged, dressed in school uniform and finishing with slippers, gloves and mask, in that order. He picked up the bag he had already prepared, collecting his red and white walking stick and departed for the academy, heading towards the first class of the day.

It was the first day of term but to rank 1001 the day was treated just like any other and in his usual way he made to journey to his first class, avoiding all the other students in what he would perceive a flawless fashion. He made his way to his classroom. The journey was almost finished as he was about to arrive outside the classroom. It would be here that the start of the change to his academy experience and life would take place.

Rank 1001 was used to navigating his way around the academy without incident; he had only ever walked into a wall on three occasions. Each time was due to him not paying attention. He never bumped into anyone by accident due to knowing the consequences. The consequences would never be good nor would he ever be forgiven for such an accident.

This incident all started with a bump, as if he was walking into a wall, a somewhat unfamiliar experience. Nevertheless, he had walked into something, so he reached out his hand to find out what it was. To his surprise it felt soft and squishy, not at all like a wall made of stone or metal. This sensation was completely unfamiliar, but it felt nice, not cold like a wall normally felt.

Chapter Four
A glimpse of truth

"Hahahaha, stop it, you're tickling me." Rank 3 was completely taken aback by this strange sensation.

Rank 21 was completely perplexed, the serious atmosphere had been shattered, and it was as if another person was standing in front of him.

"OK. OK. OK, that's enough!" rank 3 said as he spun around and swatted away his potential attacker.

With a silent thud, rank 1001 was swatted to the ground and his walking stick bounced away from his hand. Rank 3 immediately assessed the situation and felt a subtle horror at what he saw. A small trembling person acting like a small terrified creature was lying on the floor in front of him.

Rank 1001 was trembling on the floor, stunned by the shock of being forced onto the ground by an attack he could not sense coming. He couldn't see or hear very well, it felt like an invisible violent force had struck him.

Rank 3 was unable to talk or move due to what he was seeing and it was at this moment that the experienced rank 21 jumped into action.

Putting his hand on rank 3's shoulder he started to speak. "Wow, nice reaction. Nice movement too. You swatted that thing away nicely, don't know what came over him, don't care either, but that's what happens when you mess with a high ranker. Hehe, look at you, lying on the floor, you know what comes next right?" Rank 21's tone started to shift, becoming filled with malice.

"You know this person?" rank 3 asked, sounding as if his brain had just rebooted.

"Yeah, I know. Meet rank 1001. Rank 1001 meet rank 3."

"Oh? 1001? Oh no, are you OK? I didn't." Rank 3 sputtered out broken speech. He was struggling to make sense of this situation; he had never hit anyone before.

"Relax he'll be fine, he hasn't even gotten his punishment yet and because you're new, I'll demonstrate for you. Don't want you breaking any rules now do we?" Rank 21 smiled as he kicked towards the curled-up student. "Huh?" Rank 21 made a noise in surprise as he found his leg wrapped up in an unknown red vine substance preventing all movement.

"What are you doing?" rank 3 asked surprised. He didn't know what was going on, this situation seemed bizarre, he hadn't even realised that he had acted on instinct when he restrained rank 21's leg.

"Huh? Oh, I get it. You prefer to break spirits, not bodies. I should warn you in advance rank 1001's face is off limits; I can't even tell you just how badly I want to rip that mask off. Anyway we can only look to the future right?"

"What are you talking about? What's happening?" Rank 3 interrupted rank 21; rank 3 was panicking from this unfamiliar situation.

"Calm down, I'm getting there," rank 21 said as he flicked his wrist. "There it's done. Now seeing you get impatient makes my interest in you grow even more. I'll show you your seat now."

"Shouldn't we do something?" rank 3 said sounding desperate.

"What? More? You want more? No, I don't think that would be a good idea, just let it mop itself up and we'll go back to ignoring his existence. Good? Great. OK let's go." Rank 21 continued speaking as he wiggled his leg out of the red vine and dragged rank 3 into the classroom to his seat.

Rank 3 was trying to figure what had just happened. To his mind this incident had just lasted only a second. He felt like he had been watching and not participating.

"What was, I mean who was that exactly?" rank 3 asked, trying to get answers that he couldn't work out himself.

"Oh that was rank 1001, don't pay him any mind. He's a strange one that one, you'll only get distracted. So, moving on from our first fun of the term let me give you a quick introduction to this class. Our class is the top class for academic learning so obviously only geniuses like us qualify, well almost only. Anyhow, our class is also the smallest to allow us to get the best of everything, that's why there are so few of us. Eleven only, that's our class's limit, and especially with our teacher…" Rank 21 drew closer to rank 3. "Any more and he would probably kill someone, hehe."

While rank 21 had been talking, their teacher had arrived. He was tall and slim and was dressed smartly even more so than most of the other academy staff. His presence appeared weak but there were subtle hints in his aura that that was not the case. The students didn't immediately react to his presence and continued talking that was until he took his jacket off and started speaking. "Welcome back, class." The room fell silent as he spoke, his voice was crisp and sharp, his words cut into the students like a knife. The feel of his voice was enough on its own to instil silence while he was speaking. "As you all should know, we've got a new addition to our class, the new rank 3. That means two high rankers so you lot better not start anything I find distasteful."

The academic teacher walked towards rank 3 and rank 21's table; the room was split into two sides and the whole class was seated on the right, with rank 3 and rank 21 sitting at the back.

"Hello, new rank 3, I'll be your academic teacher for the foreseeable future, providing you can keep up. If you can't I'll have you kicked out. Rank 21, it's good to see you. So," the academic teacher leaned towards the two students and started whispering, "do you know anything about that outside?"

"About what outside?" rank 21 responded sounding

innocent.

"Ha. Good answer, but seriously I stepped in it, so next time make sure you clean up after your mess. And you." The teacher turned his gaze to rank 3.

"Me?" rank 3 said, worriedly.

"Don't try anything in my class. I don't care what you do outside but if I can see it, hear it, smell it or worse touch it, I'll show you the difference between a student and a teacher." The teacher stood up from their table. "I hope we get along well for the rest of the year. And that goes for everyone else. Now that everyone in my class is here, let's get started."

"Errm, teacher? Aren't we missing someone? There are only ten of us and rank 21 told me that there are supposed to be eleven, shouldn't we wait?" rank 3 asked, concerned that something was wrong.

"Er?" The academic teacher made a noise as he was shocked by the question. He then shrugged as if to say 'all right I'll answer, but I'm not sure what you're getting at'.

"OK, I've got one. Would you ask a slug to hurry up?"

"What? I don't get…"

"No you wouldn't. Would you wait for a snail?"

"Teacher, I don't…"

"No, you wouldn't do that either."

"Teacher please what are you…?"

"I guess what I'm trying to say is, it's more likely that a snail or slug will get here before that thing does, especially after what I did to it. Which, of course, was a very unfortunate and happy accident." The teacher smiled wryly.

"What? I'm confused is this some sort of riddle?" Rank 3's nerves were about to skyrocket.

"Oh, come on, it's a joke. Fine it wasn't very good, but you put me on the spot so that's the level you get, you want a good joke you have to wait for it."

"A joke?" rank 3 asked, completely puzzled.

"Yes a joke. Now let's get started, we're already three minutes behind schedule. You two pass out these sheets, let's see if you remember anything I taught you last term."

The lesson started and even though rank 3 was confused by the lack of an eleventh student, he was more concerned with earning his place in this class to dwell on it.

Most of the information that was thrown at him during the lesson was information that he had not come across so it was a struggle to complete the tasks. He did not let it get him down; he knew that he would catch up, eventually. It was just a feeling but all the information felt like a puzzle that he would eventually solve with ease and his nerves slowly started to fade. That was at least true for academics.

"Phew, that was intense. Hope you didn't struggle too much, but I guess if they thought you were good enough to be in this class with me, you shouldn't struggle for long. All right." Rank 21 banged the table.

"It's finally time for combat training, and you know what that means?"

"We'll be taught how to fight?" rank 3 said excitedly, ignoring all other thoughts.

"No silly. It means we're one step closer to lunch. OK, let's go, follow me."

'Oh?' Rank 3 suddenly thought to himself, 'I hope that rank 1001 is all right. I'm not entirely sure what happened earlier. Do I need to apologise? It wasn't entirely my fault.'

"Erm, rank 21?"

"Yes what is it?" Rank 21 answered the question but was still trying to drag rank 3 along with him towards their next classroom.

"About that rank 1001, was it OK to just leave him like that?"

"Whoa, you're a real sadist, aren't you? Didn't you give him enough earlier? Well, to be honest and to give honest advice, your only hope of that happening again is if he bumps into you like he did earlier. And, I've got to tell you, that that is not very likely. I mean he's never done that to me. Even if I prayed for it, a miracle like that would never happen. If only he would participate in the rank matches. I'm getting pretty obsessed with what's under that mask. I've been betting on horrific burns for a while now, I just want to know if I'm right or not. Why is the world punishing me so? Why must it be so cruel?"

"Hey, what's that?" Rank 3 interrupted rank 21's

rant and pointed at a stick that looked like its other half had been sliced away from it, along with bloody handprints of the same hand near it and spots of blood all over the floor.

"Huh? Oh that. Don't worry about it, we don't have to clean that up, besides sir did the worst of it. If anyone asks all we did was cut up his stick, we never touched him. Right? Riiiight?"

"Er, right?"

"Good. Now stop dwelling on one incident. If you're that desperate to hit something you better hurry up, because that was practically what the combat classes were invented for. Seeing as enthusiastic you are, you'll be sure to enjoy it."

Rank 21 again forcibly directed rank 3 towards their next destination, and once again all the other students took great efforts to avoid the two of them. Rank 3 felt discomfort from this but it wasn't an unknown feeling, the cause may be different but the outcome was the same. All except for now, he could class one other as a friend. Rank 21 was a welcome light in rank 3's new life.

The two students exited the academic building and headed towards another part of the academy, the part of which taught the combat aspects of their curriculum. They walked across the school and passed the large domed arena; the most interesting area that rank 3 had yet to see.

Rank 21 didn't give rank 3 any time to take in his

surroundings, rank 21 was only focused on reaching their next class, a trait not unique to him. All students had been taught that punctuality was the most important quality they needed to possess. This mind-set was why even though there were a thousand students walking about, they produced no noise other than that of their footsteps. Someone talking was very noticeable.

"Can you explain what our next class will be about?" rank 3 asked, attracting several gazes which were immediately retracted when his rank was noticed.

"Simply put, you're going to experience pain and pleasure, and not in equal amounts. I'd tell you more, but, where is the fun it that?"

Rank 3 asked more questions, but rank 21 kept his lips sealed; he refused to reveal any more information. The combat classes were mysterious and otherworldly compared to the academic.

The two stopped outside another stone building. This again shared characteristics with the two neighbouring buildings, none of which could be described as decorative. Like the academic buildings there was enough to make a distinction as to which building this was but that was all it could be used for. Again, the difference between the academy and the sky island was huge, but only in this respect.

Rank 21 didn't leave much time to take in the building's details, however small, and rushed into the building through the main doors. Unlike before he didn't show any caring that there were many other students sharing their space, all that mattered right now was getting to their classroom.

Again rank 3 was not allowed the luxury of detailed directions and was left to simply remember the route they had taken. Other students would surely struggle but rank 3 was lucky because he had a fantastic memory, something which his mother had given him. It was also something he was not always grateful for.

The two raced through the building and passed many other students. They travelled through many corridors and it almost seemed as if they were going to walk all the way through the building. That was until they reached the last classroom, and this classroom was where they would be experiencing their combat classes.

The classroom had no number above it. Unlike the academic classroom, it was simply identified by its location; the end of the world in the building's terms. Rank 3 took a deep breath to calm his nerves and closely followed rank 21 into the room.

Rank 21 opened the door to reveal there were no other students and no teacher in the room. It was completely empty. It was just the two of them. As rank 3 observed their surroundings trying to look for a clue as to what was going on, rank 21 turned to him and put his hand on rank 3's shoulder. "So listen. I know that you probably want to get stuck in, practising and fighting with other students but first I want to show you something."

"Show me what? Are we supposed to be here?"

41

Rank 3 responded nervously to rank 21's behaviour.

"Of course we're allowed, I wouldn't take you somewhere to just get you into trouble. You're not from here, so naturally I decided that I would take you under my wing."

"Under your wing?" rank 3 responded, confused by that statement.

"Well, following my style of combat. All the other high rankers are too proud to rely on anything other than their own bodies. They are OK with the pills but pills will only hurt their training in the long run. So first things first, are you taking the pills because if you are you have to stop immediately, and two, do you have any interest in using tools?"

"Pills? I've never heard of any pills. I've never been allowed to do combat training until I came here."

"That's even better, let me show you my combat style and train with me. Take a leap of faith." Rank 21 spoke with a sparkle in his eyes.

"I trust you so I'll follow you. I am really interested in learning how to fight; I want to be able to defend myself." Rank 3 was happy to follow this person's lead, especially now that he had come to trust rank 21 completely.

"That's great! Have no pride in your current skills. We'll start from the beginning. I'll teach you how to move properly and then you'll meet our teacher. That's when the real training will begin."

Rank 21 was overjoyed by rank 3's response, rank

21 was classed as a bit of an outcast. Not only was he the smartest of the top fifty ranks, now one of two, he also didn't conform to traditional combat roles and methods. Rank matches were strictly bare handed unless given express permission to do otherwise. No one else saw any reason to learn how to fight with a tool designed for combat, not when they would not get to use it. Even the highest ranked, planned to graduate and fight in the army with their current skills. They would never have enough shame to lower themselves to using something other than their body and abilities.

But rank 21 thought differently. No current student had displayed a prodigal or genius aptitude for combat and it was obvious to him that any student who graduated from the current one thousand and one would find an opponent they could not beat single-handedly. The only way to avoid this and survive the torment of war, would be to be prepared to use any means necessary. This made him a reckless pragmatist in the eyes of others, especially those from distinguished backgrounds.

During their first combat lesson together, rank 21 taught rank 3 the basics. Due to rank 3's memory and his body's natural strength, agility and flexibility he was a quick study. It would not take long until he would meet their teacher, someone who shared rank 21's philosophy.

After combat classes, the students were given free time for a break; in this break they were free to do as they wished. They could either cook food in their dorms or buy it from the cafeteria if they were hungry. If they weren't interested in food, they could do whatever else they wanted. As long as no rules were broken, the teachers showed no interest. And the only rule that mattered was that students didn't attempt to seriously injure or kill each other. Everything revolved around combat, everything that wasn't combat related didn't have much importance.

Rank 3 followed rank 21 learning the locations and functions of the other buildings. He wanted to see what the arena looked like, but he would have to wait. The arena was always closed on the first day due to it causing disruptions and creating confusion. This was also why students couldn't challenge each other to fight matches on the first day. All matches started on the second day despite the usual protests.

After the break for today, the students were informed through the school's speaker system that they were free to do as they wanted. Rank 21 explained this was because rank matches would normally be held at this time.

"So anything else you want to see or learn about?"

"Could you explain the rank matches briefly? I want to know about them, but I also want to get properly settled into my dorm. There has been a lot of information to take in today." Rank 3 felt his brain was brimming with new information.

"How about I explain the rank matches tomorrow

44

then, don't want you getting overwhelmed by it? Besides, there is no one stupid or brave enough to challenge you to a match tomorrow. Do you know the way back or do you need me to take you?"

"I'm OK, I've memorised the layout of the academy. Thank you for everything today, I'll see you tomorrow." Rank 3 spoke with a smile.

"Sounds like a plan. I'll meet you outside the classroom, don't be late, OK?" Rank 21 couldn't help but return rank 3's smile with a smile of his own.

"I won't, goodbye. Thanks again for today." Rank 3 thanked rank 21 a second time. It was involuntary and purely a part of rank 3's personality.

Rank 21 was slightly surprised by rank 3's attitude. Slowly throughout the day he had started to realise the truth. At first he thought all rank 3 wanted to do was hurt someone. But it seemed that that was a wrong assumption, and it appeared that rank 3 was genuine in trusting and caring about others. Although it would be comical to rank 21 and all the others, if rank 3 shared his sympathy with rank 1001.

Chapter Five
Understanding rank matches

Rank 3 returned to his dorm room and placed his bag on the floor. He walked around for a bit taking it all in. He had never experienced anything like this before; he had his own place to live on the sky island but it was secluded, deliberately placed far away from the others. It was a place designed for loneliness.

This new place, the academy, was filled with people all revolving around each other, rank 3 didn't doubt that he would make lots of friends here. His only regret was that he couldn't share any of these feelings with his mother.

Rank 3 was still feeling overwhelmed by everything and didn't feel hungry or have any desire to do anything. He had a room to train in, something he had always wanted but he would use that another time. Right now, all he wanted was to lay down on his new bed and go to sleep.

"Beep Beep. Beep Beep!" The alarm clock rang beside his bed, continuously getting louder.

Rank 3 opened his eyes and panicked for a second as he had forgotten where he was. He quickly calmed down when he remembered. He walked into the kitchen and made himself a simple breakfast, got washed and then dressed into his uniform.

Unlike yesterday, he would have to navigate his way across the academy alone. He had memorised the way, but he would have to work his way around a thousand other students. Resolving himself to deal with the pressure that came from being around so many people, he picked up his bag and left the dorm room.

As he arrived at the bottom floor of the dorm complex, the entrance was filled with students, many of whom were grouped together in conversation. Taking a deep breath so as not to get swallowed by the atmosphere, he started to walk towards the door.

Although he had experienced it yesterday, it was still surprising to experience again. As soon as the other students' gazes landed on him their expressions, happy or contented immediately turned to anxious and fearful. Any student who considered themselves to be in the way immediately moved and instantly avoided eye contact.

Unlike yesterday when rank 3 assumed it was because of some sort of fear for rank 21, today his immediate thought was that this was because of a natural disdain they held for him, exactly the way his family members had treated him. This made rank 3 remember his sadness and loneliness, and with a blank expression he walked out of the dorm complex.

Rank 300 had always had terrible luck. For someone who could always claim to see the world for what it truly is and understand why people act the way they do, she struggled to perform normal tasks. Once again she had forgotten her bag, the item that was always placed by her front door. Not only that but once again she had also tied her tie poorly and was seemingly unaware of this fact. She had good eyes but was extremely clumsy and forgetful.

So once again she was returning to the dorm complex when she came crashing into someone who was very obviously not watching where they were walking.

"Thud!"

"Ow!" rank 300 said as she bounced off the person and onto the floor; feeling like she had just walked into a wall, she rubbed the back of her head to reduce the pain.

"Are you all right?" she heard a panicked voice say.

Rank 300 looked up in disbelief. She knew that she had walked into the 'wrong' student but she never imagined that that student would be concerned about her welfare. She scrambled to her feet but wobbled and found this student's hands wrapped around hers to help her get stable.

Staggering on her feet, she settled down, the panic and the feeling of impending pain was subsiding. Normally this situation would have resulted in further deliberate bruising. She quickly glanced at his face. "I'm fine, thank you for caring," she answered and ran off as fast as she could, leaving a confused rank 3.

All the other students took no notice, they didn't want an unwelcome glance to result in something painful.

Rank 3 tried to push this incident to the back of his mind. He would ask rank 21 about it later, but for now he was only focused on getting to the classroom. Following the same route as yesterday, he made his way to the academic buildings walking past the arena. He entered the building, travelled along the corridors and made his way to his classroom, distinguishing it by the small number one above the door. To his surprise no other student was waiting outside, he had hoped rank 21 would have already arrived. Rank 3 went to take a quick look in the classroom when rank 21 came strolling out.

"Rank 21!" rank 3 said happily.

"Oh hey," rank 21 said slightly surprised. "You're early, we've still got thirty minutes until lessons start."

"I know, I was excited. Listen can I ask you about something?" Rank 3 still had concerns about yesterday's events.

"Yeah in a minute, I want to show you something first." Rank 21 gestured for rank 3 to enter the classroom. Rank 3 followed without question.

Rank 3 entered the room and saw something unexpected. The masked student from yesterday was sitting in their classroom, and unlike rank 3 and the others who sat on the right, the masked student sat in the far corner of the left side, away from everyone.

"Is that rank 1001?" rank 3 said, completely

surprised by the situation in front of him.

"Yes it is, not going to forget your first, are you?" Rank 21 spoke happily.

"First?"

"First victim silly. Now check this out, because of your little stunt yesterday, he came in earlier than usual. You see what I'm getting at?"

"No," rank 3 responded, bluntly.

"Don't be like that. I'm not trying to trick you. I'm just enjoying your handiwork. You scared him so much that he ran away and into teacher. And not only that, he was so scared by the events you caused he came into class early. You really put him in his place. He was starting to act too arrogantly, so relax it wasn't anything he didn't deserve."

"But…" Rank 3 didn't know what to say, one accident had evolved far beyond his means.

"Anyway, now that morning laugh is out of the way, what question did you have?"

"It's not important." Rank 3 was afraid to hear the answers to the questions he had.

"All right then, shall we get seated?"

"Yes. Oh! Can you explain the rank matches? I don't want something unfortunate to happen because I don't understand them." Rank 3's thoughts had instantly changed, and he was now focused on his future. He didn't want to be the cause for more unfortunate accidents.

"Yeah, sure I can, why don't we sit down and I'll

explain it to you. You brought your screen, right?"

"Screen?" rank 3 asked as they sat down.

"Yeah, it should be in your bag. It looks like a thin sheet of plastic."

Rank 3 looked thoroughly in his bag and could see all the items stored in it. It was the first time he had done this. Looking through the items in his bag, he was able to take note of what was stored in there, and wrapped in a thin black cord was something that looked like a thin sheet of plastic. He grabbed it and removed it from his bag, trying to analyse it as he did so. "Is this it?" Rank 3 asked rank 21.

"Yes, that's it. Now unwrap it and lay it out on the desk, nice and flat."

Rank 3 removed the thin black wire, unrolled the sheet and placed it on his desk. After he laid it out flat, lights started flashing from it. "What's happening?" Rank 3 panicked slightly.

"Don't worry it's turning itself on. Now I'll explain it step by step and you'll be able to have a match as soon as you think you're ready. Now wait for all the lights to stop flashing and for your name and rank to appear."

Rank 3 sat impatiently for his name and rank to appear, not only did his name and rank appear, next to his rank were the numbers of won and lost matches both currently at zero. Next to his name was a notification stating that he had no pending match requests. Seeing this fake name reminded him that he no longer had to concern himself with his old home. His only focus was now the academy.

"OK so in front of you, is your name, rank, stats and pending requests info. So with your hand swipe to the side, this is how you get to the next screen. On that screen it should show you the home page, using this page you can search for other ranks, information about upcoming matches and match replays."

"OK, so I'm swiping." Rank 3 spoke as he acted to reassure himself.

Swiping the screen did indeed remove the current information, and it was replaced with a lot more different information. In the corner there was an active newsfeed being supplied by a group of students dedicated to sharing information.

"OK, so now it's up to you to explore whatever information you want. Although because it's only your second day, you won't be able to watch any of the replay matches from last term, it would give you an unfair advantage. You'll have to wait awhile before you are allowed, you can search students' stats though. Also don't think you can challenge someone last minute, all requests are for matches to take place the next day, with today being the only exception."

"Hmm?" Rank 3 thought hard about what he wanted to learn about first.

"I would be careful not to accidently challenge anyone though, I mean anyone under my rank would refuse but the top twenty are another story."

"So who can you challenge exactly?"

"Anyone. I can challenge you and you can challenge me, of course, if you challenge me I'll refuse but if I were to challenge a higher rank than me, then they would have to accept or face the shame of losing their rank without a fight."

"What do you mean, losing without a fight?"

"Oh? You didn't do this at your old place? All right I'll tell you, to keep to students' competitive spirits, higher ranks must unequivocally define their ranks. If they refuse they lose, and between you and me…" rank 21 moved close to whisper, "that includes challenging those that have been critically injured, it's not only your challenger that benefits from crushing you. And, that's the case of the top ranks, they keep the students scared in case something like that does happen. Otherwise someone ranked ten could fall to rank a thousand haha, even if it didn't last long it would be hilarious."

"Don't you mean rank 1001?"

"No, I don't," rank 21 said with a hint of disgust.

"But he's got his screen in front of him, he must be keen to fight." Rank 3 had been looking over at rank 1001 periodically to check on him.

"No, that's just because he has nine hundred and ninety-nine match requests to refuse; all the students under rank 1 lobbied the principal to make it that rank 1001 would have to fight a match if he didn't actively refuse. If he failed to refuse, he would be forcefully dragged to the arena to fight and maybe, just freaking maybe I could see what's under that mask."

"But that doesn't seem fair, how is that right?" Rank 3 was surprised to hear something so harsh being said so indifferently.

"Fairness doesn't exist in this world. The ranking system itself isn't fair, so why should one self-important person presume to be above it."

"I don't like this," rank 3 said, feeling uneasy.

"This isn't something you have any say over, so just forget it and submit your order for a daily request like the rest of us, so he has to reject a thousand requests again. You never know one of us might get lucky."

Rank 3 had had enough of questioning rank 21 and got up from his seat. His bag search earlier had revealed one other item that was important in this moment. Using his ability in its red vine form, he had collected the one half of the red and white stick that had been left behind. It was the stick that rank 1001 had on him yesterday and the same stick that rank 21 has cruelly cut into two pieces.

Rank 3 got up from his desk and started making his way across the room to the desk in the corner that rank 1001 was sitting at. He moved carefully and quietly so as not to unexpectedly disturb rank 1001. He didn't want a repeat of yesterday's misunderstanding, especially realising how sensitive his body was to being tickled.

Rank 3 cautiously stopped by the desk and before he said anything he was taken by surprise when looking down at the screen on the desk. Rank 1001 was indeed rejecting requests. However between each rejection was a twenty second timer. Rank 3 instantly realised that it would take the majority of the school day just to reject the requests, and that was assuming you didn't get distracted for a second.

Rank 3 was starting to feel really guilty about yesterday, luckily no requests could be made until today otherwise... the thought made rank 3 shiver. The motion made rank 1001's head pop up like a meerkat to survey its surroundings. It was only brief, and it felt like he looked straight through rank 3. After which he returned to his screen, being content with his assessment.

Rank 3 didn't know what course of action to take. He wanted to apologise and give back rank 1001's red and white stick; rank 3 felt responsible for it being broken. He went to reach for rank 1001's shoulder to gently alert him to his presence when he was interrupted.

"Rank 3, get way from it and take your seat. I won't have any delays today." The teacher's voice rang throughout the classroom. Rank 3 turned around and discovered that all the other students had arrived as well as their teacher, leaving him to only guess how long he had been struck by nerves.

Rank 3 begrudgingly took his seat. He was learning slowly but surely he could very well make friends in this place, but he could just as easily make enemies and hurt and be hurt. This wasn't the safe new world he thought it would be. The lesson continued with rank 1001 focused on his screen while everyone else focused on learning from the teacher.

The lesson wasn't too much different from yesterday's and rank 3 found it easier to navigate. When the lesson ended he tried once again to reach out to rank 1001, but was unable to as he was whisked away by a very eager to teach rank 21. He would have to try again tomorrow.

Rank 21 and rank 3 made their way across the academy and into the combat teaching building. Rank 21 led them into their room at the end of the building, their own world so to speak and began the lesson.

"You're doing very well; it shouldn't take too much time until you can learn the real aspects of my fighting style. Our teacher will be very happy to meet you, you might even be a rare natural born fighter. And, following on from that, you'll be ready for your first rank match soon. I'm thinking of putting on a demonstration. It should help you understand more about the matches."

"A demonstration? Is that like a non-ranked match?"

"No, it's a rank match, but it's more like a fixed rank match."

"Fixed?" Rank 3 was confused to hear such a term being used.

"Yep, the outcome is decided before the match. These matches are common for us high ranks, it's simple really. You make a deal with a lower rank and promise to let them go all out against you until they can't fight any more. When that happens you finish them off with a big flashy move to prove your strength."

"Why would you do that, wouldn't the lower rank get hurt?" Rank 3 was concerned about the lower rank, immediately thinking about rank 1001.

"Everyone gets hurt in a ranked match. It's more of a training session. The lower rank gets proper fighting experience and you get to show off your power. It's a win-win." Rank 21 spoke with a hint of pride and sounded satisfied.

"I guess I understand, but it seems like you don't have to end the fight by hurting them, can't they just surrender?"

"Haha, you need to get rid of that mind-set; being merciful will only mean more people want to hurt you." Rank 21 found rank 3's naivety comical but was also resolved to teach him the ways of the world. Even if it took all year, rank 3 would eventually act like him.

"But why, though?"

"That's obvious, silly. That's just how the world works. Now come on let's get back into it. I want you to feel exhausted this time. You need to improve your level as fast as you can."

Rank 3 and rank 21 continued training relentlessly until the end of the lesson and just as rank 21 had wanted they were both exhausted. Although unlike yesterday where he had let rank 3 escape back to his room, today rank 21 was going to show rank 3 the inside of the arena. It wouldn't be today that rank 3 would get to see a match of his level, but he would still be able to experience a basic outline.

Rank 3 wiped the sweat off his forehead and lent against the wall to get his breath back. Rank 21 walked over to him and put his hand on his shoulder. "Come on, don't just stand still, we've still got stuff to do and see. Today you'll finally get to see the arena, you'll get to see a real fight. I bet you can't wait," rank 21 said happily. He was excited to see rank 3's reaction.

Rank 21 grabbed rank 3's hand and dragged him off somewhere once again. Walking at a quick pace they travelled from their classroom to outside of the combat teaching building. Instead of walking past the arena dome, today they headed towards the now revealed entrance. It was normally secured behind a metal sheet at night and on the first and last day of term, on every other school day it was open to any who wished to enter.

The entrance was tiny compared to how large the building was. There were only three sets of double doors leading to a small entrance which led into multiple barriers. These barriers were the means of security for the dome. If anyone was able to get into the academy without permission, an almost impossible feat, they would then be caught out by the barriers.

To get through the barriers was a very simple process if you were a student or teacher, and guests only had minor trouble as well. The barriers used a high-class system to identify individuals through a screening process. If this process was inconclusive then the person in question could use their fingerprint or blood. Their fingerprint being something that was always taken by the academy in the reception area. Both rank 21 and rank 3 would be able to use their fingerprints if necessary. Blood was only an extra method for academy staff and students; it was only used in extreme circumstances.

The barriers screened and processed the entry requests for rank 21 and rank 3 and they were allowed entry into the arena. After passing the barriers, rank 3 was finally able to see why this building was so large and the largest of all the buildings. The arena hidden underneath the plain blanket of metal was a truly wondrous sight. Given that there were a thousand and one students, more than one match needed to take place at a time and this meant more than one area designed for combat.

The solution for this problem was simple, one giant field arena which could be separated into smaller areas. So right now, there were many energy generated barriers separating multiple matches. But when it came to a tournament match, the whole field was opened up, essentially mimicking a real-life skirmish; something they would definitely experience when they joined the army.

Surrounding this giant field was a huge intricate seating area. It was clear that just by looking at it, it could easily seat double the number of staff and students. With the arena and seating area taking up most of the space, the remaining space was used in a more compact fashion.

Small booths were dotted around the arena. They had multipurpose functions; students could access their student account and see their match details, history and all other normal functions of a screen. Students could also use the booths to watch current matches while doing other tasks. They could write general or specific comments about matches, themselves or other students and lastly, they could also purchase a variety of hot and cold food.

As soon as rank 21 saw an empty booth he darted towards it, forcefully taking rank 3 with him. They both entered the booth and rank 21 let go of rank 3's hand.

"OK, so go up to the screen and access your account."

"OK, I'll try."

Rank 3 carefully placed his hand on the screen, nothing changed until he felt a small sharp pain in the tip of his finger.

"Ow!" rank 3 exclaimed as he retracted his hand. The tip of one of his fingers had a small bleeding cut on it.

"Relax, it's just a tiny cut. It needs your blood to verify who you are?"

"Why though? My screen didn't need my blood," rank 3 said with a hint of annoyance towards the booth.

"That's because that's your screen, silly."

"But couldn't I lose my screen or someone could steal it, couldn't someone…?"

"Let me stop you there before you start to panic for no reason. No student is stupid enough to steal another's screen. The punishment for that could result in expulsion from the academy, not to mention the shame of being caught. I mean if not, then any student could force another student to accept a match request."

"Are you talking about rank 1001 again?"

A wry smile appeared on rank 21's face. "Well, not just him. Oh look you're in."

The screen had flashed and changed to that of rank 3's account. It looked the same as his screen except on this one, around the edges were pop-up messages and small windows showing matches and comments.

"Whoa, there are students fighting right now."

"Yep, aren't you glad I brought you here?" Rank 21 was overjoyed when he thought rank 3 was happy and excited by the arena.

"Hey, that student looks really hurt." Rank 3 saw a bleeding student fighting in a match and became concerned.

"So, what do you expect? It is a rank match after all. Anyway, you can focus on that in a minute, press on contact administrator. That button right there." Rank 21 pointed at the screen.

"OK, contact administrator. Done." Rank 3 couldn't help but follow rank 21's directions.

"Next press on special commands and or notices."

"OK. Done."

"And press there." Rank 21 pointed at one of the options.

"Send mass order message? Can you do that? I mean what's that for?"

"That's special to us top ranks, it's used for various stuff, like match prep, boasting, or even reserving another student. You know when I told you about the training matches, you can use this system to let other students know that's what your plan is. It stops them from challenging you or that student for a brief period. If they do the top ranks punish them. We are a collective after all. Don't worry about that now, you only need to worry about that in the future. I meant press the one below it."

"Automatic match request?"

"Yeah that, it keeps sending a request until the other student accepts."

"Isn't that unfair, isn't that just bullying?" Rank 3 started to protest, much to rank 21's annoyance.

"Ah, man, you really are a worrier, aren't you? You're lucky you've got me to guide you. You'll have a better understanding after your first match, in that you don't have to be concerned with how every else 'feels'. Besides, there is only one student you can choose to automatically request a match from."

"Rank 1001." Rank 3 could tell instantly by hearing the disgust in rank 21's voice.

"Heyy! You figured it out. We'll make an academy 1 student of you yet, no doubt about it, haha."

"I'm going back to my dorm, I've had enough for one day, I'll see you tomorrow."

"Oh, OK. I guess we overdid it in training, haha."

Rank 3 left the booth without confirming an automatic request, unknown to rank 21. Rank 3 was now starting to think that rank 1001 was someone who would understand what rank 3 had gone through back on the sky island.

Rank 3 walked back silently towards the dorm building, not taking much notice of his surroundings. It was when he walked through the doors of the dorm building, that he ran into someone who was unexpectedly waiting for him. "There you are. I have been waiting all day to meet you." A female voice spoke, her tone sounded prideful and impatient.

"Who are you?" rank 3 asked as he evaluated the student in front of him. As soon as he realised she was much weaker than him, he went to walk past her.

"Wait! I just have one thing to say. Well, it's more of a warning." Rank 300's tone changed immediately, and she became timid.

"A warning from who?" Rank 3 paused to question this unfamiliar person.

"Would you start taking me seriously if I said the universe?"

Rank 3 looked at her expressionless and continued to leave.

"Wait, wait. Er… if you change yourself you won't get hurt, but if you stay the same, you'll find fame. I won't be any clearer if you're not interested in what I have to say." Rank 300 complained at rank 3 for ignoring her.

Rank 3 ignored rank 300's words and entered the stairway and went upstairs to his floor. He slowly walked along the corridor and walked into his room, not in the mood to eat again. He laid down on his bed and tried to forget everything that was happening. It didn't take long for him to fall asleep.

Chapter Six
Peace offering

Rank 3 was woken up by the sound of his alarm. It was the next day and despite having such a long sleep, rank 3 didn't feel very refreshed. He didn't want to have to think about the rank matches or the whole ranking system. Before when he first researched the academy, he didn't really understand just how ranks were decided but now he understood very well. The rank system directly opposed his primary reason for coming here; to finally have friends.

Rank 3 ate a small breakfast due to his loss in appetite and got prepared for lessons, and for the first time found his uniform to be very off-putting.

Rank 3 made his way out of the dorm complex, half expecting to see or run into rank 21 or rank 300. He thought a lot about the other student who had given him some sort of fortune-telling. He had run into her around this time yesterday; he wondered if today would be the same. However, he only got the normal avoidance reaction towards him by the other students. Ignoring them, he exited the dorm complex alone.

Rank 3 made his way to the academic buildings passing the arena building, the building he liked the least. Rank 3 walked slower towards the academic buildings than he had done before. Unlike the two previous days he was not feeling very energetic or excited. Slowly he arrived outside of the academic buildings and he stopped in front of the entrance.

Quickly rechecking his bag to make sure he had what he needed, rank 3 made his way through the building and entered his academic classroom. He had arrived slightly later than yesterday and some of his classmates were already sat down. Rank 1001 was sitting on the other side of the classroom as he had done so before. Surprisingly for rank 3, rank 21 had yet to arrive, although his absence would be helpful for what rank 3 was planning on doing.

Using a mix of nerves and conviction to do what was right, rank 3 very carefully and slowly made his way over to rank 1001. He arrived next to rank 1001's seat and surprisingly rank 1001 did not react or acknowledge his presence. In front of rank 1001 was his screen showing the number of match requests; the number was currently nine hundred and eighty-nine, showing that he had just started.

The mere thought of someone having to go through this every day greatly annoyed rank 3. What was worse, was the fact that rank 1001 was being forced to wait twenty seconds between refusals. With the technology used, it was obvious that this was deliberate, another way to bully rank 1001, and another method to try to force him to participate in the rank matches.

Now feeling even more guilty, rank 3 tried to weigh his options in his mind; he didn't want to distract rank 1001 in case he became responsible for him not being able to refuse all the match requests. It was a minute later when rank 3 made a decision; perhaps on false reasoning, he decided that the twenty second gap was useful for him, it would give him a guilt free time period in which to act.

Rank 3 reached into his bag. Rank 1001 had been motionless facing forward. He had the black wire connected to his ear; it acted as an ear piece. Rank 1001 used this to make up for his lack of vision along with his poor hearing, the ear piece sticking into his mask. Rank 1001 had no idea about what was about to happen to him.

Rank 3 retrieved the half of the red and white stick from his bag along with a small pouch filled with what he deemed an apology gift. He had attached the pouch to the stick to ensure rank 1001 wouldn't lose it. Rank 3 believed his plan to be flawless.

Rank 3 placed the stick on the table next to the screen. The vibration it made caused rank 1001 to react, again like a meerkat sensing something potentially dangerous; rank 1001's head darted to the side and he looked like he was staring at the stick. Albeit wearing the bandages and mask made it impossible for him to identify what had actually happened. After what appeared to be a brief assessment, rank 1001 returned to his screen.

'Fifteen seconds.' Rank 3 thought; he had what he would call fifteen more guilt-free seconds.

Rank 3 placed his hand gently on rank 1001's shoulder to make him aware of his presence. Rank 1001 responded by making his whole body go stiff but although he stiffened up he couldn't help tremble with what could only be described as an intense fear.

Not knowing what to do next, rank 3 went to grab the red and white stick and place it in rank 1001's hand. Unfortunately for the both of them, rank 1001 fell sideways heading towards the floor.

"What are you doing rank 3? I told you to do that outside of my class. Remember if I can't hear or see it then I don't care."

"Teacher, that's not what I'm…" Rank 3 turned back to face the academic teacher.

"Take your seat, we'll be starting in two minutes."

Rank 3 turned back to rank 1001 whom he now suspected to see in a small pile on the floor. It was clear what had happened, but the fact that it had happened unconsciously was very surprising. Rank 1001 was not collapsed on the floor. Instead, he was being rooted to his chair by rank 3's red vine like energy.

As quickly as he could he released his energy and rank 1001 was freed. Not that that affected his poise, he resumed attending to the matches on his screen. As rank 1001 reached to touch his screen with his hand, he found his hand grabbed, besieged by something. Before he could struggle against this foreign hand intruder, a thin familiar object was placed in his hand, along with a smaller non-familiar object. Instantly recognising the part of his previously used red and white stick, rank 1001 immediately placed it in his bag. Rank 3 went to walk away as he couldn't figure out what words to say in this strange moment. However, as he went to leave he felt a few small taps on his back.

As he went to see what it was, he felt a small object attach itself to him. Assuming it had been put there by rank 1001 rank 3 examined it in his hand. It was a small object, coin like but not something as fancy as a coin; it was quite boring looking apart from a small decorative outline. Deciding to assume this was both a thank you and peace offering, rank 3 happily went to sit at his seat. It was just as he finished sitting down that a distressed looking rank 21 came walking through the door.

Rank 21 swiftly moved to the back of the classroom and sat down next to rank 3. He lent close to rank 3 and whispered in his ear. "Why didn't you make the automatic request like I showed you to do?" rank 21 asked, sounding distressed.

"I'm not that type of person, I won't pick on someone who doesn't deserve it," rank 3 whispered proudly.

"It's not about that, it's just something that everyone does to show they are a conformer."

"I don't understand, what are you talking about?" rank 3 asked, confused by what he considered nonsense.

"Just come with me to the arena before we go to our

combat class, I'll explain it then. Just because you're new doesn't give you an excuse." Rank 21's frustrations were becoming very apparent.

"What are you…?"

"You two shut up! Don't make me say it again," the academic teacher said very angrily. He was getting more annoyed each second. His class was supposed to run like a well-designed machine. It had one flaw but that had been managed for him by others. Rank 1001 was in his class but not a part of it; he didn't disturb the rest of the perfect organism.

The class continued as normal, ten students studying diligently and one student rejecting match requests, both tasks done in complete silence. This silence was only interrupted by the teacher and he was the only one allowed to do so. Even if another teacher came in to their class for something, they would be met with open hostility. The reason no other teacher had yet to do so.

When the class reached its end and immediately after rank 3 had finished packing his bag, rank 21 once again grabbed rank 3's hand and whisked him away. They moved fast and rank 21 completely ignored all the surrounding others, effortlessly pushing students out of their path.

They quickly reached the arena only to find to rank 21's bitter disappointment that the arena was closed with no specific reason specified. All it said was that it would be open as normal after lessons had finished.

Rank 21 thought quickly about what they should do next and as soon as he decided he dragged rank 3 along with him to their combat classroom. "Why are you acting so weird today?" rank 3 asked curiously about rank 21's strange behaviour.

"Why couldn't you just put in the request? Why was that so hard? It's only a small thing, and it shows that you follow the rest of the academy 1 students."

"You mean all the students apart from rank 1001?" rank 3 responded disdainfully.

"I mean all the students who have pride in being an academy 1 student, rank 1 understands. You need to realise rank 1001 doesn't act like an academy 1 student or any number academy student. He doesn't participate in the rank matches, he doesn't attend combat classes and he has never entered the arena. He doesn't even watch the tournament matches. I mean how could he, he has to enter the arena to do that."

"Aren't you people overreacting, the academy accepted him as a student, that means he has the right to be here?"

"Maybe you can't understand, the rest of the top ranked students are all children of those who were top ranked when they attended the academy. Myself included. Just make the request, no one will bother you if you do it, besides it's not like your favourite rank 1001 would accept the request, anyway."

Rank 3 didn't have a response.

"All right moving on, you've got a good handle on

the basics, so you can keep practising outside of the lesson. Today I'm going to teach the basics of a rank match. I was going to wait, but I'm sure you need to learn this as soon as possible."

"Are you sure I…. Ow!" Thud!

Rank 21 without warning punched rank 3 in the stomach causing him to fly across the room.

"Lesson one, always attack when there is an opening. Now get up unless you want to learn lesson one again."

"Urgh." Rank 3 got up groggily; rank 21 had delivered a heavy punch.

"Right, now take a stance and be prepared to fight me."

"Fine, if that's what you want," rank 3 said with eagerness shining from his eyes.

"That's the spirit. Now come at me."

Rank 3 lunged straight towards rank 21, aiming to punch in the same space he had punched him. As he approached rank 21, a solid wall of air crashed into the side of him. Rank 3 was knocked down onto the floor, where he was now trapped by the wall that hit him.

"Lesson two don't be so hasty and lesson three, take extra care if you don't know your opponent's ability. All right take a break and do some basics, I get the feeling if we do any more you'll have a visible injury and we definitely don't need that distraction.

Rank 3 thought about what rank 21 had said, and in truth this was the first fight he had ever been in, so losing it was only natural. As the pressure on his body disappeared, rank 3 sat up. "How many rank matches have you been in, have you always been a top ranked student?" rank 3 asked hoping to learn more about what it takes for a student to become strong and high ranked.

"I have been in a lot of matches, you'll probably be in a lot too, so you can look forward to it. And I've earned my rank, so that's all that matters. If you're too weak you'll lose it, it's as simple as that. You can just know that I don't care for the extra responsibility of being in the top twenty, that's why I'm not going to get higher than where I am now."

"Why am I rank 3?" he asked hopeful he would now get an answer.

"No idea, I know you're not physically weak but you don't how to fight, that's for sure. All you can do is take pride in it and prove to others that you deserve it, someone certainly must believe you do. Otherwise you would have started as rank 1000 and everyone else would have been bumped up by one. Then you could have fought your way to the top if that's what you wanted. But that choice has been made for you so you should be proud of what you've got." Rank 21 paused to take a breath after his rant and to let his words sink into rank 3.

"Come on, let's head over to the arena, it might be open already."

Rank 3 had been sitting on the floor, listening to rank 21 and acting as he had before. Rank 21 whisked rank 3 into the air, grabbed his hand and dragged him to their next destination.

They arrived outside the arena and found that it had been reopened. There were only a handful of students around as most combat lessons had yet to finish. Taking advantage of the small number of students, rank 21 took rank 3 into the arena. They easily passed through the barriers, and arrived in the main entrance. Quickly scanning around rank 21 spotted an empty booth and he and rank 3 entered it.

"All right, log on to your account," rank 21 demanded.

"OK," rank 3 said frustrated.

Rank 3 placed his hand on the screen and got to experience the same sharp pain as yesterday. Using his blood, the booth identified rank 3 as himself and used this to unlock his account. With his account now in front of him, rank 3 could now access all of the booth's services.

"All right now press on the screen and send your automated match request and then I'll treat you to some food or something like that," rank 21 said trying to sound nice.

"I don't want to," rank 3 said nervously.

"It's not about how you feel, it's about conforming and keeping the peace between the top ranks. That's what's important."

"Why would something so stupid keep the peace?" rank 3 said angrily; his anger being the only thing to calm his nerves.

"Simple, that's one of the few things they can agree on. And it keeps the lower ranks quiet. Top rank status doesn't tend to come from the rank matches, it's all decided outside of the match. Top ranks are far too important to be decided so arbitrarily." A voice spoke from behind them.

"Who are you?" rank 3 asked slightly nervously from being surprised by this person's sudden appearance.

"That's rank 1's messenger boy, don't pay his rank any notice, he'll probably have a different one tomorrow, anyway. So what do you want? We're very busy." Rank 21 acted surprisingly aggressive to this unknown student.

"I can see that. Rank 3 doesn't want to pick on rank 1001, the rest of us do. Rank 3 wants to be different. Of course when you're strong enough to be rank 3 you can't have such meaningless views. Rank 1 and the unity of the top ranks and all the rest depend on conforming to simple tasks such as that one."

"Stop spouting and tell us what you want." Rank 21 was painted with his frustration towards this particular individual.

"I've come to collect rank 3. Rank 1 is holding a training session for the team participating in the tournament and rank 3's presence is requested. So chop chop."

"You can't speak like that to rank 3." Rank 21

became defensive, which rank 3 found reassuring.

"Looks like I can, he's not going to stop me. He's not a proper top rank, it seems."

"I'm confused, what do I have to do with the tournament, I never agreed to fight in a tournament?"

"Rank 1 has the privilege of being the team captain, and naturally the other top ranks are his team. Rank 1's will is our academy team's spirit, so chop chop."

"Rank 3 refuses, so leave us before I get angry." Rank 21 glared at the messenger and raised his hand.

The messenger backed away slightly.

"I'll go," rank 3 said, trying to sound as confident as possible.

"What, why?" rank 21 said, shocked and surprised.

"Excellent, follow me."

"I want to find out more about why everyone acts the way they do, so I'm going to ask the other top ranks directly. Besides, I already sent out my own mass order message."

Rank 21's expression became happy, but it quickly paled as he realised there was no way that rank 3 would have just given in.

"Wait what did you do?" rank 21 shouted panicked.

"Be back soon," Rank 3 said as he followed the other student giving a simple wave goodbye.

Rank 21 turned back to the screen, but it had already logged out of rank 3's account. Being forced to let rank 3 leave, rank 21 quickly put his own hand on the screen. Logging into his account, his expression turned to horror. It was much worse than he had expected.

The worse part was, rank 21 was completely powerless to stop what happened next. He couldn't help think this would have been avoided if rank 3 had just become like him.

Suddenly another message popped up and rank 21 felt a mix of relief, relief that he would not be directly affected by rank 3's actions and fear, fear that rank 3 would not be able to recover from what was about to happen.

Chapter Seven
A painful first encounter

Rank 3 opened his eyes, his vision was completely blurred, and he was in a daze. His whole body was in pain and the places just above his wrists and ankles hurt the worst. Those parts had received the most damage and suffered the cruellest of violence. It was these four points that hurt the most. His hands and feet however didn't hurt at all, there was no pain, no feeling at all; they were all missing.

Rank 3 tried hard to remember what had happened. He remembered going to meet the other top ranks but he couldn't remember actually meeting them. As he slowly gained consciousness, he started to remember more, but it was in the wrong order. He could remember waking up in this bed once before and all of his body parts were still attached to his body.

He woke up once before with his whole body aching, broken bones in his arms and legs, multiple if not all ribs were fractured, broken or cracked. Cuts and bruises covered the rest of his body; due to his injuries his body was barely hanging on. If not for the fact that those responsible wanted him to survive, it was highly likely that he would have died.

Despite all of his injuries, he was not defeated; he wasn't going to change just because the other top ranks wanted him to. And now that he had experienced a real fight with real stakes, he would be better prepared for the future. With his injuries and the speed of modern recovery due to various medicines and equipment he would be fully healed in a week and fully active again in two weeks.

This timeframe was unacceptable; the tournament match was in three weeks and rank 3 was not going to be allowed to be fit enough to compete.

His recovery time needed extending, and this was the reason why he had an unexpected visitor. When he had woken up for the first time, it was not due to him naturally regaining consciousness after having sufficient rest. He was forced awake. Rank 3 being awake was a bonus for what was about to happen next.

Rank 3 could barely see, but his hearing was just fine. He felt dazed but was conscious enough to notice a change in his surroundings. He could hear someone walking in. He didn't know who they were from their presence but recognised their voice. It was one of the two people who were responsible for what had happened to him.

"Hi, how are you feeling?" Rank 4 put his hand on rank 3's wrist causing rank 3 to feel a sharp pain.

Rank 4 in turn touched each of rank 3's legs, ankles and wrists and then sat down next to rank 3. "That was a fun fight though, right? Once you got going you really did some damage. I mean I might even stop in on a few of the others you put in here on my way out. I won't, but it is a nice thing to say. I get it now, you probably are strong enough to be a top rank, but seriously, you have got some crazy ideas. So, got anything to say to me?"

Rank 3 just glared at rank 4. His jaw was broken so he was unable to speak, all he could do was glare; he didn't have any words he'd like to share right now, anyway.

"No, nothing. I guess you're not so brave now, are you? It's a shame, I've kind of taken an interest in you." Rank 4 looked down at his arm and glanced at his watch. "Well time's up, see in you in a couple of months, oh and don't worry it won't spread. I'm not a monster." Rank 4 walked out of the room and as he exited he said, "Bye bye have a good sleep."

The pain was almost unbearable, the only saving grace was that it didn't last long, rank 3 felt everything that had happened. Every part of his hands and feet had been eaten away by something, it felt like they were burned off but also like they were nibbled away by thousands of tiny insects.

What rank 4 had done, whatever it was, was responsible for rank 3's loss of body parts. It didn't take long until an attending medical staff member arrived on the scene, undoubtedly directed there by rank 4. They very quickly assessed rank 3's injuries, probably knowing about them beforehand. The medical staff quickly prepared a serum and injected it into each severed limb causing rank 3 to fall asleep. His recovery would now take an expected minimum of two months to complete.

Rank 3 had followed rank 1's messenger to another part of the arena. He was brought down into the main field by travelling through the spectator area. One section of the field was closed off from the rest. It wasn't closed off in the normal fashion of a basic energy barrier. This part was enclosed on the top as well as the sides, it was also much denser stopping those from outside it peeking inside.

Rank 1's messenger led rank 3 inside. In front of them were the other students in the top twenty, with two standing in a commanding area, where they were able to easily direct the others. Rank 1's messenger hastily ran up to rank 1 and hurriedly whispered in his ear. After a brief conversation the messenger left the area completely.

Rank 1 walked closer to rank 3 and stopped ten feet away from him. "Welcome, you must be the new rank 3, I'm rank 1 the top student and captain of our prestigious academy's tournament team. Everyone you see here is in the top twenty ranks. The lower ten are the reserves while us top ten are the main team. Was that easy enough to understand?" Rank 1 spoke in a calm welcoming tone.

"I understand, but I…" Rank 3 wanted to know why he was here.

"I ask the questions!" rank 1 shouted aggressively.

"Err…" Rank 3 took a step back nervously.

"You have got some nerve, you join our academy at rank 3 no less, and yet you act like you've never met another human being before. How dare you even consider concerning yourself with anyone other than the top ranks? Rank 21 is the only exception I'll make, but just him. Do you understand?"

"I understand what you're saying, but I don't know why you feel that way."

"Are you an idiot?"

"I'm sorry I don't understand?" Rank 3 felt his situation had taken a turn for the worse.

"You are, aren't you, you're an idiot? Just one more question before we get our training underway." The aura around rank 1 became violent and dangerous. "Did you really think you could make such an outrageous statement?"

"I don't understand what's happening here, maybe I should just leave. Rank 21 is probably waiting for me after all." Rank 3 tried to end the conversation and run away. Rank 3 could find out more later, but right now all he wanted was to escape this situation.

"My little messenger, has quite a gift you know, he reminds me of a rat but even they have their uses. Rank 21 probably noticed him, but it's not like he could've done anything. Anyway, let me see if I got this right. He just told me this so I should be able to recite it perfectly but correct me if I mess up. You ready?" Rank 1 spoke wryly and his eyes were full of cruel desires.

Rank 3 didn't respond, already knowing what rank 1 was going to say. It was now clear that rank 21's warnings were justified. But that didn't make rank 21 right either.

"Hi, everyone, I'm the new rank 3. I just wanted to say that I don't think it's very nice to pick on one student or any student. I think those that want to compete against each other should do so, and those that don't should be allowed to do as well. I want to make lots of friends. I don't want others to be afraid of me or any other student for that matter. It seems pointless and mean to me, I won't force rank 1001 to have to refuse a match request from me every day and I hope everyone else will eventually do the same. It is the right thing to do. How would you feel if you were in his position? Signed rank 3."

Rank 3 just stared at rank 1. That was a perfect recital of the message rank 3 was planning on sending. The only reason he didn't send it earlier was because he was interrupted.

"How'd I do, that's about the gist of it right? I have to say all of it apart from the end makes me laugh, the end though, I agree with the end. That last statement is exactly why I expect every student to request a match."

"I don't understand, how does picking on a student who has never accepted a fight control others?" Rank 3 was panicked and confused, nothing rank 1 said seemed to make any sense.

"It's a simple fear illusion."

"It's about fear?" rank 3 asked, becoming very confused.

"It really is very simple, no one wants to be rank 1001, so they all do what they're told to avoid it. There is a reason why everyone avoids rank 1001 and it's not because he isn't able to see well. It's because there is a chance, a tiny miniscule chance that he is stronger than someone else, and no one will take the risk that it's them. Of course he isn't, but the lower ranks don't know that. You don't realise it yet. I only ask for one thing and it unites every student, even rank 1001 benefits."

"Wait. What?" Rank 3's face grew pale with the thought that rank 1001 was involved in this messed up scheme. "What does he get from something so, so...?"

"He gets the luxury of existing," rank 1 said coldly, his words filled with disdain.

"What did you just say?" The pale faced rank 3 quickly turned to an angry red-faced rank 3. His suspicion was correct, something much more cruel in his eyes was happening to someone else than what he had experienced. His experience he wouldn't wish on anyone, an experience worse than that was intolerable.

"Say that again!" Rank 3 shouted angrily, his nerves vanishing in his blind rage.

"Which part? I'll say it all again if I have to. A moron like you needs to understand, and if words don't suffice." Electricity crackled through rank 1's fingertips and lava dribbled from his feet and began to melt the floor.

"I said, say that again, say you allow people to exist!"

"I do allow people to exist. That's one of my quirks." Rank 1 smiled wryly.

"Fine. I challenge you to a match right now!" Rank 3's energy poured out from his body in response to his uncontrolled emotions.

"Ooh sorry, you need to do that the proper way besides right now we're now doing a team building exercise. I'll say this again at the end but you probably won't be able to hear me. We're going to beat you half to death and then in a few weeks' time you're going to thank me for letting you keep your rank. You'll say rank 1 thank you for being you, I'm really sorry I've learnt my lesson. Doesn't that sound just great?"

The fight lasted longer than expected. Rank 3 was able to defeat many of the lower top twenty. He discovered that his physical abilities were higher than theirs and they were weaker than he expected. Rank 21 seemed much stronger than them, using the basics only got rank 3 so far. Even when he was able to use his ability in a greater fashion than he ever had, he was only able to further incapacitate a couple others.

Most of the top ten were unscathed when rank 3 was beaten into the ground. Rank 1, rank 2 and rank 4 didn't even have to get directly involved in the fight.

After the beating of rank 3 was finished, staff were called to take him to the infirmary. Rank 1 was happy with the outcome and was also happily resolved to keep teaching this lesson if needed. It was what happened in two days' time that made him get more frustrated and angrier than he had ever been.

Rank 3 had been unable to send his message to every student, which was perfectly fine with rank 1. It was childish and uninformed. He thought something like that wouldn't happen in the future after the brutal beating of rank 3, however. Two days after the 'team training' every student received an audio recording of the conversation, the recording didn't include noises of the fight but that was unnecessary.

Rank 3 had been proven to go against the top ranks on his third day. To some lower ranks he was someone they would much rather follow, especially with the added rumours spread by a certain someone.

The person responsible for the recording and its mass release was completely unknown and they wouldn't be discovered easily. Every student ranked lower than the top twenty had someone to be truly afraid of, but that didn't mean they would willingly offer themselves up to punishment. In this situation anyone could have been responsible and that meant that either everyone was punished or no one was. Seeing how it would be impossible to punish everyone, the top ranks could only focus on reducing the impact.

Not much changed from hearing the recording, the perceptions of rank 3 were still to most, just a possibility. They had never encountered or spoke to rank 3. In the back of everyone's mind, this whole thing could be some complex deception, to what end they did not know. The only main thing that changed was that rank 21 and rank 300 weren't the only two impatiently waiting for rank 3 to come out of recovery.

Rank 1 sensing the discourse quickly came up with a solution. One main problem for him would be if rank 3 was able to properly utilise his strength and gain fame and popularity at their first tournament match. If that happened it would be guaranteed to split the academy with his and rank 3's supporters. To rank 1, the unity he had achieved was everything. So he got rank 4 to perform a special task for him.

Chapter Eight
A tournament to remember

Tournaments events were the most important and most prestigious event students could participate in, naturally though only the top students were allowed to enter. Another reason to train and fight as many rank matches as possible, a culture of competition bred strong participants after all.

Academy 1 stood at the top of the other academies. It was the first one to be founded hence its name and it had been able to constantly attract the upper echelons of the state. A lot of the current top ranked students occupied the ranks their parents did, and it was because of their inherited ability. They were also given a higher standard of care and teaching when they were young, resulting in individuals with the ability to succeed and triumph over others.

This was a symptom or benefit of the state's current model of governing. The people at the top stayed where they were. The academies were no different, they all tended apart from a few brief disruptions to attain a rank that corresponded to their founding.

Tournaments ran continuously throughout the academic year. Monthly contests were the norm, but special extra matches could be arranged at any time. The first tournament of the second term was arranged to happen on the fourth week and it was to be academy 1 versus academy 2. This match was the most exciting as only academy 2 had come close to knocking academy 1 off of its perch.

The day of the tournament arrived quickly, for most the excitement was almost immeasurable. The arena filled quickly with all the students watching to support their academy. Due to incidents in the past, no academy 2 student supporters were allowed in the academy, only those in the main and reserve team were permitted entry.

Rank 300 was watching the tournament from the furthest point at the top of the viewing stands. Unknown to everyone else she was waiting for someone to arrive.

The tournament unfolded before her eyes; she didn't expect any of what was happening to take place, she only had a clue of what was about to happen next. She had seen a future involving the meeting of two individuals, one of which was already in the arena. She was still waiting for the other to arrive.

Despite the fact she couldn't care less about those in her academy's team, she was still a proud academy 1 student so she couldn't help get irritated by the events taking place in front of her. Although unlike the other students she wasn't openly voicing and shouting her opinions, all of which were in opposition to what was happening; it was a very unexpected upset.

He appeared from behind her, entering the arena

from the direction she knew he would. He had no idea what was taking place; he could hear shouting but he had yet to see it with his own eyes. Rank 3 stopped when he recognised rank 300, they only met once properly but he wouldn't forget the face of someone he had talked to before.

"What are you doing watching from up here, isn't there a better view from down below?" rank 3 asked with a smile on his face from seeing someone familiar.

"I could ask you the same, by all rights you should still be lying in a hospital bed."

"Ah, well I guess I heal faster than most, haha. Do you mind if I sit with you? We've met before, haven't we?" rank 3 answered trying to change the subject.

"I knew you would make this choice."

"What choice is that?"

"The one where you got beaten half to death and had your hands and feet cut off."

"How did you know about that?" Rank 3 took a step back from rank 300.

"Well everyone knows about the fight but only I know about what rank 4 did. I've got good eyes, I can't control this function, and it only happens rarely but it happened with you. I saw two futures, and you chose this one, good for you."

"Thank you for telling me the truth when we first met, I just didn't listen properly," rank 3 said sounding thankful and with a hint of regret.

"Don't thank me yet, you've got a job to do."

"No I'm just to going to watch the tournament, anything serious can wait." Rank 3 had only just fully recovered and didn't want to do anything too strenuous.

Rank 3 came out of the entrance to the seating area and moved to sit next to rank 300 and that was when he saw it, a scene of complete destruction. He couldn't see the real damage though because most of it was covered in a thick layer of dust but many unconscious student bodies could be made out.

"That is unexpected, not that I'm interested in the outcome." Rank 3 tried to dismiss his feelings about the situation.

"Don't act like you don't care, you may not like them but this isn't right. You know that, don't you?" Rank 300 looked rank 3 directly in his eyes.

"But what can I do, I can't force my way in there."

"No, but you can enter as a participant, we've still got one person left to enter."

Rank 300 put something in rank 3's ear. It was small and as soon as it was placed in, he could hear her voice coming from it.

"I'll communicate with you through this, this way you won't be on your own. I'll be an extra pair of eyes, trust me I'm a brilliant analyst." Rank 300 spoke full of pride but was being completely honest.

"OK, I'll put my trust in you. Which ones are academy 2 students and which ones are ours? It's a ten vs ten right, I don't want any of our students to get hit by me by accident."

"Don't worry about it, I'll point out your target when you get in there, I forgot you don't know what many students look like, haha. Oops, looks like I'm keeping you too long, rank 1 looks like he's about to lose." Rank 300 pushed rank 3 into the exit.

"Fine, give me the directions," rank 3 said accepting his fate.

Rank 300 directed rank 3 to the waiting area on the side lines of the arena. It was from this area that students on each team on opposite sides entered the arena. When rank 3 reached the academy 1 side, he met someone he wasn't expecting.

"Rank 3! How are you here?" rank 21 blurted out, he couldn't contain his surprise.

"Rank 21, why are you here? I thought you didn't like the top twenty," rank 3 asked. He was surprised but not as shocked as rank 21 at seeing his appearance.

"I don't but I have to represent the academy when it is asked of me, I'm a proud academy 1 student after all."

"I'm still uncertain I understand what it means to be proud of something, I don't think I've ever held pride. But that still doesn't mean I would throw away doing the right thing for pride," rank 3 said with a hint of contempt.

"What can I say, I like having an easy life. I won't judge you, just don't expect me to support you. I like things the way they are."

"Then why haven't you already entered the arena?"

"Hey, what do you take me for? We're both in the top academic class, I know a pointless fight when I see one, I couldn't beat that guy in these conditions," rank 21 said dismissively. He had lost interest in the tournament.

"Is it just one left? I'll take your place if only to show the students that I'm trying to be one of them, even if I don't like how they act towards rank 1001."

"Are you still going on about him? I guess you'll have to take my place if you want anything to change regarding him. He hasn't been in for two weeks now, I'm guessing something happened to him. Hehe, if only that weirdo would show his face, if I could see that even I would remove my request. Hey I might even acknowledge his existence from time to time."

"Why is that so important to you?" rank 3 asked full of contempt.

"It's simple, I only have a few goals for my life, all of which are easily achievable by my great self, everything else, rank 1001's face included, is just for my own entertainment."

"What category do I fall under?" rank 3 said, while starting to doubt his assumptions about rank 21.

"Both. Although you probably wouldn't understand why."

"What does…?" rank 3 asked, hesitantly.

"Stop talking to him and get in there, I almost don't want to watch this, you need to make this stop!" Rank 300 said while pointing into the arena. She was getting agitated.

"OK I'm going, you don't have to shout. How bad a shape could our team be in, aren't they the top team?" rank 3 responded, completely unaware of what was taking place.

"Just get in there. And as soon as you are in, follow my commands without hesitation," rank 300 interrupted. She knew it was time for her vision to become reality.

"I'm going now, see you later, rank 21." Rank 3 spoke with a smile, despite their differences in opinion rank 3 still considered rank 21 his first real friend.

'I don't like this place, but it is my home now so I'll do what I want, and right now I want to see what it feels like to be a top rank student.'

Rank 3 entered into the arena field. It was filled with dust and rubble, all sorts of damage; all evidence of the fighting that had taken place. At first it was hard to see, but it didn't take long for the dust to settle. This was because the fighting had ended a few moments before rank 3 had entered.

Rank 3 had no idea what had just happened unlike the audience who were all now gripped in fear and terror. The staff at the top of the academy could only feel shame and a sense of disgust at the students and their teachers. They were currently being humiliated by an academy that they felt was far beneath them.

Rank 3 could only be described as a late arrival, so late that he hadn't been able to properly witness the events that had taken place. And because of such a fact he had no idea just what and who he was about to face.

"First things first, your ability. Tell me its range and how well you can control it."

"I'm not sure about either, all I know is that it's much more a part of me than it was before. I can feel it more clearly now."

"Then I guess I have to play the odds. Listen carefully and don't panic and definitely do not hesitate," Rank 300 said with her voice full of conviction. She had complete faith in them both.

"Wait tell me which students are ours, if anyone recovers I need to know if they an opponent," Rank 3 spoke quickly. He needed to know who to watch out for, if he hurt someone he didn't want to, he would have a hard time forgiving himself.

"The dust is settling so I'll tell you. Everyone on the floor is an academy 1 student, all of them apart from rank 1 and rank 4 are in the emergency cocoons. Your first task will be, using your energy to retrieve rank 1 and rank 4 and activate their cocoons. They are currently both incapacitated approximately thirty metres from your position. I would be more accurate but that seems unnecessary. Just look ahead, spot them and save them." Rank 300 spoke distinctly and precisely.

"That's a lot of information," rank 3 responded, starting to feel overwhelmed.

"Don't talk, just follow. Now act quickly, you should see them any second now."

The dust settled and cleared rank 3's view. The audience had been able to look down into it, but he had had to wait. It was both a blessing and a disadvantage.

"What is happening?" rank 3 said in disbelief. He was completely taken aback.

"Grab them now!"

Rank 3 immediately released red vines made out his unique energy from each of his fingers. He made them wrap around rank 1 and rank 4 and pulled them towards him. He threw them behind him for their own protection. He then moved to activate their cocoons and it was then that he saw the extent of their injuries. He did almost all of this based on sheer instinct: it was as if his body was reacting faster than his mind. His mind however was the one who had to face this horrible sight.

It was unclear and if he thought about it, his imagination would have run wild. Their injuries were different from normal injuries. Although different was not a word that did their injuries justice; they were covered in blood, bruises and broken bones that were visible where the flesh had been torn. These injuries were fairly common but the horrific injuries came from their torsos, wrists and ankles, something had been carved in their chests and it was obvious the tool that had been used. The tool was in fact still with them, it was their ribs, with one rib impaling each wrist and ankle.

It was a miracle that they were still alive, it had to be by design. Because why would anyone go to such lengths to torture a dead person. Rank 3 felt a mix of emotions. On one hand he felt that they deserved to suffer for what they did to him, but not like this. So on the other side he felt an intense rage for the culprit. It didn't matter who they were, people who were unnecessarily cruel would be stopped by him.

After all, he was planning on changing the academy students' way of thinking, this was just another step to that goal.

"He's coming towards you, blast him," rank 300 ordered.

Rank 3 turned around without hesitation. The person coming in his direction was headed straight for rank 1 and rank 4. It didn't even look like this opponent had even noticed rank 3. Rank 3 gathered his energy into a sphere and blasted his opponent away with it. His opponent crashed against the energy shield barrier that was surrounding the arena field. Only participating students could enter through it, and they could only leave once the fight was over.

His opponent stood up without flinching. He must have been injured though. Everyone in the crowd agreed that an attack like that must have hurt him even a little.

The opponent looked over in rank 3's direction. Rank 3 had quickly activated the emergency cocoons and the safety and lives of rank 1 and rank 4 was now guaranteed. The opponent walked slowly; with every step he left a fresh bloody footprint.

"What's with his feet, is that his ability?" rank 3

asked, desperate to understand his situation.

"No, it's an injury he got earlier. He's a monster that walked through lava to get to his target. With your attack we can now say his injuries are semi-destroyed feet and some definite upper body bruising. There's definitely a chance that you can win. Keep going."

"OK let's do this," Rank 3 said with renewed vigour.

"Stay where you are for now, let him come to you. Aim for his face, he's wearing some sort of mask, destroy it and we'll see what's underneath." Rank 300 spoke while constantly analysing the opponent.

Hearing this comment instantly reminded rank 3 of rank 1001. After this fight he would most enthusiastically search for rank 1001 and make sure he was all right. He had thought about rank 1001 quite a bit when he was recovering. Rank 3 was certain that his background would give him an insight into how rank 1001 felt. Like when he first arrived, rank 1001 probably had never made a friend either and rank 3 would take it upon himself to remedy that.

Right now, though, he had to focus on what was in front of him. He had to ignore the thought of helping someone using kindness and replace it with the thought of violence is the only answer.

Rank 3 was doing his best to hide it, but he was filled with nerves. If it weren't for rank 300 helping him and talking to him, he would be stuck trembling in fear. He could only focus because of her commands.

Rank 3's opponent stopped after ten steps and reaching behind him he pulled out a short and incredibly sharp looking blade. "What is that? That can't be allowed," rank 3 asked rank 300 nervously, thinking he had been thrown into another trap. Maybe rank 1's and rank 4's injuries were fake, an elaborate trick.

"Relax, slow your breathing, everything is fine. The rules were changed at the last minute and every student was allowed to use one item: one tool. Yours is this earpiece, his is that weapon. He first took out our ten starters by spraying a liquid that that blade was covered in. I think he's run out but still be careful for a ranged attack." Rank 300 soothed rank 3. She was certain he would react the way he did and acted to fix it.

"Ten? How many academy 1 participants have their been?"

"You're the twentieth."

"And how many of them are there?" rank 3 asked starting to panic.

"Focus on the opponent in front of you, this fight between you two was what I saw in my vision. You'll be OK." Rank 300 spoke with a hint of pride in her ability.

The opponent was standing still; apart from brandishing his blade he was making no other big noticeable movements. He moved his head side to side, as if he was scanning his surroundings, checking the opponents he had crushed around him.

"Do I go to him?" rank 3 asked. His nerves were

staring to overwhelm his patience for rank 300's commands to be given.

"Blast him again!" rank 300 shouted as she ordered another attack.

Rank 3 did as he was commanded and blasted his opponent with an even bigger sphere of red energy than before. His opponent was forced into the ground by the attack. His opponent grasped his stomach and was forced to drop his blade which was then flung away from him. He patted the ground around him trying to find it but he was unsuccessful. It was when he was in the middle of patting the ground that his head shot up and he stared in a single direction.

'EMERGENCY! EMERGENCY! ALL STUDENTS EVACUATE THE ARENA IMMEDIATELY!' An incredibly loud automated alarm started sounding.

The emergency announcement rang through the whole arena. In an instant the energy barrier was dropped and all the teachers and even the upper academy staff descended into the middle of the field.

"You need to get out of there too. Get out any way you can, I'll find you later."

"What's happening?" rank 3 responded, panicked and confused

"JUST GET OUT NOW!"

Chapter Nine
The aftermath

All the students quickly gathered outside of the arena. Not a single one of them knew what was going on. Most of them had no idea that there was even an emergency warning system.

Most students were already shaken by what they had seen happen in the arena; it was unlike any of the past tournament matches they had witnessed. Losing to academy 2 was unheard of, just as much as them being forced to evacuate.

Many students had grouped together and were all discussing the possibilities that caused this situation, most felt safe despite the emergency warning. Nothing had ever happened in the academy that the academy had no knowledge of or had not given permission for. The academy was almost completely autonomous, entering its walls was like entering another world. Most of the people who had never entered it, considered it as such.

Rank 300 slowly walked over to rank 3. Rank 3 was the last student to exit the arena.

"Hey you." Rank 300 smiled as she spoke to rank 3.

"Do you know what's going on? Is something bad

happening?" Rank 3 ignored her smile and tried focusing on what was happening around them.

"Heh, you worry too much, I don't know what is going on but it can't be that serious. My guess is that this is something between academy 1 and academy 2. Us students needn't get involved." Rank 300 used a soothing and confident tone.

"Is rank 1001 here? Was he inside?" Rank 3 was now starting to shake as his whole body filled with panicked thoughts.

"Hmph. You should already know he doesn't follow the rest of us, he's a fake academy 1 student," rank 300 responds in disgust.

"Then is he in his dorm room? I need to go to him." Rank 3 ignored rank 300's disgust and continued to seek information regarding a person he was worried about.

"Ha, don't make me laugh, I only want to help you because my ability tells me it's the right thing to do. That doesn't mean I share your charity. Rank 1001 lives off site, no one knows where, if they did he probably would have been convinced to quit the academy by now. We have things to do, forget about him." Rank 300's disdain for rank 1001 was glaringly obvious and rank 3's expression showed that he was starting to get annoyed by it.

"Yeah if you're not careful people will think you're obsessed and lose interest in you. You probably haven't realised yet, but everyone will soon see you as something of a hero." A confident and witty-toned voice spoke from behind them.

"Rank 21! Do you know what's going on?" Rank 3 was happy to see rank 21 but was also still very concerned by what was happening.

"Nope and I don't care. I was enjoying the show until this annoying thing happened, looks like you've gotten stronger?"

"I feel stronger. Wait, that's not important. How do I find rank 1001?" Rank 3 put his hands on rank 21's shoulders.

"Give that up already." Rank 21 brushed rank 3's hands off of him. "You're going to be more popular than ever now and this time it won't be for a bad reason, you should enjoy it. Don't worry about anything else." Rank 21 spoke, trying to brush off thoughts of rank 1001 along with rank 3's hands.

It wasn't long after the emergency alarm until one of the senior members of staff exited the arena. Immediately the students gathered stopped talking and turned to face the senior member of staff.

"All students, there is no need for concern at this moment. The tournament has to be postponed due to an incident caused by academy 2. I would now ask you all to return to your dorms, while the members of staff tend to the arena. Now off you go, and as a reward there will be no planned lessons tomorrow, so please spend tomorrow relaxing. You'll be updated on further information when it is seen fit to do so." Every word the staff member said was filled with authority.

Without protest the students all headed inside the dorm complex, except only now they had even more questions than before. They would have to wait for now.

Rank 3 and rank 21 said goodbye to rank 300 at the entrance area of the dorm complex; rank 300 lived several floors below the two top rankers.

Their floor was missing many of its occupants. All the top twenty minus rank 3 had all been sent to the infirmary. Only the top thirty lived on this floor, so they had much more breathing space than usual.

"Hey rank 3, want to hang out or something? We haven't got anything to do. I'm not in the mood for anything tiresome. How about I make you something to eat, I guarantee you'll enjoy it?" rank 21 asked with a smile on his face.

"I want to, but I have to figure something out first. Next time," rank 3 responded apologetically but also very candidly.

"What is wrong with you? I'm being nice here, isn't that want you wanted?" Rank 21 was very obviously annoyed by rank 3 declining his invitation.

"I don't want people to change for me, I want them to be nicer because it's the right thing to do." Rank 3 spoke, feeling every word resonate with his soul.

"You are a real mystery to me." Rank 21 turned to leave and said, "I guess I'll see you later." Rank 21 walked off without saying anything further and not letting rank 3 say anything to him.

Rank 3 didn't like how rank 21's behaviour was

different from before. He wasn't expecting rank 21 to change how he acted. Seeing what happened in the arena must have affected rank 21 more than rank 3 had realised. Nevertheless, rank 3 had another, more pressing matter to tend to, and as he had feared it was going to take much more than his own efforts.

Rank 3 walked into his dorm and looked around. It had been several weeks since he was last here Unsurprisingly everything looked the same as before. It was a refreshing sight to what had been a long day which was set to be longer still.

Rank 3 stood still for a moment, gathering up the courage and resolve to do what he thought was the only choice he had left. He had to know even if that meant revisiting his past.

He picked up the phone in his room and was about to type in a phone number when his phone started ringing. Startled, he answered it without thinking. "Hello," rank 3 answered nervously.

"Rank 3, is that you? It's me, rank 300."

"Oh, hi. Are you all right? Rank 21 seems to be a bit shaken, at least I think he's acting differently because of what he saw," Rank 3 asked, concerned for someone he had come to see as a friend.

"I'm fine, my sister has told me worse stories. She is a state investigator, so she's seen the real worst of it. Anyway, I wanted to call you to tell you that my sister will be the one coming here to investigate the incident. She won't want to talk to any students straight away so you'll have a few days until she comes for you, haha." Rank 300 spoke with an oddly optimistic tone.

"You called to warn me?"

"Nah, that's just extra. I called you because I want you to make me your official analyst. I want you to tell everyone that you're mine."

"What's an official analyst? And won't we give the wrong impression if we say we belong to each other?" Rank 3 was filled with doubts surrounding this idea.

"Why are you being so stingy? An official analyst is like your support team and coach rolled into one, all the top rank students have one, excluding rank 21 of course. He also possesses analytical qualities." Rank 300 started to sound slightly upset.

"Then I think rank 21 might already be mine," Rank 3 responded, hoping to change the subject.

"Don't talk nonsense! He's helped you out a bit sure, but I helped you survive that monster. I looked out for you." Rank 300 spoke as if rank 3 owed her.

"I guess that's true. Please be my analyst." Rank 3 did feel like he owed a lot to rank 300 and happily agreed to make her his analyst.

"And of course I accept. Well nice talking to you, call me if you need anything. OK, bye!"

"Wait!" rank 3 blurted out desperately.

"Whoa, what is it?"

"Err… well you said your sister is someone who knows things right? So could you please ask her to find out rank 1001's living address please?" Rank 3 asked, filled with nerves and hope.

"Haha, I thought you might ask me that, couldn't hold it in could you? Unfortunately, no she doesn't nor can she find it out, I already asked her to access rank 1001's information but you need a higher level of clearance. She's not important enough haha. He's probably part of one of those families who look down on the rest of us, another reason to dislike him. Anyway, unless there is anything else I can do for you, I'm going to get going now." Rank 300 quickly dismissed rank 3's question.

"No, I don't need anything else, thank you for your help."

With rank 300 revealing the hardship of uncovering information about rank 1001, rank 3 was certain he had no other choice to make an uncomfortable phone call.

"Hello."

"Hello." Rank 3 paused stiffened by nerves. "I need to ask you for a favour."

Chapter Ten
Surprise visitor

Rank 3 had been walking for over an hour. He was far away from the academy and after leaving the city he was now far away from anything that resembled civilisation.

He was using his screen to navigate; it was no longer connected to the academy's servers, but the map he had loaded up on it earlier was still being displayed. He walked through fields and took careful notice of all of his surroundings, even every individual tree could be vital in helping him reach his destination.

It had only been an hour so rank 3 wasn't feeling dejected just yet. His enthusiasm was still strong even if his doubt in his navigation abilities was slowly increasing. It was slowly eating away at him until he saw a small white box in the distance.

It was obvious at first glance that this white square object was not a naturally occurring phenomenon, although it was also not something that stood out as particularly interesting. However, it was rank 3's intended destination, at least that was what his map was telling him. It was the first out-of-place thing he had seen, so he was hopeful and was very eager to investigate it.

The white square structure was identical on three sides. It was twice the size of a normal person's height and even though it was white like marble, rank 3 could tell it was made of metal. This structure was unbelievably reinforced.

The one side that was not like the others, was only slightly different. It looked less together than the others as if it was a panel that could be removed. Surprisingly as well, there was a small button on this side. With extreme caution rank 3 pressed the button but he could sense no response, he didn't even know if the button activated anything. Unbeknownst to him a small camera was currently looking down and carefully analysing rank 3.

Not knowing what else to do rank 3 kept pressing the button. After a few minutes he gave up on that endeavour so instead he started banging on the metal wall. Despite it putting up resistance he did not find his hands injured by it. It hurt to knock but it also seemed his regenerating speed had increased. He had no idea why nor was aware of this change happening, but he felt like he could keep knocking forever if necessary.

A further five minutes had passed, almost fifteen minutes in total since he first reached this white metal square. Rank 3 was still not giving up. He had to make sure for certain that this was or wasn't rank 1001's place of residence.

It was a minute later when rank 3 heard a subtle metallic clunk. Soon after that the majority of the metal wall in front of him slowly descended into the ground. Standing behind it was a person he thought he recognised as rank 1001, but admittedly it could have just as easily been anyone else.

The person standing in front of him wore a mask, but it was different to rank 1001's usual and just like his opponent in the arena, anyone could be behind a mask. Along with the mask, the person in front of him was wearing gloves, a robe which covered his entire frame and slippers concealing his feet and ankles.

The doubt was quickly erased in rank 3's mind that this person was rank 1001. Apart from the masks being different and a robe instead of the academy uniform everything else about this person reminded him of rank 1001.

Suddenly becoming very nervous, rank 3 spluttered out speech. "Are, are you rank 1001?"

The person in front of him suddenly ripped holes in the sides of his mask freeing his ears. He threw bits of mask and bandages on the floor next to him. Rank 3 could also slightly notice the person's mouth moving, but the speech was muffled by the mask and bandages.

"Are you rank 1001?"

The person in front of him nodded yes.

Rank 3 sighed a sigh of relief. He had found the one he was looking for.

"Are you OK? Rank 1 and rank 4 didn't hurt you, did they? Or any of the other students, I now know how cruel they can be," rank 3 asked, his words filled with concern and the worry that he had caused unnecessary pain to another.

Rank 1001 shook his head.

"So you are OK? Phew, I'm glad, I thought I might have inconvenienced you. I brought you something, I still hope you'll accept it even if it isn't needed for an apology like I had planned." Rank 3 felt a wave of relief flow through him.

Rank 3 reached into his pocket and pulled out a small circular object. In response to an object being removed rank 1001 took a step back. He didn't trust any unknown objects.

"Oh please don't be afraid, I would never want to hurt you; it was an accident when we first met. I didn't know anything back then and I truly apologise for my actions. I can assume you've experienced many hardships." Rank 3's tone changed from delight at finding his target to one of a deep sadness. "I've had a hard time of it too, not that you'd think that seeing as I'm rank 3, but before I joined the academy I was forced to feel what it means to be alone. I could only talk to my father and when I say talk, it would only be a couple words a year, and that's if I could meet with him in the first place. All the others avoided me and, when I was younger, they picked on me, called me names and beat me. This small token I made is for you to remember, know and understand that there is someone who wants to be your friend and not hurt you. You don't have to be alone any more." Rank 3 paused for breath and hoped that rank 1001 would respond.

Even as rank 3 spoke these words, he could remember every time perfectly when in the past he dreamt of someone saying the same thing to him. How great, he thought, would it be if someone magically appeared, solely purposed to be his friend?

"So please take this." Rank 3 held out his hand to rank 1001.

Rank 1001 took a step forward and stumbled slightly. He reached out his hand only to miss rank 3's. Instead of grabbing the small badge, he started to fall towards the floor.

"Here I've got you!" Rank 3 instantly reacted and quickly caught rank 1001, lifting him back up with both of their hands now holding on to the other. Rank 1001 slowly took a step back into the white box. Seeing him walk backwards and glimpsing into rank 1001's home, all rank 3 saw was darkness.

Rank 3 released rank 1001 leaving the badge in the other's hand. Rank 1001 tried to feel the badge thoroughly but it was clear he was dissatisfied with his poor assessment. He held it up into the air and paused. After a brief wait, he put his arm down and placed the badge in his pocket.

Looking at rank 1001's motionless body and expressionless face was very vexing for rank 3. He didn't know what he should say or do next. He started to feel very awkward, especially as rank 1001 had yet to say anything, that was if he could speak.

"Oh, you're probably wondering how I found this place. Don't worry no one else knows about this at the academy and I wouldn't betray a friend. But I also can't tell you exactly who told me, just please believe when I say you won't be inconvenienced."

As soon as rank 3 mentioned the word friend again rank 1001's head twitched.

"We are friends, right. I mean of course I regard you as such. You don't have to, but I'll always let you rely on me. Anyway, as I was saying the person who gave me your information is very important but has no interest in something as small as this so please don't be concerned. Like I said, I'm a friend."

Rank 1001's head twitched again and this time he raised one of his hands to his face and ripped off a chunk of his mask, uncovering his mouth. Instead of the mask and bandages he now used his hand to obscure it but it was much more exposed than before.

"Should I accept everything you say to me as the truth or as a lie?" Rank 1001 spoke through his hand, slightly muffling his speech.

"Whoa, your voice is just like…" Before rank 3 could finish his statement he immediately stopped himself. He almost said another male student's voice sounded like an angel's. "Truth, as I said I want to be your friend."

"And friends tell each other the truth? So if you don't tell someone the truth you can't be their friend?" Rank 1001 tilted his head as he spoke.

"Yeah, that's basically how it works. Of course just telling the truth isn't enough, you have to care about the other person too."

"Care? Oh, as in look after their needs?" Rank 1001 responded happily as he felt he had answered the question correctly.

"Yes, that's why I came to check on you. I was afraid you had been injured, hurt or worse. I was worried."

"Hmm? OK you can be my friend," rank 1001 said after quickly weighing things up in his mind.

"Hey! That's great. Well, it's starting to get dark so I should go back to the academy. Will you be in tomorrow?"

"What's the date tomorrow?"

"Err…? It's the eleventh."

"Hmm? Forty days would equal? Tonight is the night, right?" Rank 1001 mumbled to himself.

"What's that?"

"Not tomorrow but I'll be in the day after."

"Why not tomorrow? I want to see you," rank 3 said concerned but was instantly made embarrassed by his exact wording.

"I'm normally very busy tonight and tomorrow. Hmm, if you want to see me so badly come here again tomorrow but at the same time, that's roughly four hours after lessons finish. That should be manageable."

"What about your match requests? How will you decline them? You may have been missing lessons but you must have been in to decline them otherwise I would have heard about it," rank 3 asked. He wouldn't forget anything important.

"It's fine, I'm allowed to connect to my account from here if I need to. So tomorrow evening then?"

"Yeah OK. I'll be looking forward to it." Rank 3 was completely distracted by the thought of seeing rank 1001 again tomorrow.

"Great, see you then, rank 3."

Rank 3 smiled and waved goodbye to rank 1001. Rank 1001 turned around and went back into his poorly lit home. The metal door closed behind him and when it closed completely, he started to panic.

"Babe! I need help. Can you please help me by telling me how I should treat a friend guest person? I don't know what to call them, just find out and tell me everything about both please. It is urgent," rank 1001 called out as he raced down the corridor.

Chapter Eleven
White lily

Rank 3 woke up with a smile on his face. Yesterday had gone better than he had planned and it had been confirmed that lessons would be starting back up again. The arena was still sealed off while the academy investigated and would soon be open to the state investigators, one of which would be rank 300's older sister.

Rank 3 got out of bed and got ready for the day. He made himself a small breakfast as he still had a small appetite; during his recovery he was unable to eat whole foods. He then showered and put on his uniform. Looking down on his rank he felt indifferent towards it, but looking at the uniform as a whole he started to feel a small sense of pride.

As usual, as he went downstairs to exit the dorm complex the other students all actively got out of his path, but this time a few did try to interact with him, with a couple asking him questions about the fight, even a few requests to follow him around. Rank 3 tried to communicate that he had no desire to talk about what happened in the arena nor did he want other students to follow him around as he was not someone who demanded, or needed to be followed.

Rank 3 stopped trying to leave and at the entrance he took a deep breath. "Erm, excuse me, everyone!" Rank 3 raised his voice, quieting down the surrounding students. "I just want to say that I entered the arena because I thought it was the right thing to do. I don't like the views of the other top twenty but I still couldn't just sit back and watch others get hurt, whoever they may be." Rank 3 meant the words he said even if he didn't truly feel that way at the time. If he had acted differently he would have regretted it.

Rank 3 went to leave as he finished speaking, ignoring any comments from the surrounding students, but right before he exited, he turned back. "Oh and I also want everyone to try and be nicer, but that's up to you, I won't force my views on anyone and please, please don't be afraid of me." Rank 3 smiled at the crowd as he finished speaking.

Rank 3 left the entrance and travelled to his academic classroom. The other students there gave him much less attention. All the students in the top academic class were highly intelligent and were all ranked above rank 250. All were indifferent about student politics, especially as all of them were mostly unaffected.

It was the lowest ranked students that felt most concerned, they were most affected if a top rank or high ranked student were to 'bump' into them. A seemingly accidental incident with painful consequences was something that would be very unwelcome. It was definitely something to be feared and lower ranks had to be very aware of their surrounding students to survive.

Rank 21 sat next to rank 3 but refused to say anything; he didn't even return rank 3's greeting. Rank 3 didn't press him further as he still felt that rank 21 was still feeling off.

The academic teacher was present and conducted himself in the same manner as always. The students felt easy with this atmosphere. The academic teacher felt very unconcerned with the events of the past few days. When he was in the army, he worked alone doing covert tasks so the importance of team tournaments was still something of a mystery.

As classes finished rank 21 turned to rank 3 and said, "I'm not in the mood to train today and our teacher is occupied with the arena business. So I suggest you act as you please. You can use the room if you wish or you can do as I do and go back to dorm. I'm going back to bed."

"Are you OK?" Rank 3 finally voiced his concern. He couldn't hold it back any longer.

"What? I'm fine of course, it's just that I think I'll wait for teacher to return, she has other things to attend to right now. She has been back to the academy for a while now though, you would have met her if you didn't get yourself into that mess. Anything else?" Rank 21 quickly dismissed rank 3's question.

Rank 3 wasn't sure how to respond. He didn't know

if rank 21 was avoiding his question, he didn't sound or look OK.

"OK, that's good, I'm glad you're all right. Call me if you need anything, if not I'll see you tomorrow, hopefully the combat teacher will have finished her business." Rank 3 smiled, trying to cheer up rank 21.

"Yes, hopefully. I'll be off then, see you later." Rank 21 left quickly leaving rank 3 behind.

Rank 3, after thinking briefly about what he should do, decided that he would also return to his dorm. Once he did, he realised something and started to panic. Rank 3 didn't know what gift to bring rank 1001, and he didn't know what to wear either. It was only now he realised that he was visiting in the evening. He couldn't really wear his uniform like last time, especially now when he realised that his uniform would have a negative impact on rank 1001.

Rank 3 paced around his room trying to come up with a solution. He started to sweat and his paces increased until he was almost jogging in a circle. And then suddenly, it hit him. Rank 1001 couldn't see anything, well maybe a little. Rank 3 wasn't sure but he was certain that his clothing wouldn't have any meaningful impact.

Next was a gift. Even though he brought something yesterday, rank 3 still felt like that wasn't enough. It held meaning, but he didn't know if rank 1001 would value it. He didn't want to give rank 1001 just anything, he didn't know what but just something more thoughtful and valuable than a handmade badge.

Hours passed and rank 3 had finally decided on his outfit. He wore the clothes he had first worn when he landed in the academy. It was a simple outfit; it was a larger version of the clothes his mother had given him when he was a child. It was formal, similar to the academy uniform. The outfit consisted of a shirt and a pair of trousers along with a long thin jacket. It couldn't be called fancy or well-designed but it was comfortable and always felt warm. Along with this outfit he wore a pair of white shoes.

Looking down at his shoes, rank 3 had the inspiring idea to buy a pair of slippers for rank 1001 but this idea broke apart quickly when rank 3 realised he was ill-equipped to do so. He didn't even know where to buy replacement uniform, let alone non-academy clothing.

But choosing this outfit did remind rank 3 of his mother and a string of happy memories flooded his mind, until they were crushed under the weight of the sadness they caused. Nevertheless, he found further inspiration, even if it was daunting and brought up painful memories.

Rank 3 walked over to the room with the closed door, the second of his any purpose rooms, the first containing a fully functioning gym and the second containing something else, something that he first thought shouldn't exist. He still felt that way, but today it would have a use.

Rank 3 grabbed the handle tightly and closed his

eyes. He opened the door swiftly, then he slowly and carefully walked in. He waved his hands around trying to get a feel of his surroundings. He stopped when he felt the presence of a flower, he picked it and hurriedly exited the room.

He slammed the door shut behind him. He checked the handle to make sure it was completely closed and sighed a sigh of relief when he decided it was. He opened his eyes and looked down at the flower he had picked, oddly enough it was his mother's favourite, a white lily.

Chapter Twelve
First time being a guest

Rank 3 left the boundaries of the academy and headed out of the city into the area minus civilisation. He walked a more direct route than last time and arrived five minutes earlier than agreed. Surprising himself, he was able to subdue his nerves and excitement and he waited the five minutes before he pressed the button.

Rank 3 pressed the button and waited patiently. It only took a few seconds for the door to lower and rank 1001 was standing behind it. Rank 1001 was wearing the exact same outfit as last time, although unlike last time, his ears were already slightly showing and his hand was covering his unwrapped mouth.

"Rank 3, you arrived right on time, that's very kind of you. I've discovered that guests often arrive at their own convenience, but I'm glad you're here now. I was afraid you wouldn't show." Rank 1001's angelic voice was welcoming but also sounded a bit forced.

"I didn't want to miss this. I want to get to know you. No one else seems interested in what students are like underneath their ranks. But I am, especially in you since you don't follow the directions of the others." Rank 3 spoke in a soft tone and was constantly trying to gauge rank 1001's reactions.

"I find you fascinating as well, isn't that a fortunate coincidence? So please, dearest guest, won't you accept the invitation into my home?" Rank 1001 continued to speak in a forced tone.

"Err...? Yes I'll accept your invitation, but you don't have to treat me as if I'm someone important. You don't have to keep your distance from me," rank 3 responded, trying to get rank 1001 to stop forcing this persona.

"So you accept and you'll willingly join me in my home, my guest?" Rank 1001's tone did not change.

'Oh? It must just be the way he talks. Maybe it's the way his family is, I've never thought much about it until now. I guess I'll have to get used to it.' Rank 3 decided to accept rank 1001's tone and continued to enjoy their conversation.

"Yes, thank you for letting me in. Before you take me inside, I have something for you."

"Another precious gift?"

"Well, it has value to me, but it's not something that would be labelled precious." Rank 3 surprised himself by how he described the flower.

"I've discovered that all gifts given with good intentions are precious. Of course, real gifts from you are the only ones I've ever received. But I'm certain some others share that point of view. Your gifts don't contain any bad intentions, do they? I doubt your gift could hurt me, besides I've got some things for you too, so even if you see it as a trade that will work. Trades are built on trust after all."

"Well, I can't say my gift is purely without ulterior motives. I still feel bad about what happened when we first met. My gift is simple. My gift is a white lily, and it holds a very special meaning to me. Please accept it." Rank 3 held out the flower in his hand.

"Yesterday you said you would never lie to me, so I already trust you completely. I am also fascinated by you, so I don't think I could find a gift from you lacking in anything. Please won't you follow me inside now, my friend?"

"Yes, of course I will, but first please let me put my gift in your pocket, I want you to hold on to it. I won't force you to try to take it while not being able to see it."

Rank 1001 nodded at rank 3. Rank 3 very carefully moved towards rank 1001 and very delicately placed the flower in the robe's pocket, only the top of the flower was showing and it was a pretty sight.

Rank 1001 whispered something that rank 3 was unable to hear and then surprisingly, rank 1001 grabbed rank 3's hand. Due to rank 1001's perfect precision and no hesitation, rank 3 was taken aback by it but didn't feel any desire to reject it. He was used to being dragged around by rank 21 after all.

Rank 1001 led rank 3 inside. Unlike last time the entrance was well lit and rank 3 could see deep inside. He could see a small slope leading down to a long corridor that was full of lights. He couldn't see much else, but realised that this place was much larger than it seemed.

Rank 1001 pulled rank 3 beside him, ensuring that they were now walking side by side and hand in hand. Rank 3 felt comfortable like this, even though it seemed unnecessary for them to hold hands, it felt warm and nice.

"Wait aren't you going to close the door?" Rank 3 asked concerned.

"Not yet, I'm getting some of your gifts delivered. I've arranged for hot meals to be delivered in an hour."

"That's not necessary." Rank 3 was flattered, but he didn't want to be a nuisance.

"Please don't worry, friend, I didn't know what you liked to eat, so I just ordered one of everything." Rank 1001 sounded very unconcerned about it.

"That seems a bit extreme. Are your family OK with you spending money like that?" Rank 3 was concerned he was forcing rank 1001 into an uncomfortable position with others. Rank 3 was especially concerned when it came to families due to his past experiences with his own.

"Of course, how would they object? Please don't talk to me about those people called family, they don't care about my actions." Rank 1001's tone sounded oddly cold for a moment.

Rank 3 got the feeling that rank 1001's family and rank 1001 must have a bad relationship.

"Anyway, please do not worry about anything else,

friend. Let me give you what they call the 'grand tour'. I've learned that this is the most common first activity." Rank 1001's tone returned to how it was before.

Rank 3 was certain that rank 1001 had never had a friend before, let alone anyone to properly interact with. Rank 3 could clearly see the students of the academy had been too cruel and too quick to judge rank 1001. The rank 1001 rank 3 had met didn't act any differently to how any of them acted.

As rank 3 thought about the hardships rank 1001 had faced, his own seemed to pale in comparison and lost in thought he loosened his grip of rank 1001's hand. Their fingers were at risk of not being interlocked. Rank 3 didn't notice at all until rank 1001 very quickly and concisely pulled rank 3's hand back into his own, freeing rank 3 from his worry-filled train of thoughts.

"Don't let go of me, OK? I don't want to lose you, friend." Rank 1001 was very concerned with them being connected.

"Oh, I'm sorry I forgot what I was doing for a moment, I won't let go of your hand unless you let me or need me to." Rank 3 didn't want to pry into the reason why, so he happily agreed to do whatever rank 1001 needed him to.

"That's great to hear. OK, where to start? Do you have any preferred choice of tour start? I plan to finish where I set up an area which you can use for eating."

"No, please show everything you want in the order that you decide."

"I'll just go in order then, as it's easiest. So we'll walk slowly and I'll explain each room as we get to it."

The corridor was long and seemed unending. If not for a light pointing in their direction, it would definitely seem so. The walls were all painted completely white and again rank 3 could tell they were made of metal. Their thickness, he was unable to ascertain.

"Who designed this place?"

"That's not important," rank 1001 said with a hint of embarrassment. "Anyway, this is the first two rooms, their doors are opposite each other to allow for an easy exchange between the two rooms. I did some rearranging yesterday so these two rooms are now for guests. One room has all necessary facilities for a guest or friend to be comfortable. There is a bed, bathroom, kitchen and an area to relax and an area to eat. The other room is more open. I've only put in a table and some furniture to prepare your meal."

"Yesterday? Did you say you did this yesterday?" Rank 3 was completely surprised by the idea that someone would go to such lengths for him.

"Yeah, I didn't have anything for someone else so I had to make arrangements. It wasn't too difficult, the furniture, the plumbing and wiring took the longest, the other stuff didn't take very long."

"But isn't that doing everything? You didn't need to do this; I don't need you to completely change any part of your home for me." Rank 3 was starting to feel like he had put too much pressure on rank 1001.

"What are you saying? I wanted to do this, it's polite to let your guests use your guest room. I didn't have a guest room, so I made one. It's very simple, you don't need to think too much about it." Rank 1001 spoke again, very unconcerned about doing something that seemed strenuous.

Rank 3 wanted to keep protesting rank 1001's decision but realised it would be pointless to and anyway rank 1001's home was well hidden. Not just to an outside observer, but it was extremely difficult to get any information about it in the first place. This meant it was highly likely rank 1001's background and most likely family could arrange something like this easily. Rank 3 was certain his own family could do something like this.

"Thank you very much for your consideration." Rank 3 was starting to relax and just let everything unfold in front of him.

"You're very welcome, friend, I am glad you find it to your liking. Do you wish to see more or would you like to relax in the room provided?"

"I'm very happy to do whatever you choose. Show me everything and anything, this is your home after all. I don't want to intrude or overstep; I wouldn't want to upset you or your family."

"Do you want me to show you everything? Do I have to show a friend/guest everything?" rank 1001 said with a hesitant and doubtful tone.

"Oh no, I don't want to make it sound like I'm

forcing you to do anything. I can just spend time with you here. I just came today so I could learn more about you." Rank 3 revealed his true intentions.

"Learn more about me? You mean you want to know what's under my mask like everyone else, don't you?" Rank 1001 started to panic. "Just because I find you fascinating doesn't mean you get to do to me or see something of mine that I don't want to be seen or done. I have the right to be myself." Rank 1001 took a step away from rank 3, but rank 3 kept holding his hand. "Show everything, you're just like the rest. I am not something to be laughed at!"

"Hey, no I'm sorry please don't panic, remember you can trust everything that I say. So please listen, I'm not here to hurt you or manipulate you I just want to be your friend." Rank 3 desperately tried to calm rank 1001 down. He had said something in a way he shouldn't have.

"Why do you want that? I'm tired I didn't get to sleep because I was worried about you visiting today. If you came here to hurt me just get it over with and leave. This was a mistake." Rank 1001 sounded sad and dejected. Rank 3 could tell rank 1001 had been hurt a lot before.

"Err...? Here." Rank 3 wrapped his arms around rank 1001. Rank 1001 expected rank 3 to crush him or do something painful but instead the hug felt warm and gentle.

"Do you get it now? I just want you to not feel

alone. Just focus on how this feels." Rank 3 spoke softly and his kindness could be felt in each word.

"OK, I'm sorry I overreacted, I'll trust you," rank 1001 responded positively. He was holding on to the promise that rank 3 wouldn't lie to him and this new warm feeling was taking over his emotions.

Rank 1001 slowly released rank 3's arms around him. He grabbed rank 3's hand tightly and started walking at a fast pace down the corridor. They walked right up until the end of the corridor. "Promise you won't tell anyone about this. I really want to show this to you now." Rank 1001 spoke excitedly but rank 3 could tell rank 1001 was nervous.

"I promise," rank 3 responded but was unsure about what was happening.

"OK good and remember you are the first person I've ever shown this to."

Rank 1001 pressed against the wall in a certain spot. He pushed into the wall and a small clunk noise was made.

"Wait." Rank 3 pulled rank 1001 backwards. "You don't have to do this." Rank 3 didn't feel like he had earned this privilege.

"No I want to."

Rank 1001 released the pressure pad, and the wall disappeared to the side revealing an elevator. He led rank 3 into it and pressed one of the buttons, then a small metal fence covered the gap left by the wall and the elevator descended.

"Wow, I didn't expect this," rank 3 said in surprise. This place was much more mysterious than he had first believed.

"Yeah, there is currently two floors below the first one. The first floor is mainly for storage and has some facilities for training and exercise and now guest facilities. The second floor has my room and my favourite place in the house."

The elevator stopped after a short period and rank 1001 led rank 3 out of the elevator. They exited the elevator and entered into another corridor. This corridor was shorter than the other one above.

"This floor is my favourite, the floor below is for all the serious business and other serious stuff but this floor, is much more personal. If you follow me, you'll see that this corridor leads to an open space the size of the top floor. My room is connected to the two doors at the back, one on the left and right-hand corner, but this is what I wanted to show you."

Rank 1001 walked over to the wall and pulled a large switch which illuminated the entire room, revealing a large metal and stone object. It was a large forge. Various metals were all placed around the room along with moulds for weapons, nearly all of which were blades and swords. Along with the moulds, hanging along the walls were multiple blades, the handles, sheaths and open blades were all elegantly decorated. Other moulds and items were scattered around but they weren't as eye catching as the decorated blades.

"What is this place?" Rank 3 had never seen such a sight.

"This is where I spend most of my free time. Do you like it? I can make all sorts of things in here, all handmade, and all designed by myself. It's my own world."

"It's really impressive. I think it's great." Rank 3 couldn't help admire something that he had never had the chance to do or even thought about doing.

"So you like it? I'm really glad."

Rank 1001 as if by instinct hugged rank 3 with both hands revealing his mouth for a moment before he buried his face into rank 3's chest.

"Does it really mean that much to you that I like it?"

Rank 1001 didn't respond. Rank 3 wasn't sure what to do, so he did what felt most natural and hugged rank 1001 back. After a full minute had passed, rank 1001 gently pushed rank 3 away and covered his own mouth again.

"I am really happy that you like it. I've never even told anyone about this before. No one knows that I make these things. My favourite are the swords, in particular I like the short thin blades the best, they are the most relaxing to make."

"I think you would have to be really skilled to manage something like this, you should be proud."

"Thank you for your kind words. I don't like having

to hear criticisms or complaints. Oh?" Rank 1001 tilted his head upwards in the direction of the front door. "The food is arriving early. I'll take you back up and show you where you'll be eating."

"OK, thank you again for sharing this with me."

Rank 3 led by rank 1001 holding his hand was taken back up to the top floor. They exited the elevator and rank 1001 sealed the elevator behind them. They then travelled back along the corridor until they arrived at the first two doors.

"If you need to wash up or use any guest room facilities beforehand, please say now and I'll direct you to the room to our right and wait for you out here."

Rank 3 was interested to see what was in the guest room but couldn't shake the feeling that rank 1001 would be uncomfortable if they were separated.

"I'm fine, thank you, I don't need anything like that."

"Great! Please come with me into this room." Rank 3 made rank 1001 happy when he heard rank 3's response.

They entered the room to their left. It was a large room in the shape of a square. It was well lit with lights on the walls and in the ceiling. In the middle of the room was a finely decorated and intricately designed table made out of high quality and highly valuable wood. The chairs were the same giving the appearance that they were designed and crafted by an expert.

The table was covered in a plain looking white

sheet. At the opposite end of the table to rank 3 and rank 1001 was a laid-out table setting with a golden candlestick with a lit candle along with a golden chalice. The cutlery was also golden along with the plates, both items were very much in excess; it looked like preparations for a large dinner party were being used for two people.

"I'm going to pick you up now."

"What? Why?" Rank 3 immediately reacted nervously to this statement.

"I read that that's what two people do when they share a meal. But promise you won't look up."

"Ah, well that sounds like two people who are..."

Before rank 3 could finish his sentence, he was swept up into the air and was now being held in rank 1001's cradled arms. Rank 3's expression changed to that of extreme embarrassment. He didn't know what to do or even how to respond.

"Is this right? Does it feel right?" rank 1001 asked, concerned. He had read all sorts of information about how to host a party for two and this was one of the things that stood out most.

"Erm? It feels fine, just carry me over there please," rank 3 said while continuously looking down. He couldn't look at someone who was carrying him in such a position. Rank 3 could also tell his cheeks were now bright red.

Rank 1001 carried rank 3 over to his seat and gently placed him on it. Rank 1001 then pushed rank 3 in so that he was sitting at a comfortable distance from the table.

"What do you think of everything? I made it all myself," rank 1001 asked, eager to hear a compliment.

Rank 3, assuming rank 1001 was talking about the metal tableware responded, "It's all very pretty, do you make a lot of these?"

"Not really, we make lots of things similar but everything you're experiencing is a custom-made item made by myself. Now this next part is very important, you have to make a promise?" Rank 1001 spoke in a serious tone.

"Promise about what? I'm not going to reject your hospitality. I'm looking forward to seeing what you're going to show me next," rank 3 responded truthfully and didn't even consider answering dishonestly.

"Well, the food is here and I need you to promise not to leave. I won't be able to tell if you leave, I'm not very good when it comes to you."

"I won't leave, I promise. You don't think I would abandon you, do you?" Rank 3 felt that rank 1001 had put up another wall between them.

"I wouldn't notice if you did," rank 1001 responded in a slightly sad tone.

"Please don't think like that, I told you everything I say to you is the truth," rank 3 said as rank 1001 left the room.

It was at this moment that rank 3 asked himself why he was so desperate and was putting in so much effort in trying to be rank 1001's friend. Rank 1001 was still being distrustful of rank 3. It wasn't necessary any more and yet he was still acting distant. Even after showing rank 3 something he had never shown anyone, it was more of another thing rank 1001 still wanted hidden. It was now clear that rank 1001 was so used to being alone that he was more afraid when he was with someone than when he was on his own. This was something rank 3 struggled to understand.

Rank 3 wondered how someone could come to be so distrustful of others. He had always resented the way his family members had acted towards him. Even when his mother was alive, they still acted the same, but it was because of his mother that rank 3 learnt that relying on others, even one person, made life much brighter.

Rank 3 thought that rank 1001 would be delighted to have a friend, but in fact it didn't seem exactly like that. Rank 1001 had put in a lot of effort for their meeting but it didn't give rank 3 the feeling that it would happen again. In fact he thought rank 1001 would make him promise to keep it a secret and that would be the end of it. After this thought, rank 3 made certain in his mind that he would do everything he could to make this evening as enjoyable as possible for the both of them, and he would do everything he could to make rank 1001 want to acknowledge him as a true friend.

Rank 1001 entered the room pushing a large metal object. It was filled with multiple shelves all full of different foods and meals. Rank 1001 then wheeled it round the table and placed it near rank 3.

"So, as I mentioned earlier, I didn't know what you liked, so I ordered one of everything. There is a couple more of these outside if you don't like anything in this one. It seemed more efficient to get you to check them one at a time."

Rank 3 admittedly didn't quite believe rank 1001's earlier statement concerning food options. Rank 3 just assumed there would multiple options and they would be nowhere near this extent.

"Well, I'm not actually very fussy, do you have any favourite foods?" Rank 3 was hoping to find out more about rank 1001's personal tastes.

"No, I don't eat much," rank 1001 responded blankly; he was clearly indifferent when it came to food.

Rank 3 didn't have much of an appetite when he was at the academy, similar to when he lived on the sky island. His appetite had been increasing slowly since he was starting to feel more comfortable in the academy, but it was still small. Right now, however, either due to rank 1001's presence or maybe the sheer quantity of food rank 3 felt like he could eat forever.

"If you've gone to all this trouble, then I'll try a bit of everything."

"OK, I'll arrange that for you."

Rank 1001 left the room and brought back in turn three more heated food storage devices. In total there was over two hundred different plates of food.

"Wow, this food tastes delicious. Thank you for

this." Rank 3 was eating everything in sight and he enjoyed every meal.

"I'm glad you're enjoying it," rank 1001 said as he stood next to the eating rank 3.

Rank 3 ate several meals and after he took another plate of food off of one of the trays, he realised rank 1001 was stuck in place not leaving his side.

"Aren't you going to have some?"

"No, I don't eat much and I would never be comfortable fully revealing my lips or tongue to another person."

"Can I ask you a personal question?" Rank 3 decided he needed to take a risk.

"Hmm?" Rank 1001 thought intensely, he needed to decide if revealing more information about himself would be 'safe' to do so. He thought for five minutes in silence while rank 3 waited and continued eating. "As long as I get to ask you one and it can't be too personal."

"That seems fair, I haven't really told you anything about me other than the fact that I definitely want to be your friend. Do you want to ask your question first?"

"Actually can I ask two?" Rank 1001 spoke nervously; he didn't want to scare rank 3 or cause rank 3 to want to hurt him.

"How about this, you can ask me as many as you want and I'll answer all of them, and I can ask you as many as I want but if you don't want to answer you don't have to?"

"OK. Why are you doing all of this? What does me

being your friend mean to you? And how did you recover so fast from your first fight?" Rank 1001 asked his questions in quick succession stopping rank 3 from interrupting him to answer.

"Oh I was expecting the first two but not the last one, so I'll start with that but it's one of my secrets so please don't tell anyone else. I have the rare ability to regenerate unaided. I'm roughly level 3 and I can go close to level 4 if I focus. Was that the answer you thought you would hear? I hope you're not scared by it; I've heard all the rumours about regenerators, lots of people believe it makes me insane. Haha, I'm not though." Rank 3 paused to try to gauge rank 1001's response.

Rank 1001 didn't respond to rank 3 so rank 3 continued with answering the other questions. "Regarding the other two questions, the answers are quite simple, I simply desire your friendship and I'll take it in any form it comes in. I can't let myself stand by while a person gets singled out for no reason. I don't think anyone should live a life alone."

"So you want to be my friend because you pity me?" rank 1001 asked hesitantly.

"No not pity, I think I can empathise with you, not entirely but I know how it feels to be alone trapped by those around you. Alone even though there are people everywhere you look. I think I understand."

"To be honest, I don't like being around people."

"You invited me to your home though because you

feel lonely, right?"

"It's more accurate to say I wanted to meet you. I want to be near you. You interest me. It feels nice when I'm near you." Rank 1001 responded as accurately as he could, saying everything as it came to mind.

Even though rank 1001 didn't say he desired rank 3 in any clear tone, rank 1001's angelic voice couldn't help make rank 3's heart skip a beat.

"Empathy is complicated. I'm not sure how I feel about any of the others. You are different. You are interesting and I find you fascinating," rank 1001 said, causing rank 3's heart to skip another beat.

Rank 3 didn't say anything to respond, he was caught off guard by rank 1001's non-confession but something that sounded like a confession. Rank 3 realised that in this moment his interest in rank 1001 was increasing in a way he wasn't expecting.

'Is he saying I'm special?' This single thought shook rank 3's mind.

"Did you leave?" rank 1001 asked sadly as he waved his arms around searching. Rank 3 hadn't responded and rank 1001 feared rank 3 had run away.

"I'm still here," rank 3 said while grabbing rank 1001's hand. "Can I ask you my question now?"

"Yes, I'll try to answer it if I can." Rank 1001 was starting to let rank 3 in, but was still not ready to reveal any information that he deemed too personal.

"Why do you hide behind that mask? I can sense your internal energy isn't disrupted. I don't think you're blind. Are you really scarred or that ashamed of your appearance? Even when you have the voice of an angel? Why would you hide? Will you help me understand? You like me, right?" Rank 3 panicked and his mind struggled with every word. Still, if he could help rank 1001, then he would do whatever necessary even if that meant asking uncomfortable questions.

"It's getting late, you should be getting ready to leave." Rank 1001 spoke distantly.

"Oh you're right, it is late, I should be getting back now." Rank 3 swallowed his desires and resolved himself to be patient.

Rank 3 stood up from the table and was now able to admire what he had done. He had easily eaten over half the dishes. He was so caught up in his conversations with rank 1001 he hadn't realised he had been eating the entire time.

"I can find my own way out if you don't want to say goodbye to me. I'm sorry if I overstepped, but if possible, I would like for us to…"

"Let's meet again in two days at the same time," rank 1001 interrupted.

"You're happy to see me again?" Rank 3 was happy and surprised in equal measure.

"Of course I am, we're friends now." Rank 1001's angelic voice and soft tone made rank 3 feel a warm feeling in his chest that he hadn't felt for a long time.

Rank 1001 led rank 3 out of his house and said goodbye as rank 3 waved to him as he left walking in the direction of the academy. Rank 1001 closed the door and took a couple of steps down the slope. He ripped off his mask and continued down the corridor.

"Babe, did you get all that? Let's go over it before I get settled, and run my bath please, I need to catch on my sleep. Although for the first time I might not be afraid to dream, not if rank 3 is in it. Something interesting seems to be happening to me."

Chapter Thirteen
The combat teacher and the red vine

Rank 3 had arrived home, with a happy smile on his face and a sense of accomplishment along with an odd feeling of being content. The evening had gone far better than he could have hoped for. Rank 1001 had accepted him, and even feelings that rank 3 didn't know he had, had started to surface.

Rank 3 fell asleep almost immediately and fell into a deep sleep. In it he didn't dream of anything fantastical or nightmarish. Normally he dreamt of the happy times when his mother was alive, his mother still being alive or the rough times of his past exaggerated or not.

Rank 3 woke up feeling as if only a moment had passed. He felt completely relaxed and refreshed. He got washed and dressed and happily travelled to the first class of the day. The only downside was that he would have to wait until tomorrow to see rank 1001 again.

The class got settled in and rank 3 realised that rank 21 had more colour in his face than the last few days. "Are you feeling better, rank 21?" Rank 3 asked, hoping that was the case.

"Yes I am. I realised I got caught by the shock of

what I saw in the arena, but my sister came back and she explained everything to me. I'll let her tell you after class, she is our combat teacher after all."

"I'm glad you are feeling better, I'm excited to meet your sister, is she like you?"

"I'll let you decide that for yourself." Rank 21 smiled as he answered.

The academic teacher walked in with an angry expression on his face. He was very obviously irritated by something.

"All right, you brats, better shut up and pay attention. What I'm about to tell you is very important so leave all your questions until I'm finished, is that clear?" The teacher spoke with authority and an intense aura of fear.

All the students including rank 3 nodded.

"Good. Now I'll begin."

"Crash!" When the academic teacher was about to start speaking, rank 1001 stumbled in and crashed into an empty desk and a chair.

"I'm not in the mood for you today," the academic teacher said violently and raised his arm.

"Rank 1001 watch out!" Rank 3 shouted as the academic teacher moved to strike rank 1001.

"Eh? What's this?" The academic teacher for the first time in many years was surprised.

"That was close," rank 3 said relieved, he had made it in time.

Wrapped around the academics teacher's arm was

rank 3's energy in the form of red vines restricting the teacher's movement.

Rank 1001 completely ignored the teacher and sat down. As usual, he pulled his screen out of his bag and began rejecting match requests.

The academic teacher looked even more agitated than before. Rank 3 stood up to show his protest of the teacher's previous action. Rank 3 released the teacher's arm, and the teacher looked directly at him.

"Urgh." The academic teacher grunted a noise of frustration and disgust. He was already stressed enough as it was. "Fine, I'll ignore rank 1001 for now, sit down and I'll continue what I was saying. Another outburst like that and I won't hold back no matter which student it is." The teacher looked directly at rank 3.

Rank 3 sat down in his seat and using the part of his ability that let him sense others' energy and especially their internal energy, he checked to see if rank 1001 was hurt. There was no strain or interruptions in his energy so rank 3 was confident that rank 1001 was unharmed.

"This is an announcement about the events that took place the day of the arena match. The match was supposed to be between our academy and academy 2. This was not the case."

The students murmured in confusion. What other possibility was there?

"Yes, it's come as a big shock to us as well. The academy was completely unaware. The unidentified masked person is now designated as an outside intruder.

The intruder through means we are unsure about entered the academy and even convinced our staff they were from academy 2. They even made a sudden change in the match rules, with all twenty of our participants competing each allowed one tool."

"Teacher, I don't understand, surely academy 2 should have still arrived?" rank 21 asked because what the teacher said was completely unheard of.

"Yes that should have been the case, but it is precisely because they didn't we weren't able to detect the intruder's presence in time. It has become apparent that the intruder first defeated the academy 2 team, their ten main, ten reserves and the teachers accompanying them. I shouldn't need to express this explicitly. The intruder was definitely someone a student would have no chance to defeat. Rank 3?"

"Yes, teacher?"

"You should consider yourself lucky, you and the other top twenty it seems weren't fated to die, but you would have had no means to oppose it if that was the intruder's intention. Do you understand?" The teacher's tone was deadly serious.

"I understand," rank 3 said weakly. His confidence had taken a big hit.

"Good, all of you should know and understand your limits and being able to tell the difference between you and others is an essential skill, a skill that I will help you learn."

"Sir, isn't that a combat skill?" rank 21 again asked.

His sister had been the one to teach him those skills.

"Yes, it is. Until further notice we will be studying combat skills and data analysis. All of you, well you ten by the time we're finished will all have a better sense of danger. Any questions before we begin?"

"What about rank 1001?" rank 3 asked, concerned about how rank 1001 would learn skills to keep himself safe.

"Rank 1001 has the luxury of being in this classroom, but I won't put myself out by teaching him. I haven't earned that punishment yet."

"Then is the academy taking extra steps to improve the safety of all the students?" If the teachers wouldn't teach rank 1001, then rank 3 believed they should at least promise to keep him safe from outsiders.

"That information is not being given to students, the students should trust the teachers and other staff. That's all I can say about that. Now everyone get your screens out, I'll then direct you to archived matches and other sources that we will be using."

Throughout the lesson, the students were made to watch past matches and other combat scenarios, all with the intention of analysing the participants. The greatest analytical skill is to know who will win before a match ends and an even greater skill, the ultimate skill, would be to know before a match starts.

"All right that's a good intro, keep practising outside of class, you're all dismissed." The teacher looked stressed and was already tired of this change in pace.

"Come on then, rank 3, let's go meet my sister."

"OK," rank 3 replied happily.

Rank 3 and rank 21 left the academic building and walked past the arena. They noticed it was all sealed off, not just by academic staff but noticeably by state staff as well. They stopped to see if they could notice anything themselves. It was a very intriguing site when rank 3 felt something bump into him.

"Huh?" Rank 3 turned around to see what had happened and this time he moved carefully to avoid the previous incident. "Rank 1001, why are you here?" rank 3 said, shocked. He had never seen rank 1001 outside of the classroom apart from at rank 1001's home.

Rank 1001 reached into his pocket and pulled out a piece of paper with something written on it. It read, *Have to attend every day and stay until all classes finish until it is decided otherwise.*

"Oh, OK. Come with me." Rank 3 spoke to rank 1001 but was unsure if he could actually hear him. Rank 3 grabbed rank 1001's hand and proceeded to walk with rank 21 to their combat classroom.

"What are you doing?" rank 21 asked, agitated.

"Rank 1001 says he has to attend all classes so I'm taking him with us, it's not like he wants to or is going to participate. Besides, I wouldn't trust anyone else to look after him," rank 3 said, making it obvious that he wouldn't tolerate rank 21's protests.

"I don't see the point in arguing with you, as long

as he doesn't get in the way of our training then I won't care."

"Thank you, that's very kind of you."

"Hmph. You might be having a strange effect on me."

Rank 21, rank 3 and rank 1001 all made their way to the combat classroom. As rank 1001 was with rank 3 no other students harassed him for being in the combat teaching building.

The three entered the classroom and waiting in there for them was someone who looked like they were definitely related to rank 21. She was much older but their faces were very similar and rank 3 could notice all the similarities immediately. It was the way she moved that was different to rank 21. Every step she took towards them looked like she was walking on air, elegantly gliding across an invisible cloud.

"Hello, students. Little brother, is this the friend you told me about?" Her voice was soft and calm, it felt like she wasn't speaking and the air itself formed the words and sounds for her.

"Yes, this is rank 3, he fought the intruder." Rank 21 spoke proudly as he was showing off his friend to his sister.

"It's nice to finally meet you. I heard about what had happened before with the other top twenty. It's good they didn't break your spirit. What about the one holding his hand, who is this?" The teacher was wary of and interested in this unknown third person. She couldn't help think that she had heard of someone wearing a mask.

"Teacher, this is rank 1001. I'm looking after him while combat classes take place, please allow him to wait at the side." Rank 3 spoke politely but he wasn't going to accept no as an answer.

"Rank 1001? I've heard about him, and not just through my dear younger brother. Fine, I'll let him stay, I wouldn't feel good if he got hurt outside in the corridor. Nor will I teach anything to a weak student, so just shove him in the corner until the end." With her memory jogged, she knew exactly how she would deal with rank 1001's presence.

Rank 3, leading by the hand, led rank 1001 to the corner of the room and sat him down. Rank 1001 didn't put up any resistance and rank 3 manoeuvred him easily. However, as rank 3 went to leave rank 1001 refused to let go of his hand, gently but firmly gripping to not let their hands separate.

"What's taking so long?" rank 21 asked, impatiently.

"Nod if you can hear me," rank 3 said to rank 1001.

Rank 1001 didn't reply.

Having failed the first attempt, rank 3 moved his lips next to where he sensed rank 1001's ear to be and spoke into it. "Nod if you can hear me."

Rank 1001 gave a slight nod but also trembled slightly.

"Oh sorry, it's me, rank 3. I should have started

with that, haha. I need you to let go of my hand but I won't ask for something for free."

Rank 3 lifted up rank 1001's other hand and wrapped it delicately in his red vine like energy and wrapped it around his own wrist. "Just pull on this and I'll immediately come and check on you. Nod if you understand."

Rank 1001 nodded and let go of rank 3's hand. Now feeling settled rank 1001 retrieved his screen, put in the ear piece and did what he always did: declined match requests.

Rank 21 watched the whole bizarre scenario with confusion and started to feel disgust. The teacher however had a different expression. "Have you finished tending to rank 1001?"

"Yes, sorry about that, I want him to feel comfortable."

"That's fine. You know having pity and applying kindness is rare, every other student no doubt turned pity into disgust. I've heard many stories from my brother about rank 1001, but I won't make any judgements about a student that aren't combat related. I am first and foremost a combat teacher, my only concern is that the concentration to maintain that red thread will impair your combat skills." The teacher was oddly indifferent about rank 1001.

"Thank you for having me as a student, as long as you do not judge rank 1001, I'm sure we will get along." Rank 3 was pleased to find out the teacher didn't wish harm on rank 1001.

"Rank 3, don't be rude, just because you treat rank 1001 special doesn't mean you can get angry in his place." Rank 21 was angered by rank 3's attitude towards his older sister.

"Relax, little brother, I'm sure rank 3 wouldn't go too far. Besides wouldn't you be happy if he said something like that about you?"

"That's not important." Rank 21 quickly dismissed that line of questioning.

"Good, now that is out of the way, let me explain what we're going to be doing. I've heard that you know the basics of hand-to-hand combat and I've seen that you have a good handle on your ability. We'll continue developing those skills, along with finding out what tools you're compatible with. Just to give you a brief example, purely outfit wise, me and my little brother benefit from light clothing, with low wind resistance. That's just a brief outline on outfits, there are many other tools used out on the battlefield. Combat in the academy and outside of it are the same as night and day. You've probably already been warned that you couldn't beat the intruder. That's one of the factors why. Any questions?"

"Why doesn't every student go through this training?"

"Little brother asked the same thing. It's quite simple, nearly all of those who reach the top fifty survive their military service. On average ninety percent of the top ten survive and eighty percent of the rest survive, as they are the main representatives of the academy. Their families also don't advocate the use of tools. They are far too proud in their abilities, so the weaker ranks are made to suffer."

"Why don't you try to train more students?" Rank 3 still thought that some students would accept this type of training.

"I plan to, but before I can get the attention of students and their families, I am going to make little brother my main representative. I've been training him with tools for a few years now."

"Wow, rank 21, you do have something you believe in. I'm glad I thought you didn't care, but you must care about weaker people if you want the mass introduction of tools. You're definitely the nice person I thought you were."

"I care about surviving military service, anything that increases my chances is all that matters to me." Rank 21 made it clear that he was acting selfishly even though rank 3 didn't believe him.

"That's good enough for me, little brother. Now we don't have any budget for the purchase of tools, but through our family you can get a custom-made item from the crafting company. Think of it as free credit, a gift from a high family to you. Our family has a good relationship with the crafting company so why shouldn't we let you take advantage of it."

"Crafting company?" Rank 3 had never heard of

the main companies.

"Don't worry too much about that yet. Let's begin today's lesson. I want to gauge your combat abilities and get a proper feel for your ability."

"OK, what do I need to do?" Rank 3 was excited but also nervous to make a good first impression.

"Just attack me however you like, don't worry I'm much stronger than you."

"OK, but please be careful." Rank 3 worried that he could hurt someone who was not fully paying attention.

"I'll tell you what, if you can land a solid hit on me anywhere you win, and if I can make your thread dissipate you lose."

"What happens if I win or lose?" Rank 3 glanced at rank 1001 as he asked this question.

"You'll find out when that happens, now attack me before I attack you."

"Yes, Teacher." Rank 3 was eager to experience a combat lesson from an expert.

Rank 3 got into a ready stance, allowing him to move at a moment's notice. He tried carefully to read his opponent but found that the surrounding air distorted her figure. Even the atmosphere in the entire room became heavy and felt thick. Without hesitation rank 3 lashed at the teacher with his energy in the form of a whip. He targeted where he could see her but the whip passed straight through.

The teacher had dodged effortlessly. By manipulating the air around her she moved with incredible ease. She flicked her wrist at rank 3, and he felt a sharp pain like a blade slicing into his flesh.

"Ow!" Rank 3 was shocked by the pain. He now had a cut on his side.

"Looks like you're not trying hard enough," the teacher said happily. It was as if she was enjoying seeing rank 3 in pain.

"Focus on where the energy is being emitted from and strike there, the surrounding energy I'll just have to ignore for now." Rank 3 tried quickly to come up with a plan.

Rank 3 took a deep breath and focused. He had to focus completely on the teacher's energy emissions and her internal energy, and also on the red vine that he was keeping intact to keep rank 1001 calm.

Looking after someone who was constantly being targeted by others was the most important task rank 3 was performing right now. Rank 3 had decided that no matter what happened, he would not let the connection between him and rank 1001 break. Rank 1001 being able to feel safe was a constant priority for rank 3.

Rank 3 kept his position and targeted the internal energy of the teacher. He lunged his whip in her direction and to his and the teacher's surprise rank 3 landed a solid hit. However, the teacher was completely unharmed, the whip was too weak to break through the teacher's defences.

"Hit me properly if you can. You hit the intruder with a much more powerful attack, didn't you?" The teacher planned to push rank 3 to his limit.

Hesitantly rank 3 focused and condensed his unique energy into the shape of a ball in his hand. It emanated and shone brightly with red energy. It was much more powerful than the whip but it was slower and harder to maintain. It wasn't an attack he could replicate with ease during a single combat.

"Your energy is really something, I can't get a feel for it, it must really be unique. I've fought many opponents in my life, many of which could create and manipulate various types of energy and matter but none like yours. Let's see what you can do." The teacher was starting to get excited by rank 3's unique ability.

While the teacher talked, rank 3's ball of energy had gotten slightly weaker.

"Why did you let me talk? Stop being polite and attack me already!"

"Ah! Sorry. Ouch!" Rank 3 apologised for his hesitation and when he did, he felt another cut to his side.

Rank 3 immediately responded by firing his ball of energy at his opponent. It was slow and the teacher easily avoided it. She thought that she had easily beaten rank 3's strongest attack. Now this fight would end after her next attack.

"Behind you!" Rank 21 shouted.

The teacher turned around and the ball of energy travelled towards her, she dodged again but it persisted tracking her every movement.

"Wow, this is really something, I've never seen energy that can be controlled like this before."

"It is connected to you and will follow you as long as I maintain my focus, I'm confident I can make two at a time but only one right now."

"Tch! To think you would dare go easy on a teacher."

The teacher wanted to target rank 1001 to punish this behaviour but feared that she would kill him, so instead in a rage she launched multiple blades of wind at rank 3.

Rank 3 quickly realised he wouldn't be able to dodge in time. He had been too focused on controlling his energy that he had forgotten to be prepared to move.

"You've beaten me," Rank 3 said humbly. He knew he couldn't even land a solid hit on his teacher.

Expecting the blades of wind to vanish, rank 3 relaxed, that was until one buried itself deep into his side. The rest were about to strike until he suddenly found himself pulled across to other side of the room.

"Hmm?" The teacher was surprised by what had happened but was not shaken by it.

"What did you do?" Rank 21 shouted angrily at rank 1001.

Rank 1001 had used the red vine to abduct rank 3 and make it so that the air blades buried themselves into the wall instead. Seeing the damage to the wall rank 21 was confident that rank 3 would have needed urgent care.

"My bad," the teacher said almost playfully.

"I'm not talking to you, I'm talking to that thing." Rank 21 was incredibly annoyed despite the fact that rank 3 had been saved a trip to the infirmary.

"Calm down, little brother, thanks to that action I avoided paperwork." The combat teacher shrugged off this incident. She was powerful but could be carefree when it came to students' welfare.

"I'm not impressed," rank 21 said grumpily. He knew he wouldn't win an argument with his older sister.

"Urgh." Rank 3 groaned in pain; the bleeding had already stopped but it was a very deep cut.

The teacher walked over to him and stopped several steps away. "Are you all right?"

"I'll be fine." Rank 3 wasn't in a serious condition but from his tone you could tell he was in a lot of pain.

"I'm sure you will. Do you know where you went wrong and surprisingly I wouldn't blame you focusing on the vine?"

"I only focused on attacking and not defending," rank 3 said while struggling to suppress groans from the pain.

"I did both. At all times you should be prepared to defend, you can't only attack. No matter what always be ready."

"I will remember, thank you for the lesson."

Rank 3 slowly tried to stand up when he realised he was placed firmly in rank 1001's lap. He tried to get up but each time he did rank 1001 prevented any

158

movement. Surprisingly rank 1001 reached into his uniform and pulled out a chunk of bandages along with stitches.

Rank 1001 ran his hand along rank 3's torso, sides and stomach but was unable to locate the wound due his gloves and lack of sense of touch. Annoyed he grabbed a small screen from his bag and furiously typed into it and then started waving it around waiting for rank 3 to read it.

Rank 3 struggled against rank 1001's other arm and hand that was keeping him in place. Spotting the screen he pulled rank 1001's hand closer towards him. Reading it, it said, *If injured please treat now, even if regenerating blood will still spill.*

Oh? He's worried I'll lose too much blood before I heal, I guess that makes sense. That's kind of him, but I'll be fine.

Rank 3 grabbed the first aid equipment and rank 1001 released him from his grasp. Rank 3 stood up from rank 1001's lap. He didn't use the first aid equipment but kept it on him so that rank 1001 would assume he had used it. He put it in his pocket to conceal it.

"Are you two finished?" the teacher asked impatiently. She had turned around before because she was unsure whether she should be witnessing something like that. Turning back around when she heard rank 3 move, she questioned him on the matter. "So are you going to explain?" The teacher spoke as if she was accusing rank 3 of wrongdoing.

"Explain what?" rank 3 responded nervously.

"How rank 1001 was able to pull you to safety just in time."

"It was probably luck. He pulled me away because I most likely tugged on the vine when you cut me. Rank 1001 probably assumed, rightly, that I needed help." Rank 3 wasn't going to let any accusations be placed on rank 1001.

"Fine, I'll ignore it for now, it's not too important right now. We'll end the class here for today, I'll continue to train you though. Little brother, you're still energetic, right?"

"Hmph!" Rank 21 turned his head in frustration.

"Thank you for today, we'll see you tomorrow."

Rank 3 picked up rank 1001 by grabbing his hands and placed him next to himself. Then leading rank 1001 by the hand they left the classroom. Rank 3 lent closer to rank 1001 so his lips were near rank 1001's ear.

"I'm sorry if you got scared back there. There is still time before lessons properly finish, is there anything you want to do. How many requests do you have left to decline?"

Rank 1001 pulled out his small screen and started typing on it, rank 3 read it as he typed.

"I'm glad you're not too badly hurt. I can probably leave now. Do you want to come with me?"

"Oh I do. But, I really should do some studying after everything that's happened. I need to get myself organised. Can we arrange another day to meet, tomorrow maybe?"

"That's fine, do you need anything? I can get you anything that you're missing."

"I'm fine thank you, besides teacher said that she can get me what I need."

"Oh OK, I understand. See you tomorrow."

Rank 3 surprised himself, he acted as if by driven a natural instinct. He hugged rank 1001 to say goodbye. Rank 3 did it so quickly that at first he didn't realise what he had done. Regardless, he felt the same warmth as before.

"Goodbye, I'll see you tomorrow. Be careful." Rank 3 said goodbye but also made sure that rank 1001 knew that he was worried about him.

Rank 1001 nodded in agreement. Unknown to rank 3, rank 1001 was smiling and blushing under his mask and bandages. They had both felt a warm refreshing wave wash over them.

Chapter Fourteen
Caring about those close to you

Rank 3 spent the whole of yesterday afternoon and evening, watching combat footage and attempting to improve his analytical skills. While doing so, he also went over what had happened in the training earlier that day. Every so often he found himself distracted, a side effect of his increasing interest in rank 1001.

Rank 3 attended the academic class as usual, and like the day before the students continued to study combat footage with prompts from the academic teacher. Rank 1001 sat silently rejecting match requests and surprisingly they had decreased. It was only slight; a couple less than normal, but that in itself was very substantial. It held great meaning in the sense that some students were possibly making their own decisions on this matter.

The class went without incident and afterwards rank 21, rank 3 and like yesterday rank 1001, forced by the senior staff, attended their combat class. Rank 3 was excited to see what would take place today. He was eager to keep learning and grow stronger.

They entered the classroom and the combat teacher was already waiting for them. Today she was wearing a completely different outfit. It was loose and light; it moved easily in the wind, not only did she wear this outfit, in her hand was a small thin object, its purpose was unknown.

Rank 3 guided rank 1001 to the corner of the room leading him by his hand. He whispered the same words as yesterday and wrapped his energy in the form of a vine around rank 1001's hand. With rank 1001 feeling content and safe, rank 3 greeted his combat teacher.

"Hello, teacher, thank you for yesterday and I hope today will be just as informative." Rank 3 was happy and eager to learn more today.

"I learned some interesting things yesterday as well. From today I'll teach you in two steps, firstly you'll spar with rank 21, but you can't use your ability to attack, only to defend. I want you to increase your mobility and the second step, you'll have another match with me only this time I'll let you use a tool of your choice. Begin when you are ready."

Before rank 3 could respond to the teacher's command, rank 21 punched him in the side of his face and he fell to one knee.

"You can be really hopeless sometimes," rank 21 said goading rank 3 to make a false move.

Rank 3 responding by releasing his energy in the form of spikes sprouting from his body.

"Just how many shapes can you make with that energy? That energy really is ridiculous," the teacher commented; rank 3 didn't seem to have a limit with what he could do with his energy.

Rank 21 gracefully avoided all the spikes and used a similar attack to his sister. He launched blades of wind at rank 3. They were weaker and slower but could still cause significant damage.

Rank 3 did his best to avoid the attacks. The blades that collided with his energy caused both to vanish. After the attack finished rank 3 was left with minor cuts to his sides.

"Nicely done," the combat teacher said, praising both.

Rank 21 lunged towards rank 3. This time he wrapped air around his arms in the form of spirals and directed it to a point and the end of his hands. Rank 3 braced himself, but he was hesitant though as he still couldn't make a quick decision whether to defend or dodge.

As rank 21 moved close to rank 3, he was caught mid rush and held up in the air by his older sister. "Let's stop there for now. I've seen enough."

"But why, neither of us has received a proper blow yet?" rank 21 complained in protest.

"Little brother, stop your complaining. You haven't forgotten what it was like when you started my training, have you?" The combat scolded rank 21.

"No," rank 21 said weakly. The early years of his training were extremely tough and not something to be remembered fondly.

"Good, now sit down and do ability strengthening

and focus training."

"OK." Rank 21 grumbled and moved away from the others.

"Now you."

"Yes, teacher!" rank 3 responded quickly. He was slowly becoming aware of how dangerous this teacher was.

"I've been too gentle with you; I was too interested in your ability that I skipped the basics. It's obvious to me that you can't make quick decisive decisions while in combat. So for your next lesson, I'm going to continuously attack you with blades of wind; they will vary in strength some will not be able to hurt you and some will almost kill you. What I want you to do, is to avoid the ones that will hurt you and block the ones that won't. You will learn to choose between dodging or defending. If you focus too much on one you'll lose. Now go stand other there."

"Yes, teacher," rank 3 said hesitantly. He was nervous, the only time he had felt like this before he was reassured by rank 300. This time he was on his own.

As soon as rank 3 took his position he narrowly avoided a blade of wind. He was fortunate he moved in time because the blade sliced into the wall behind him.

This lesson was going to be a long and quite possibly a very painful one.

"Huff, huff, huff." Rank 3 was breathing heavily, his body was all cut up and his blood had been spilled all other the floor.

"You look better than I thought you would." The teacher gave some praise that to rank 3 sounded very empty.

"You lied. 'Cough'." Rank 3 felt like his body had been torn apart, the main reason, not a single blade could be blocked with his current combat abilities.

"Yes I did. But you still attempted to defend, you were convinced that some blades must be weak enough to block. You should have dodged all of them. I know I said don't only use one or the other, but that was a white lie."

"I don't understand, what is the lesson here?" Rank 3 spoke while trying to bear the pain of injuries.

"If you can't block, dodge and if you can't dodge, block and if you're against an opponent who is too strong for you, you'll fail to do both and lose either way. If you think you can't win, you're probably right."

"I don't understand, is the lesson to accept defeat?" Rank 3 was trying to make sense of the pain.

"Yes and no, yes because you need to understand that very few people stand at the top of the world with ability alone. And no, because with my philosophy you can bridge the gap between you and those who are above you."

"How?"

"Haven't you been listening to what I've been saying, you'll bridge the gap using tools."

"Are they really that important? Are you saying a tool could let me beat you?" A ray of hope flashed before rank 3's eyes.

"Not necessarily, you might not be able to completely bridge the gap between you and me, but it can give you a chance."

"That would be much more than I have now. But I'm still not sure how? What tool could do that?"

"I have two main weaknesses, learn and understand them, little brother shares them too. I'm not very durable and I'm limited by my eyesight. In short, if you land a hit through my defences or go around my defences I'll be injured easily, and two I don't have any extra sensory abilities. I can detect changes in the air, but not enough to solely rely on it. I need my eyes to fight. Your weaknesses are your hesitation and you still need lots of physical training but I'm confident your physical limit is far higher than mine, so you can turn your body into a strength. Your last weakness is you're too kind, but that is not up to me to help you with. Your energy is already your greatest strength, keep training it and improving your control. Now have you understood what I just told you?" The teacher was staring directly into rank 3's eyes.

"Yes, I think so, teacher."

"Good, now I'll leave it up to you to come up with an idea for a tool or tools to give you a fighting chance against me. Of course that will mean that you should be able to beat my little brother in a fight where only you use a tool."

"I'll think carefully about it."

"Tell me tomorrow and I'll order it for you."

"Tomorrow?" rank 3 responded, surprised. That didn't give him much time at all.

"Yes, you'll have to think carefully and fast. Custom items from the crafting company can take a long time to be delivered. All right that's enough for one day, go and clean yourself up, and if you need to, don't hesitate to go to the medical centre."

"Yes, thank you for the lesson."

Rank 3 bowed to his teacher and then walked over to rank 1001. Rank 21 was sitting down in the opposite side of the room. His eyes were closed and the surrounding air was swirling in circles.

Rank 3 limped over to rank 1001 and bent down. He pushed his lips to the side of rank 1001's head and said, "Hey, it's me. I'm finished with the lesson now so we can leave."

Rank 1001 nodded and with the help of rank 3 he stood up. Rank 1001 noticed the difference instantly; rank 3 was acting sluggish and his body wasn't moving in its usual way. The movements weren't obvious, but rank 1001 could tell there was a difference.

Rank 1001 waved his hands around searching for rank 3. He waved his hand directly into rank 3 locating him but it also caused rank 3 to step back in pain. Rank 3 quickly pulled rank 1001 close to him and placed rank 1001's head close to his. "Please be careful, I'm a bit injured at the moment."

Hearing these words, rank 1001 trembled and jolted

two steps backwards, surprising rank 3. What was even more surprising to rank 3 and even the combat teacher was that rank 1001, trembling, was grasping at his mask. He was grasping the part that was covering his eyes. It looked as if he was about to rip it off but at the same time, it was as if his body refused to act that way.

Rank 1001 was experiencing an unknown sense of discomfort. He didn't care too much about the lives of others, that being said he knew plenty about how others live. What he didn't know much about was rank 3, despite the fact that rank 3 had become a person that he was interested in and cared about. Hearing him say he was injured only ignited a passion, a sense of unavoidable concern.

Rank 3 had thought he was onto something when he accused rank 1001 of not being blind. Rank 3 had blurted it out accidently but it was always a prominent thought in his mind. Rank 1001 was stuck in place, both hands shaking as they grasped his mask. For the first time, rank 3 was able to act decisively. Rank 3 rushed rank 1001, picking him up and lifting him over his shoulder. Rank 3 knew he would be too embarrassed to carry rank 1001 the same way he had carried him before.

"We're leaving now, goodbye, teacher."

"Er... yes, goodbye."

Rank 3 exited the combat building as quickly as he could while carrying rank 1001. There were a few other students around but due to rank 3 being rank 3 all they

169

could do was observe and judge from afar.

Rank 3 was continuing to make snap judgements. Instead of the closest most obvious choice, his dorm room, he instead made the decision to take rank 1001 back to rank 1001's home. Rank 3 wrapped rank 1001 up in his energy producing a gentle but firm energy blanket.

Rank 3 then quickly left the academy not stopping for anyone and made his way to rank 1001's home.

It was a journey that normally took around an hour to make, and that was only if you knew the most direct route. Today rank 3 had made the journey in under twenty minutes. Rank 3 had pushed the limit of his regenerative abilities to ensure that he could keep going. He was now very tired but knew that he wouldn't have made any other choice, he couldn't have made any other choice, his instincts wouldn't have let him.

Rank 3 raised up rank 1001 into the air. Rank 3 retracted his energy releasing rank 1001 from his blanket of energy and surprisingly rank 1001 had fallen asleep. Even with the fast and bumpy movements of rank 3, rank 1001 had been able to sleep comfortably throughout their journey.

Rank 3 placed rank 1001 in his arms, in the embarrassing pose as the one used by rank 1001 to carry rank 3. Rank 3 cradling rank 1001, pressed the button on the door. The camera above scanned meticulously the two people waiting outside and after careful observation it was satisfied with their identities and the door opened.

Rank 3 walked in and remembered that rank 1001 had described the first room on the left as a guest room with a bed in it. Rank 3 felt it would be too rude for him to go down to the lower level and into rank 1001's bedroom.

Rank 3 opened the door on the left and revealed the guest room. Rank 3 paused for a moment when he saw it, it was a scene that was hard to take in with one glance. After a few seconds of gawking, rank 3 made his way across the room and placed rank 1001 down on the bed.

The bed was incredibly soft. It was large enough for more than three people, and it had a large wooden frame filled with many intricate and delicate carvings. Everything in this room looked like it was made to the highest quality; all the materials used were rare and beautiful and all of the items' designs gave the impression they were made by an expert. How many experts it took was a mystery, but it truly was a room that rank 3 definitely thought he wasn't worthy of.

Rank 1001 rolled onto his side and slowly opened his eyes. When he did all he could see was pitch black; this wasn't right. When he woke up, it was to a different sight; the sight was always the same, the ceiling of his bedroom and the object placed there.

Disoriented rank 1001 grabbed his mask and gripped the bandages underneath and as he was about to rip it off, he felt a sensation. Rank 3 had pulled rank 1001 towards him and once again put his lips close to the side of rank 1001's head. "Calm down, you fell asleep. It's me rank 3, I brought you home after you panicked at the academy."

'What happened at the academy again?' Rank 1001 thought quickly to himself and panicked.

"Thud!"

"Ouch." Rank 3 was pushed into the floor by rank 1001.

He looked in front of him and saw countless ripped up pieces of mask and bandages. Rank 3 caught some in his hands. Without looking up he asked, "What are these?"

"Are you hurt? Did she hurt you?" rank 1001 asked in an accusatory tone.

"She? She, who?" rank 3 asked as he looked up. What rank 1001 had done made him pause; rank 1001 had ripped multiple holes in his mask and bandages. Right now his eyes, ears and mouth were all uncovered, he covered his mouth with his hand but all the others were clear to see.

"The one who calls herself a combat teacher!"

"Oh, teacher only taught me things I didn't know, but I needed to and now I do. I just happened to get injured. If I didn't get injured, I wouldn't have learned. You don't need to worry about me, I regenerate remember."

"Hmm. You don't look too injured but shouldn't you have healed completely by now? If you regenerate, a few cuts no matter how deep shouldn't take long to heal."

"I'm only a low level right now, so it will still take an hour or two. There are only a few people with regenerative abilities but that doesn't mean that the ability is all powerful."

"It seems that that is the way it is. You should learn to be more careful. I don't like being forced to feel powerless." Rank 1001's honest angelic voice was invigorating for rank 3.

"I'm sorry for making you feel that way, but I do feel glad even if that's selfish. Can I ask you a question?"

"Yes, of course, we agreed we can ask each other as many questions as we want," rank 1001 responded, his tone indicating that he thought rank 3 had asked a pointless question.

"You were going to rip your mask to check on me in the academy. What stopped you?"

"That's simple, you stopped me, I was going to give in as you grabbed me. You are the reason, lately you are always the reason," rank 1001 said honestly, his words a complete truth without any secrets.

"Why do you keep your eyes hidden? They look like everyone else's, and you can see. I mean they are golden but it's good being different." Rank 3 was almost bewitched by rank 1001's golden eyes.

"You're good different. I'll only reveal them to you."

Rank 3's heart skipped a beat but he wouldn't get

distracted. This was important.

"Why though? Why don't you want to see what surrounds you?" Rank 3 struggled to understand why rank 1001 would isolate himself from the world.

"I want to see you, and I see everything in my house, is that not enough?" Rank 1001 spoke while he started to pout.

"When you say it like that, then it's more than enough," rank 3 said embarrassed. Once again rank 1001's angelic voice reached into his soul. Rank 3 couldn't resist when rank 1001 complimented him using his angelic voice.

"That's good. Do you want to stay here for a while?" Rank 1001 was hopeful that rank 3 would want to spend time with him.

Rank 3 thought about it carefully. He wanted to stay, but he also needed to think about how he would progress in his training. If he wanted to be strong and be able to protect what he deemed precious, then he would need to be focused.

"I'll stay for a bit." Rank 3 couldn't refuse his desire to spend more time with rank 1001.

"I've got something for you and I'm working on another one. Do you want to see it? Also if you're willing can I ask you to do something?" Rank 1001 became unusually excited.

"You were making something for me? You don't need to do that." Rank 3 felt uncomfortable receiving gifts without giving something in return.

"So you don't want it, you don't even know what it is yet? It's not as bad as you think it is." Rank 1001 was forced to defend his crafting pride.

"No, I'll accept any gift from you, I just feel bad I haven't got anything for you."

Rank 1001 took off his glove and placed his bare hand on rank 3's cheek, rank 3 couldn't help but tilt his head into this warm connection. After a few seconds it looked like rank 1001 had come to a conclusion. "You really are fascinating. Just being genuine in caring for me is enough."

"I don't really know how I feel about you yet, I'm getting confused." Rank 3's mind was flooded with all sorts of confusing thoughts.

"We are friends though, right?" rank 1001 asked shakily.

Rank 3 turned his head even further into rank 1001's hand, confirming that what he felt in this moment was real.

"Of course we're friends. Please show me anything you want me to see." Rank 3 had to keep in his confusing thoughts. If he voiced them, then their friendship could be affected.

"OK, let's go," rank 1001 said excitedly. He grabbed rank 3's hand, and they set off.

They ran to the end of the corridor and rank 1001 pushed into a part of the wall to reveal the lift. Using the lift they travelled to the second floor, the floor that had rank 1001's bedroom and his personal crafting area along with his giant metal forge.

Rank 3 noticed a big difference compared to last time. Last time everything had been put in something of an ordered setting, but now everything seemed out of place.

"Sorry it's a bit messy at the moment, I've had lots of inspiration recently. We can get a bit disorganised sometimes." Rank 1001 apologised out of politeness.

"Oh don't feel like you have to explain something like that to me, I'm just happy that you're comfortable enough to show these things to me."

Rank 1001 let go of rank 3's hand and walked into the room. He walked past several boxes filled with all sorts of metals, and various crafted objects. He eventually stopped when he arrived next to an unopened, wrapped metal trunk. He grabbed the handle and dragged it to rank 3.

"What's in there?" rank 3 asked curiously. With his sudden change in mind-set, he couldn't help but be completely interested in rank 1001.

Rank 1001 didn't respond right away and instead ripped off the trunk's wrapping and using a small but incredibly sharp blade, he broke the lock on the trunk. He then opened it to reveal a trove of every gem, precious stone and precious metal that the world had to offer.

"This is entirely up to you, but if you let me, I think I can make you something really special. I have a small understanding of your ability. I know you use energy-based processes so what I want to do, is to get you to see if any of these materials conducts and/or stores your energy."

"I can do that, but for what purpose, that is, if you don't mind telling me?"

"Can I keep it a surprise?" rank 1001 asked nervously; he wouldn't refuse if rank 3 asked him further.

"Because it's you, I'm certain it will be fine." Rank 3 could sense that rank 1001 was feeling uneasy.

"Thank you." Rank 1001 thanked rank 3 happily. He was looking forward to seeing or hearing rank 3's initial reaction to what he had planned for him.

"I'll get started right away, but first could I ask you a question?" rank 3 asked hesitantly.

"You don't need my permission remember, we can ask anything and share anything.". Rank 1001 concealed a smile as he thought about how true his words were.

Rank 1001 had left rank 3 with the trunk and had started rummaging around the room. Rank 3 starting picking up items and injecting his energy into them, most were destroyed instantly, others lasted a little longer.

After gathering up more courage, rank 3 asked his question. "You know about tools and stuff like that right?"

"I know a bit about them, that being said no one in this world could be called an expert."

"Do you think it's possible to bridge the gap between individuals' combat abilities with tools?"

"That's an easy yes. Of course I do, have you heard the crafting company's slogan? I wholeheartedly agree with it."

"No, I'm afraid I don't know anything about the crafting company apart from knowing that rank 21 and the combat teacher use it to create tools for them."

"Well, its slogan is: we'll keep on crafting until everyone has what is desired even if it makes the world a bit mad."

"That's intense." Rank 3 was slightly stunned by the slogan.

"Yeah it's tricky though, because it omits the part where it's not what people desire but what the company has chosen to set the limit as."

"What limit would that be?" rank 3 asked in a somewhat accusatory tone towards the crafting company.

"Have any of the materials responded positively yet? Also didn't you have a different question, it seemed like you wanted my advice on something?" Rank 1001 asked new questions to change the subject of the conversation.

Rank 3 accepted that rank 1001 didn't know the answer or didn't want to say but rank 3 was perfectly satisfied with rank 1001's behaviour. They weren't too close to not have secrets from each other.

"The materials keep getting overwhelmed and

succumb to the destructive nature of my energy, I'll keep trying though. Anyway my question is this, do you have any idea as to what tool I could use to beat rank 21 and have a fighting chance against the combat teacher? They both manipulate air."

"Hmm?" Rank 1001 pondered, only murmuring to himself.

Rank 1001 after a few seconds seemed to burst to life as he began quickly moving around the room and started opening various boxes searching for something.

After several minutes and many materials later rank 3 finally got a response he was looking for. "Rank 1001 this one seems to be holding on!" rank 3 shouted triumphantly. He had succeeded in rank 1001's task.

Rank 1001 reached into a box and pulled out a small metal item attached to a small metal container. "This should do it," rank 1001 said while smiling to himself.

Rank 1001 ran up to rank 3 excitedly. He was expecting an intriguing reaction. "This should work," rank 1001 said while holding up the device.

"This stone is able to store my energy without breaking." Rank 3 held up the gem, both wanted to impress the other.

"Trade," rank 1001 said as he switched his device for the gem; the gem was glowing bright red.

"What is this?" Rank 3 was completely dumbfounded by the device in his hands.

"It is what will help you win, although depending

on the nature of your energy, you shouldn't need a tool to defeat an air manipulator. The device I'm giving you is a highly powerful vacuum device; it will suck all the air out of a room in less than a minute. It then stores the air in this part and using its secondary function you can shoot condensed air back out. In terms of your problem, as long as you hold your breath, you'll win as soon as all the air is sucked up."

"When did you come up with this?" Rank 3 was fascinated that someone could invent something like this.

"It's an early design for pumping air into the forge. It's basically junk that I've held onto so you can have it and I'll gladly see it go to where it's needed." Unknown to rank 3, rank 1001 was lying.

"Wow, to think an item you think is junk could help me win in a fight. But what did you mean, I don't need a tool? Oh, wait never mind, I'll ask rank 300 she should know all about my combat abilities by now."

"Rank 300? What is she to you?" Rank 1001 was starting to feel concerned.

"She says she's my analyst, she helped me fight the intruder in the arena."

"So that's how it is. Anyway if you're satisfied could you please leave now, I'm tired and I need to sleep. I have to cut it short because of the new imposed rules on my attending lessons. Falling asleep earlier reminded me how tired I am."

"Oh OK, sure."

Rank 1001, still not completely comfortable with rank 3 roaming around the house on his own, took rank 3 up to the first floor and out of the doorway. "I'll see you tomorrow then."

"Yes, tomorrow. I'm looking forward to seeing you," rank 3 responded, blurting out something he was trying to suppress.

Rank 1001 closed the door and looked up and held the glowing gem in the air. "Babe, order another two boxes of this gem, correct me if I'm wrong but I think its order number is gem-502. Please place an order immediately."

Chapter Fifteen
Deciding how to act

Rank 3 woke up with a smile on his face. It was becoming the norm as he was becoming much happier with his surroundings and was enjoying the company of those around him much more than before.

As rank 3 was preparing for the day, he heard his phone ring. "Hello," rank 3 answered in a polite tone.

"Rank 3, it's me rank 300."

"Rank 300, how are you? I haven't seen you since the tournament." Rank 3 was happy to hear rank 300's voice.

"Not important, my sister has arrived and she's started her investigation, and that's not all she's been partnered with someone from one of the superior families. That means that families with similar power to the state are taking an interest in the academy. You should be careful, you're a high ranker who's not connected to a high family, let alone a superior family. They might try to recruit you and take you away. As your analyst I forbid you to be swayed by them. OK? That's it, talk to you later."

"Wait!" rank 3 said desperately, before rank 300 hung up the phone.

"Yes, what is it? Was I not clear enough?"

"I don't care too much about the investigation, it's not my concern. I need your analytical advice."

"Oh. It's about time you called me then, isn't it? Ask away," rank 300 replied proudly.

"How can I beat rank 21 without using a tool?"

"Ooh that's an interesting question. Let me guess you haven't been able to beat him yet, have you?"

"Not yet."

"I thought that might be the case, his analytical ability is only a bit short of mine, and he has strength as well. But your ability is quite unique, depending on your energy's nature this tactic should work, and I'm confident your energy's nature is determined by you not in of itself. That's what makes it unique. It's a simple strategy, but it is complex in its execution. Adjust your energy to flow at the same rate and match the nature of the air and redirect attacks sent against you. Instead of blocking or dodging you redirect and use your opponents' attacks against them. Failing that, attack the ground to throw dust all over the area to obscure rank 21's vision; he is a vision-based combatant after all."

"Wow, you really do know a lot, thank you for your help. I'm glad you wanted to be my analyst."

"Be sure to ask me for help anytime, that's what being your analyst means. I got to go now; I get to be my sister's guide while she's here. Have a good day, rank 3."

"Yes, you too, bye."

Rank 3 thought carefully and intensely about the advice that rank 300 had given him. Her ideas seemed much more advanced than everything he had come up with. Happy with what he would be attempting today, rank 3 finished his preparations and left to go the academic classroom.

It was just like normal, rank 1001 was already rejecting match requests and the rest of the students had all taken their seats. Rank 21 was sitting happily next to rank 3 when their teacher arrived. It was an instant reaction; all the students became silent.

"Urgh," the teacher grumbled angrily and was full of disgust. "All right listen up, the state investigators are here, avoid them best you can and don't answer their questions unless a teacher or member of staff is present. They shouldn't be here so don't give them an easy time; they're trying to interfere with academy business and they have no right. If academy 2 wasn't so useless, we wouldn't be in this mess, don't forget whose fault this really is. All right that's it, continue analysing old data and do it silently, I'm in a bad mood."

The students were very cautious when it came to their academic teacher. He was a genius but was also very reputable as someone who was violent and easy to anger. The students were not prepared to take any chances with him.

The lesson continued in silence and when the lesson was over the teacher left. He stormed out and any student unlucky enough to cross his path would undoubtedly receive a painful blow.

"He was on edge, wasn't he?" rank 21 said in a half joking manner.

"The state investigators must be important people," rank 3 responded. He was nervous about his eventual interrogation.

"Well yes and no, they kind of act like they can do what they want but they have limits. They are more annoying than anything. Think of them as flies that won't leave you alone." Rank 21 wanted to reassure rank 3 and calm his nerves.

"Have you met one before?"

"Not properly but my sister told me about them, and talking about her, let's get going."

"OK, I'll just collect rank 1001, also I've got a surprise for you today."

"A surprise for me?" rank 21 said, startled.

"Yes, you'll find out soon, be prepared." Rank 3 smiled as he spoke.

Rank 3 walked up to rank 1001, whispered in his ear that it was him and wrapped his red vine energy around him and grabbed his hand.

The three of them then travelled over to the combat building taking particular notice of the changes to the arena building. The entrance was no longer blocked but no-entry signs with the state's symbol were placed outside.

They tried to take little notice and also get out of the area before they drew attention to themselves. They quickly arrived at the combat room, where the teacher was waiting for them. Again her outfit had changed.

This was undoubtedly her most complex outfit, designed solely for combat. It was similar to yesterday, but it was much more enhancing. The material was lighter and her main outfit there was a gown concealing tight fitting clothing. The outfit made moving easy and also allowed for easy flight. On the back of her outfit was more loose wrappings of cloth, designed to help manipulate air resistance. In her hand she held a fan, and most noticeably, she was barefoot.

"Come in, you two, urgh three. Come in and get ready, today we're really going to push your limits." The teacher wasn't as tolerant of rank 1001 as she had been before.

Rank 3 ignored the teacher's comment about rank 1001, but only because he thought it was polite to do so and she had spoken without thinking. He placed rank 1001 in the corner of the room and made sure he was comfortable and only then did he greet his teacher.

"Hello, teacher, please instruct me today," rank 3 said smiling. He was excited to test the advice he had received.

"Why do you keep bringing him with you?" the teacher asked coldly.

Instantly recognising that she was talking about rank 1001 and sensing her hostile tone rank 3 responded, "That's none of your business, teacher, he's not here to be instructed by you. I am, so please do so."

"Very well, but there is a limit to my tolerance and I can only be patient for so long, be careful bringing him in the future." The teacher spoke softly but rank 3 easily recognised the violence in her tone.

"I say we make him join us; everyone could do with some combat advice. Even that thing," rank 21 commented wryly.

"I already said leave him alone. That's the end of it."

"If I have to make him join, I will," rank 21 said while making the air around him swirl.

"Crash." Rank 21 narrowly avoided a bolt of red energy.

"Ooh, looks like you are learning," rank 21 said, finally acknowledging rank 3 in combat.

"All right then, boys, whoever wins this next fight gets to decide what happens to rank 1001. I'm the teacher and I make the rules here so rank 3 I don't care how much you protest. I will give you some advice if you fight with the vine as you have been you won't win. I for one am very interested in what my brother will do to that thing."

Rank 3 was angry; this situation was completely unnecessary and unfair. Rank 1001 had nothing to do with their combat training. If it wasn't because of the academy's response to the intruder, rank 1001 wouldn't have even been here to be harassed. Rank 3 felt angry and guilty.

"I refuse to get rid of the vine, but I won't lose."

Rank 3 spoke full of vigour. Underneath it was obvious his words were filled with violence.

"Very well it is your choice after all," the teacher said indifferently, she wouldn't be giving out any more advice.

"Ha, this will be easy. Watch out, rank 3!"

Rank 21 immediately launched multiple blades of air at rank 3, rank 3 dodged them and starting launching attacks of his own in the form of a red whip. Rank 21 dodged rank 3's attacks and didn't let up and started integrating more complex attacks into his attack pattern.

Not only were fast blades of wind attacking rank 3 but also slower and large whirlwinds with the same slicing capabilities were headed towards him.

Rank 3 was slowly being pushed back and attacking less and less. He had to change tactics. He stomped on the ground as hard as he could, creating a crater in the ground. The dust from the attack filled the air and started to mix with the air attacks, weighing them down and slowing their speed.

It also slightly obscured rank 21's vision interrupting his attacks for a moment. Rank 3 used this distraction to attack rank 21. Rank 3 used his extra sensory ability; the ability to sense internal energy to pinpoint rank 21's location. He launched his whip at rank 21 and started lashing him. Unfortunately for rank 3 his whip was too weak to break through rank 21's air-based defence.

"You're getting better, I'll grant you that, but

you're still too distracted to win," the combat teacher said with a hint of pride for her student.

The dust started to settle and rank 3 didn't have a chance to do that move again as rank 21 unleashed the full extent of his ability. The blades had all different varying speeds making it hard to judge their trajectories, not giving him much time. Rank 3 was only able to dodge.

Rank 3 was started to get overwhelmed when he thought about the other piece of advice he had received. He didn't know if it would work or if he could do it, but he had to try.

Normally he let his energy act on its own based on its own innate properties, he directed it but didn't control it on its base level. That was what he had to attempt to do right now.

Rank 3 reached deep into the depths of his body with his mind, attempting to find the source of his energy. He had never done this before, if he continued to doubt himself, he would never find it. Luckily, rank 1001's presence was enough reason to never give up.

Rank 3 had to concentrate. His movements became sloppy and while he was searching for his energy's core his body was slowly being cut to pieces.

"Found it!" rank 3 shouted triumphantly.

Unfortunately the next hit he took forced him to the floor. It was now that he realised the grim state he was in; his body was covered in countless cuts and blood was spilling from each one.

Despite all this rank 3, stumbled up to retake his combat position. His body was trembling but that didn't matter, to win this fight he could now do so without moving.

"Give up, rank 3, you already need medical aid," the combat teacher said indifferently. She didn't care too much about his state, and she certainly didn't care about rank 1001.

"I can still fight!" rank 3 shouted in protest and to suppress the pain.

"I have no objections," Rank 21 said happily. He was only a few steps away from seeing what was under rank 1001's mask.

Rank 21 launched multiple blades of wind at rank 3, all fast and deadly. Rank 3 was in no obvious shape to avoid them. This attack would be the decider.

As the blades drew near to rank 3, rank 3 let his energy flow out of his body. It poured out like a river and danced through the air. It reached out and joined with the blades of wind shifting their trajectory, making them completely miss rank 3.

"You can't hit me now. Give up," Rank 3 said fiercely.

"Ha, even if you think you can defend you're going to pass out any second now. I can just stay here and wait."

"I won't pass out and I won't lose." Rank 3 glared at rank 21, his resolve shining from his eyes.

Rank 3's energy moved like a blade of red water

and targeted rank 21. Rank 21 attacked the red river with air attacks but they were drawn into the river and launched in different directions. One blade of wind was almost launched back at rank 21.

"Tch! Fine!" rank 21 exclaimed in anger, the fight was going to last longer than he had expected.

Expecting this red river to follow him, rank 21 leaped backwards several metres to buy himself time. Instead of following him the river crashed into the floor causing a dust cloud to erupt in the room obscuring rank 21's view. Rank 21 started to panic. He only needed to land a hit on rank 3 to finish this fight but that was becoming increasingly difficult.

It was rank 21's innate personality that gave birth to his next idea. If he couldn't get to rank 3, then he would make rank 3 come to him. Rank 21 knew exactly where rank 1001 was sitting. He took the risk and travelled through the dust cloud. The river scraped his side only being slightly repelled by his natural air armour.

Rank 21 pushed through and shouted, "Can you stop this!" as he launched a huge blade of wind at rank 1001. It contained the last of rank 21's strength; he was too exhausted to keep fighting. It was, however, the strongest attack rank 3 had faced so far.

Rank 3 acted exactly as rank 21 thought he would, well almost. Rank 3 was forced to block the attack but he did so with his body leaving the red river to pierce through rank 21's stomach. Rank 3 suffered a deep cut to his cheek, torso, left arm and left leg. Even with these injuries he still maintained the red vine connecting him to rank 1001.

"I win," rank 3 said, breathing heavily and looking directly at rank 1001 to make sure he was unharmed.

"I don't think so, we'll call it a draw seeing as neither one of you can stand up properly. I guess that will be all for today. Come on I'll carry you both to the medical centre."

"I'll be fine, take rank 21, I need to check on rank 1001."

"Don't be so stubborn, you're starting to act stupid because of him. Now come with me." The combat teacher was showing open disdain for rank 1001 and rank 3 was not impressed by it.

"I'm staying to check on rank 1001!" rank 3 stated defiantly.

The combat teacher carefully picked up her wounded brother and went to pick up rank 3 off of the floor when his energy targeted her. She swatted it away but was shocked by how it felt. It felt much heavier and much more dangerous than before. This energy was truly unique.

"Fine act like a brat, if you end up in worse shape don't complain about it to me!" the teacher shouted, frustrated. To her mind, her student was making a foolish and possibly extremely dangerous choice.

The combat teacher, deciding that there was no time and no point arguing, raced off to the medical centre carrying her younger brother. Rank 3 laid on his back completely and took a deep breath and sighed in relief. He looked directly at rank 1001 who was behind him. It was clear that his actions had spared rank 1001 unnecessary and unwarranted pain.

Rank 3 was happy with this outcome; if rank 1001 was unharmed then he would consider this fight a win regardless of his current state. He had proven to himself that he was definitely going to get stronger, and not just his resolve but his potential had been revealed to him. He now felt closer to his own energy than he had ever felt, it was truly a part of him now and it was something he readily accepted.

Rank 3 was distracted by these thoughts that he didn't initially realise the tugging on his wrist by the red vine connecting him and rank 1001. As soon as rank 3 realised his whole body jolted, and he gasped in pain. Nevertheless, he quickly sat up and turned to rank 1001.

Rank 1001 continued to tug on the vine, he also waved his other arm in the air trying to locate rank 3. Rank 3 doing his best to ignore the pain, pulled rank 1001 towards him, doing so made him want to pass out but it was necessary and he wouldn't fail.

Rank 1001 was slid across the floor and stopped next to rank 3. Rank 3 was breathing heavily due to his whole body being exhausted; his regeneration was keeping him from passing out from the blood loss but it couldn't erase his exhaustion.

Rank 3 lent towards rank 1001 and landed in his

arms Rank 1001 was surprised by this feeling but it felt nice so he didn't oppose it. He wrapped his arms around rank 3 and he felt his gloves become heavy. Unbeknownst to rank 1001, his gloves were being soaked in rank 3's blood.

Rank 3 was healing, most of the bleeding was stopping but some remained. The small cuts had already started to close but some cuts were deep, so deep that they even scratched his internal organs. The pain and bleeding would have been unbearable if not for rank 1001's presence.

Rank 3 was unsure how long it would take to heal on his own. Unlike last time he had no major or large body parts to regrow; most of his wounds were superficial with only a few being serious. Still it wasn't the severity of the wounds but the number of them that was the problem, and the other problem was that his consciousness was fading and he healed faster when he focused.

Rank 1001 was starting to panic. Rank 3 would normally announce his presence and say something about his current state, but he had remained silent. Rank 1000 could only barely make out the shape and presence of the person in front of him. If he wanted to know more about rank 3, he would have to rip holes in his mask and bandages.

Rank 1001 weighed the options in his mind. Never before would he have ever contemplated something like this. He covered his entire body for a reason. Rank 3 may be an exception, but that didn't change the fact that they were currently in the academy.

Before rank 1001 could decide, rank 3 sensing rank 1001's distress, pulled rank 1001's head close to his.

"Sorry, it's me, rank 3. I just need to stay like this for a while. Rank 1001 will you please watch over me?"

Rank 1001 had been protected by rank 3. No one else in his entire life had ever done anything remotely kind for him, nor did he want or expect them to. Rank 1001 was happy being alone, but things had changed. Just as rank 3 had realised, rank 1001 was discovering that his fascination with rank 3 might not be from a purely researcher's point of view. Rank 1001 was starting to view rank 3 as someone precious. Rank 1001 would and could no longer consider himself the centre of his own universe.

Just as rank 3 had asked him to do, rank 1001 kept rank 3 wrapped up in his arms. Rank 3 slowly fell asleep. It was unavoidable and not just because of his injuries. Right now he felt that he was in the safest and most comfortable position he could be in.

When he eventually woke back up, rank 3 realised that rank 1001 had also fallen asleep and that they had ended up lying on the floor wrapped up in each other's arms. Rank 3 gently woke up rank 1001 and rank 1001 woke up in a panic. Once again he was waking up to the wrong sight and sensations.

Only now he wasn't sure if it was wrong, but rank 1001 instantly felt embarrassed. He stood straight up and left the room. Rank 3 wasn't sure how to act in this position so he felt he had to let rank 1001 go.

Chapter Sixteen
State investigator

Rank 3 was pacing impatiently outside of the arena. Rank 300 had called him up in the early hours of morning, a couple hours earlier than which he was used to waking up. He felt a bit groggy; he still hadn't fully healed from yesterday, but it would only take a few more hours until he was back to normal. Rank 21 however would still need a couple more days.

"Rank 3, you came. Just like I asked, thank you. My sister is very eager to meet you," rank 300 said brightly while smiling.

"Yes, you said it was very important," rank 3 responded, trying to suppress his nerves.

"Oh it is, here they come now."

Rank 3 turned in the direction of the state investigators, one male and one female. As he did, he saw the two of them had stopped. They were talking to each other resulting in one of them walking off.

After their split, the female state investigator headed in rank 3 and rank 300's direction. It became clear immediately that she was related to rank 300; they had exactly the same eyes.

The state investigator was wearing a very obvious

state uniform. It had a very large state emblem on the front and back showing her connection to the state, and it was proof that she wielded the authority that came from that connection.

It was a smart outfit, but was also clearly designed for combat. It was made from light but durable fabric and offered quick mobility. She carried multiple weapons all on display. These were two pistols at her sides and a knife strapped to her thigh.

"Is he rank 3?" The state investigator spoke only to rank 300.

"Yes, he's the one you asked for. As promised, I delivered." Rank 300 spoke politely to her sister, but it was obvious they were both very comfortable around each other despite the importance of this situation.

"Good. Go after that one, I don't want him getting into trouble or getting lost."

"Don't you want me to be here?" rank 300 protested. She trusted her sister but was not naive enough to underestimate the orders of the state.

"No, interviews should be private, you know that."

"Fine. I'll go keep that guy company, but I'm not happy about it." Rank 300 walked off as soon as she finished speaking, leaving rank 3 feeling confused and vulnerable.

"OK, you're coming with me." The state investigator grabbed rank 3's arm and dragged him into the arena.

They entered the arena. It was strangely quiet and

no one else was around, everything apart from the lights had been switched off. The state investigator dragged rank 3 into the main arena field. It was here that the majority of the incident had taken place and rank 3 was finally able to see the aftermath.

To rank 3's surprise, he saw a shocking sight. In the direction that the intruder had entered the arena to face their team was a large hole, it looked like it extended deep into the ground. It was unexplainable given what he remembered about the incident.

"All right, this spot will do. I am allowed to tell you that the intruder escaped and no one was killed. What I need from you is your account of events. I have already received all the witness statements from the students in the audience. I haven't been able to talk to other top twenty ranked students because they are still not in a fit conscious state. So, I now want to hear from you. My sister has given me her account, but you experienced the intruder first hand. Start."

Rank 3 was expecting to give his account, but it didn't stop everything from feeling so sudden. He had to think quickly he didn't want to leave anything out.

"I came to the arena to watch the match but after rank 300 advised me to participate I went down to the arena field. I spoke briefly with rank 21. It was during our conversation that I realised the extent that our academy students had been injured. I quickly jumped into the ring, and I discovered both rank 1 and rank 4 were the only two left to activate their emergency cocoons. Using rank 300 as an additional set of eyes, I quickly rescued rank 1 and rank 4. It was clear that they had received the worst injuries. I immediately activated their cocoons and afterwards I engaged the intruder until the emergency alarm sounded."

"Hm. Good that lines up with the combat footage, now I need you to answer as truthfully as possible the following questions. Do you understand?" The investigator's tone was cold and sharp.

"Yes, I understand." Rank 3 was already prepared to be as honest as possible.

"Have you ever met anyone with the intruder's skill set before?"

"I don't think so, I couldn't even work out the intruder's ability, so I can't say with a hundred percent accuracy but I am certain I've never met the intruder."

"I believe you. It is true that no one knows the intruder's ability. Next, what do you know of rank 1 and rank 4's injuries?"

"Not the whole extent, but it looked like they suffered badly."

"The majority of their bones were broken or fractured, cuts and lacerations to the torso, arms, legs and face with some areas completely devoid of flesh. Particular notice was the five ribs ripped from them each, four of which were used to impale their wrists and ankles, the fifth was used to carve a message into their chests. The message stating, 'you deserve this'." The state investigator recited their injuries perfectly.

Rank 3 didn't know how to respond to the extent of their injuries nor did he know what to say to the message.

"You were attacked around three weeks prior to the incident, were you not?" The state investigator's tone was filled with accusations.

"I was, but that was just a training accident." Rank 3 desperately scrambled to prove his innocence.

"I have a written statement from rank 4 stating that after the confrontation by him, rank 1 and the other top twenty, he paid you a visit in the medical centre. He stated he acted under orders from rank 1. Is that correct?"

"That is correct, but that had nothing to do with the intruder. When did he write that?" Rank 3 was very confused and was starting to panic.

"So is it just a coincidence that their injuries were not too dissimilar to yours, or are you denying rank 4's statement that he took away your hands and feet? Before you answer, I also have your medical report."

"That did happen. It happened exactly as you've heard, but I had nothing to do with the intruder. Why do you know all of this? My previous injuries had nothing to do with the intruder."

"I have no reason to doubt you at this time, but I am still very suspicious. There is currently no evidence against you apart from a series of coincidences so I am still not satisfied and would advise you to behave while being around rank 300."

"I think I understand most of it." Rank 3 said this, but he was unsure about where the state investigator had gotten all of her information from. He was also extremely nervous and wanted to leave as quickly as possible.

"Good, she seems fond of you, but you're in a precarious position so you better not let anything happen to her. I'm a state investigator and you're just a student so remember who has the power here."

"Do you need anything else from me?" Rank 3 was desperate to escape this situation.

"No, I've had a good look at you and I'm satisfied for now. I'll send for you if I need anything more, you can leave now." The investigator spoke dismissively and coldly.

Rank 3 turned around and went to leave.

"Wait!" The investigator stopped rank 3, her voice piercing his soul.

Rank 3 immediately turned around to see what else the state investigator might need. He wouldn't risk leaving without permission.

"Do you recognise this blade?" The state investigator was holding the blade used by the intruder, the blade that rank 3 had separated the intruder from.

"That looks like the blade wielded by the intruder," rank 3 responded honestly.

"Hm, good. We're done now, please leave."

Rank 3 left the arena. There was still over an hour until lessons started but seeing as he had nothing else to do he went to the academic classroom.

Rank 3 didn't enter the classroom but chose to wait outside. He wanted to wait for rank 1001. After their sudden separation yesterday, he was eager to see how rank 1001 was feeling, especially as rank 3's feelings were starting to fall all over the place. He was unsure how he felt about rank 1001.

The other students arrived and when they reached rank 3, they silently passed him. They were still wary of him despite his attempt to change their attitude. Rank 21 didn't show. This was likely due to him still needing to recover in the medical centre. When the academic teacher arrived, he glared at rank 3 but didn't say anything. He ignored rank 3 as he passed. He no longer had any patience for rank 3 and rank 3's fanciful opinions.

Rank 1001 was not in the classroom nor had he arrived outside. Rank 3 was starting to worry about him. At first he felt angry because he easily assumed that someone else was to blame but that anger turned inwards when he started to doubt himself. He had no intention of ever hurting rank 1001, and yet he couldn't help but worry that he had done just that.

After the lesson had begun and ten minutes had passed, rank 3 quickly made the decision to go straight to rank 1001's home. No matter how unwise he thought it might be, he had to check on him. After all rank 1001 was much weaker than him. If it was serious, rank 3 would never forgive himself if he failed to help. Rank 3 couldn't help but view rank 1001 as someone who needed protecting from the world.

Rank 3 walked at a fast pace so as to not draw too much attention. He carefully scanned the area for the state investigators. When he was satisfied the coast was clear, he made his way out of the academy and out of the city.

Rank 3 ran most of the way to rank 1001's home, only stopping when his body's injuries forced him to. Running like this had stopped his advanced healing, so he was starting to feel the pain as some of his wounds reopened and started to sting. Still, they were of little importance at this moment in time and he endured by focusing on his task and thoughts of rank 1001.

Rank 3 finally saw the white box in front of him. He ran up to it and started pressing the button as if he was in a mad fury. He wouldn't stop pressing it until someone answered.

He continued until a while had passed with no response, so he started banging on the metal door as well as pushing the button. The camera above was carefully inspecting him the entire time.

The door wouldn't budge nor did rank 3 have the physical strength to move it. He could try to use his energy, but he was unsure of what the aftermath of that would be. Also rank 1001 could come from behind the door at any time, and rank 3 was afraid rank 1001's delicate and fragile body would get damaged.

There was no response until rank 3 shouted, "Rank

1001, are you OK? Let me in!"

"Voice recognised, basic order confirmed," an electronic voice responded to rank 3.

"Clunk!" The metal door started to lower.

"Huh!" Rank 3 made a noise in surprise.

The door opened, rank 3 walked in through the entrance. The corridor lights were already on and it was apparent that rank 1001 was home.

"Crash! Whoosh!" Rank 3 heard a loud explosion and the crumbling of rock. Along with the noises he felt a strong gust of wind rush past him.

Rank 3 was now feeling nervous. He didn't know of anything in this place that could cause that response. Rank 3 pushed his nerves to the bottom of his mind and walked forward full of concern and courage.

He didn't have to walk very far though as rank 1001 walked out of one of the rooms in the corridor. It wasn't the guest rooms but one much further down, a room that rank 3 had yet to see inside. In rank 1001's hand was a small metal device with the red glowing gem that rank 3 had given him.

Rank 3 was most surprised by rank 1001's outfit. He could only see him from the side but it was obvious that he was missing several items. Rank 1001 wasn't wearing a mask, his gloves or slippers, even his robe was shorter. Much of his flesh was exposed.

Rank 1001 hadn't noticed rank 3. It was only when he turned around that their gazes met and rank 1001's face turned bright red, along with rank 3 who immediately turned around when he noticed rank 1001's robe was undone and he wasn't wearing anything underneath. Rank 1001 quickly wrapped himself up and went to run away when rank 3 stopped him. "Wait! I'm really sorry!" rank 3 shouted, making rank 1001 pause.

Rank 3 was now staring at the back of rank 1001's head. He had only glimpsed rank 1001's face but he was now certain it was that of an angel. Even now when he could only look at rank 1001's golden hair, that was enough to make his heart skip a beat.

"What are you doing here? How did you get in?" Rank 1001 was making it sound as if he was accusing rank 3 of breaking the rules.

"Someone let me in. I asked to be let in and the door opened." Rank 3 answered as honestly and as quickly as he could.

"Damn it, babe, it was just a suggestion." Rank 1001 moaned at the ceiling above him.

"What was that?"

"It's nothing, I made a mistake yesterday. I didn't think you would show up here again so soon, and now that you've seen my true appearance feel free to laugh and leave. Don't ever look at me again. If you call yourself my friend you'll give me that much." Rank 1001 spoke quickly and loudly, his speech filled with sadness and disgust for himself. He took a step forward when rank 3 called out to him.

"What are you saying? I came here because you

didn't show up for lessons. Is it that much of a problem that I've seen what's underneath your clothes and bandages? I mean I might have accidently seen a little too much, but it's not like you look different to anyone else. In fact with your features I'd say you're more beautiful than most others, if not the most beautiful I've ever seen. I really want to keep being your friend." Rank 3 started nervously saying anything that came to his mind.

"Why are you lying? Of course I look different to everyone else. Did you not see it before? Here!" Rank 1001 angry but depressed turned around and threw his robe on the floor.

"What are you doing?" Rank 3 blushed while partially covering his eyes.

"Well, which colour is your favourite?" rank 1001 asked rank 3, every word filled with hatred and disgust.

"Colour, what are you talking about, what colours are there to choose from? Are you all right? You're acting different, not weird but different." Rank 3's concerns were multiplying. He worried that someone had hurt rank 1001.

"What are you talking about?" rank 1001 said as he looked down at his bare skin. "Oh? Fascinating."

"Are you starting to calm down?" Rank 3 sensed the calm in the air was starting to return.

Rank 1001 covered himself back up with his robe but rolled up the sleeves to leave his arms exposed.

"Sorry I overreacted, but everything really does

look normal even though you're standing in front of me."

"Well, to me everything about you is normal and everything about you is something that I would always accept. That's how friends are. I'm sorry for scaring you and I'm sorry if I made you feel uncomfortable. I really did only come here to check on you, but it seems I've hurt you again. I'm truly sorry, I'll leave now." Rank 3 was happy that rank 1001 was unharmed by another but was saddened when he thought he himself had hurt rank 1001.

"Wait, you don't have to go. I mean as long as you don't want to. I can show you what I've been working on if you'd like."

"Are you sure? Even yesterday you ran away from me?" Rank 3 spoke with sadness in his words.

"Oh that." Rank 1001's face turned bright pink as he started to blush. "I felt something unfamiliar, so I ran. I didn't know what else to do."

"So I didn't scare you?" rank 3 asked feeling relieved.

"I felt surprised, but that was caused by me, not you. Well you were the trigger but it was my thoughts that I was confused by. I'm even more confused now. You really are different. I've never met anyone like you before."

"I'm glad, I've been struggling with realising my own feelings too. Is that why you didn't come in today?" Rank 3 wondered if rank 1001 was being confused by his feelings as rank 3 was.

"No, I was busy, so I didn't get to finish your gift. I didn't want to go in without it."

"You say that like it's so natural."

"You don't want a gift from me?"

"Oh no I do, I mean I would really like that, thank you, I feel bad though because I didn't get you anything." Rank 3 still believed that if he received something he had to give something back in return.

"You being you is more than enough," rank 1001 said completely truthfully and unashamedly.

Hearing those words set rank 3's soul ablaze. "I'm sorry, I have to know right now."

"Know what exact... ly?"

Rank 1001 was unable to properly finish his sentence. Rank 3's energy wrapped around his body and very gently and very carefully carried him over to rank 3.

"I'm sorry, I'm being selfish but I have to know." As soon as rank 3 finished speaking he put both of his hands on the back of rank 1001's head. Rank 3 placed all his fingers in rank 1001's golden hair.

Rank 1001 was stunned and confused by what was happening but didn't resist. He was intrigued by this unknown situation.

Rank 3 might not have stopped even if rank 1001 had resisted. His desire to know if this was the right course of action was stronger than any feeling he had ever felt before. It was even stronger than his desire to leave his family's sky island. If rank 1001 responded positively both of their lives would be changed for the better; rank 3 firmly believed this would be the case.

Rank 3 took a deep breath and looked deep into rank 1001's eyes. They were golden just like his hair; to rank 3, he really did have the face and voice of an angel. But even if he didn't rank 3 was certain he wouldn't feel any other way. Rank 3 felt it in his soul that he and rank 1001 were connected. The only question was how deep that connection would go. Rank 3 slowly pulled rank 1001's face closer to his own.

When they were millimetres away from each other, rank 3 kept rank 1001 in place. Using his desire to offset his nerves, he pushed his lips closer to rank 1001's and kissed him.

Rank 1001 had no idea what was happening. He knew about these sorts of occurrences but had never experienced any in his lifetime. He didn't know what to do, so he followed rank 3's lead and kissed him back, both of them pushing their lips onto one another, intentionally and unintentionally revealing their true feelings.

Rank 3 became unbelievably happy when not only did rank 1001 let him kiss him, but he kissed him back. This had to be proof that they felt the same way. Rank 3 would have stayed in this embrace forever, but he feared rank 1001 might pass out from breathlessness.

Rank 3 pulled away and gently released rank 1001 from his hands and energy, both their faces bright red with embarrassment. However, they couldn't look away from each other, both sets of eyes staring deeply into each other's.

"I'm sorry, that was selfish and impulsive," rank 3 said embarrassed but not with regret due to the outcome.

"I liked it," rank 1001 said bluntly.

"Really? Me too, I'm so happy that you feel the same." Rank 3 was overjoyed to hear rank 1001's words.

"Well, I don't think I'm able to resist you. Like I said before, you are different."

"Yes, you did say that. To me you are perfect. I don't want you to have to feel like you have to be afraid of others' judgement. Please only care what I think about you, because I accept every part of you and all of you is something I consider precious and hold dear."

"Does that mean you're going to stay here with me now?"

"Yes, of course, I want to spend as much time with you as I possibly can," rank 3 said with the tiniest hint of sadness.

"Great, come with me I've got something to show you."

After rank 3 and rank 1001 had finally figured out how they viewed the other, all the tension in the air had completely vanished and they both felt very relaxed. Now that rank 1001 wasn't going to run away, the two of them entered the lift and travelled down to the second floor.

"What happened here?" rank 3 asked, shocked at the scene in front of him. The whole room apart from the forge which was unharmed looked in a much worse state than the combat classroom and even the arena.

"Don't worry too much about it, I'll have it cleaned up when I've finished my work. I'm getting quite close now."

"What could be so important? This looks dangerous." Rank 3, looking at this scene, was worried for rank 1001's health.

"It's fine. Stuff like this happens, it's not something we're not used to," rank 1001 responded positively. He didn't seem to care about the risks.

"Right, but you should still be careful." Rank 3 didn't like the thought of anyone or anything hurting his precious rank 1001.

"Yeah, I guess. Anyway, this is what I've been working on." Rank 1001 looked around the room until he picked up another metal device with a red glowing crystal.

"What is it?"

"I've been trying to make a device that can store and release your energy. I'm close to creating a storage device, but the release output is tricky. Using only crystals to regulate the energy flow is harder than I thought it would be, especially as your energy nature is complicated and I can't get a complete feel for it."

"Why are you trying to do this? I don't need a device like that." Rank 3 was shocked that rank 1001 would even attempt something so dangerous.

"Don't you want to always be prepared? What if you run out of energy and need more? Even with your regeneration you might not run out of energy, but that doesn't mean much. For example, even if you let your energy continuously flow, if its power was weak then its capabilities would be weak. Like a wave-less ocean trying to destroy a pebble. But using a device to concentrate and focus your power you'll be able to protect yourself better."

"I'm not sure I understand, but it's clear to me that you are doing it for my sake so I'm very grateful."

"I'm sorry I haven't finished sooner; I had a lot of orders and demands come in recently. It seems like something big is happening. I had to make a lot of custom and personalised equipment. That stuff takes the longest, everything else is blueprints and mechanised mass production. I don't have to care too much about that stuff."

"What are you talking about? Is someone forcing you to do these things?" The word demand felt uncomfortable to hear.

"Of course not, well yes if I say I never refuse an order, well I won't refuse as long as it's not a weapon of mass destruction. I only create equipment to protect individuals, I won't be responsible for deaths without combat. I get paid to do it. I wouldn't do it for free, and I definitely wouldn't spend the time to build custom items with no payment. You're an exception of course;

you keeping me company is more than enough."

"I had no idea that someone like you existed." Rank 3 was unaware of how the world worked, especially with the mass production of basic and complex goods. "Are you happy doing this? Won't you always be serving others?" Rank 3 was unsure about rank 1001's situation and wanted to make entirely certain that rank 1001 wasn't being trapped or forced.

"Are you saying academy students aren't serving and are not destined to serve? Soldiers, state workers, everyone who is not in charge of themselves is a servant to another. I'm not because I'm in charge of my affairs. I choose to create things; I can always refuse if I wish. It's my production; all of my affairs are my own. I am in control of myself. I control my own world." Rank 1001 spoke proudly of himself and made it clear that he had an inherent dislike of those who would give up on the chance to have what he possessed.

"I'm sorry I didn't mean to offend you, I've felt trapped before. I certainly don't want to follow in my father's footsteps but that is the most likely path I'll walk."

"Aren't you exaggerating a bit too much? You can be free if you want to."

"What are you saying? I don't think you understand."

"I mean you are rank 3, you must have a high family background, the high and supreme families usually produce the highest ranked students. Are you a member of one of those?"

"I guess I am, but I cut ties with them when I left. I don't want to go back so don't ever worry about me leaving."

"If you say it, I won't worry. You already said you won't lie to me. But don't ignore those who care about you. From what I know, families can be useful."

"Oh, maybe now that we're more than friends, we should make each other a promise."

"What promise? What do you mean more than friends? What is more than friends? Is it something dangerous?" Rank 1001 started to panic he hadn't done any research on the stages of relationships that evolved from friendship.

"No, calm down. You're not in danger, I didn't mean to scare you, I should have explained properly first. Now that we've kissed I just thought that we could be closer than friends, that we care about each other more than friends. Isn't that what kissing means?" Rank 3 was hopeful that their kiss meant what he interpreted it to.

"I guess that makes sense, the way I feel about you no longer matches up with my research on friendship. Here, catch." Rank 1001 threw the two red crystal devices to rank 3. He had connected them together.

"Wait before we get distracted. I promise to always look after you, not just protecting you from pain but also I promise to always make you happy and not hurt you."

"I already planned to do that for you. I'm not sure

my understanding of happiness is as at the same level as yours, but I'm sure I'll learn more from our time together. Now test it out."

"How do I do that?" Rank 3 stared at the unknown contraption in his hands.

"The left side is for injecting energy and has a large storage crystal. The right side stores and releases energy using small crystals placed in a special alignment. The device can't regulate it very well between the different sides, but if it's you using it, you can do that yourself. You'll have to act as the mechanism that fixes the only flaw."

"OK, I'll give it a try." Rank 3 started to inject his energy into the left side.

"Not here!" rank 1001 said, panicked. "We should go up to one of the testing rooms. Follow me."

"Sorry I got a bit too impatient," rank 3 said trying to laugh off his embarrassment.

Rank 3 and rank 1001 went back to the upper floor and entered the room opposite to the one rank 1001 had first appeared from. It was a large empty room; it was brightly lit and all the walls were bright white with a layer of clear material covering them.

"This room should handle your energy, although no promises. That device is tricky after all."

"I think it might be easier if I empty it out first so I can get a feel for the flow. The nature of my energy has changed since I last injected it. I think it acts however I decide when I release it, it changes depending on what

I need from it."

"OK remove the glowing crystals, then inject your energy into the right side until the crystals start glowing. When they are glowing, press the button and fire at the wall. Focus on using a destructive nature, that should have the biggest effect on inorganic matter."

Blast! BOOM! CRASH! The opposite wall started crumbling and was filled with deep holes.

"I'm sorry, rank 1001, I didn't mean to!" rank 3 shouted, panicked. He felt incredibly guilty for damaging rank 1001's property.

"What? It's fine, it's all part of the testing process. So let me ask you a question, can you produce that level of power on your own?" rank 1001 asked curiously, his only concern was rank 3 and the device.

"Not yet, but I'm confident that once my body grows and my power matures further, I'll be able to."

"That's why for now, I want you to keep this device on you. Just for emergencies."

"I will thank you very much." Rank 3 gripped the device firmly. He knew it was something that he could treasure. "But, is it really OK for me to have this without giving you something in return?"

"Well, you could always thank me with a kiss. I enjoyed that other one."

Chapter Seventeen
Fighting and feeling

Rank 3, after making his payment, convinced rank 1001 to return with him to the academy. He waited patiently for rank 1001 to get dressed; he realised it took rank 1001 much longer than he did to get prepared for the day. Rank 3 also thought about just how rank 1001 was able to wrap his whole body in bandages by himself.

Thinking about that process caused the image of rank 1001 without his robe on to flash in rank 3's mind causing him to blush a vibrant red. Rank 3 hurriedly tried to distract himself from that memory before rank 1001 returned.

By the time they reached the academy it was almost time for the combat classes to start. Rank 1001 was unusually reluctant to go with rank 3, but after rank 3 caressed his cheek his resistance faded.

"Don't worry, it won't be like yesterday. I've got both of the devices you gave me, so I'm sure rank 21 couldn't possibly hurt me."

Rank 1001 shrugged; he agreed with the statement about rank 21. However, rank 21 wasn't the one causing rank 1001 to feel worried.

They travelled to the combat building and made

their way to the back of the building. To rank 3's surprise there were many other students waiting outside. Rank 3 instantly tightened his grip on rank 1001's hand to make sure that they both felt reassured.

Rank 3 still wasn't used to talking to strangers. Both rank 21 and rank 300 introduced themselves to him first. His confidence and willingness to talk to these students was also taking a hit as all of their gazes were fixed on rank 1001.

"Can we help you?" Rank 3 tried his best to sound confident, but his voice was shaky.

The other students looked at rank 3. After he had spoken their gazes had shifted, and some of them took a step back when they realised exactly who he was. Some of them were afraid, but that didn't change the fact that they were curious as to why rank 1001 was there. It was long established that rank 1001 didn't go into, nor was he allowed in the combat building. If he refused to fight rank matches, then he didn't deserve academy combat training.

"Good, you're all here." Rank 3 turned around to see whose voice that was. He instantly recognised it but couldn't be certain, and as he had guessed, it was the combat teacher.

"You're probably wondering why you're here. Go into the room and I'll explain."

All the students entered the room. Rank 3 and rank 1001 entered last and as usual rank 3 guided rank 1001 to the corner of the room and sat him down. Rank 3 wrapped rank 1001's hand with a red vine made out of his energy and connected it to his wrist. Like normal he did this to give rank 1001 a way to make sure he could communicate with rank 3 and it wasn't just for rank 1001's sake.

As long as they were connected rank 3 was confident that rank 1001 felt safe and content. Rank 3 didn't want rank 1001 to just leave and run off. Rank 1001 to rank 3 had become as much a source of strength as rank 3's abilities. As rank 3 went to leave rank 1001 pulled rank 3 close to him. Rank 1001 pulled out his mini screen and started typing on it.

Rank 3 read the message and blushed. "I can't do that, not in front of everyone else. What if it makes them target you more?" rank 3 responded with embarrassment and concern.

Rank 1001 heard rank 3's response and turned his head away from rank 3, to show his annoyance and displeasure at rank 3's words. "Don't be like that, I'll give you two later to make up for it."

Rank 1001 turned his head back and reached out his hand. Rank 3 caught it in his own and said, "It's a promise. Please pull on the vine if you need me. I'm going now."

Rank 1001 nodded. He let go of rank 3's hand slowly and gently and relaxed. He then pulled out his screen and started rejecting match requests just like he always did.

"Are you finally done?" the combat teacher asked,

annoyed. "All of us don't have time to indulge you in your weird hobby."

"I'm finished doing what I wanted to do. It's as simple as that, so I won't tolerate complaints even from you," rank 3 stated confidently and proudly.

"Ha, you're getting overconfident, aren't you? I'd teach you a lesson but right now you're more valuable than usual. Now as to why you're all here. I have good news and bad news; the state investigators have agreed to leave and repairs are being made to the arena. The crafting company drones are doing most of the work so don't mess around with them. Secondly, the match between academy 1 and academy 3 is still taking place. The bad news is that you lot will have to compete. All of you are still top rank students even if you are ranked between 20 and 40. Any questions before I continue, or any complaints? I'll hear them now."

The students murmured to themselves in confusion. They had never even dreamed or had nightmares that they would have to fight in the tournament matches. None of them had ever achieved a rank higher than rank 22. Still, none of them were confident enough to complain about their new situation. That was until rank 1001's presence was remembered.

"Are you including that thing over there? If you are, then I may have a complaint." It was rank 22 that had the courage to speak up, but only because he directed most of his speech at rank 1001.

"No, I wouldn't let that happen. Rank 1001 is here

so I can keep him safe until we can spend time together away from this place. I'm the only one who needs and wants combat training. So don't even think about involving rank 1001!" Rank 3 responded in a loud voice and annoyed tone.

"Yes yes, calm down, rank 3. Rank 1001 is not included, if he was it would make for a very enjoyable sight but like rank 3 says, no one would let it happen. And if they did, rank 3 wouldn't be any position to stop them. Just like this."

"Don't!"

The combat teacher, before rank 3 could respond, attacked with rank 3 barely sensing it. The teacher attacked rank 1001 with a small powerful sharp blade of air. It cut across his face, damaging and tearing his mask, but it was unable to pierce through his bandages.

Rank 3 quickly moved to rank 1001 to make sure he was all right. Luckily he was unharmed; the attack hadn't broken through the bandages to his flesh. It was either luck, or the teacher held back, but rank 3 thought knowing her temperament it must have been luck.

"What was that for?" rank 3 shouted angrily, his energy started overflowing from his body.

"That's your punishment for being so disrespectful. Put your energy away or something worse will happen. Even if you thought you had a slither of a chance against me, you can't fight me and protect rank 1001 at the same time."

Rank 3 was about to explode in a rage when rank

1001 pulled rank 3's arm towards him. Rank 3 couldn't resist being drawn to rank 1001. Rank 1001 gently held rank 3's hand and waved his small screen with a message written on it. The message said: *Are you OK, you were pulling on the vine a lot?*

Surprisingly, the message had no mention of what rank 1001 had just suffered. It only had words concerning rank 3's state of emotions.

Rank 3 pulled rank 1001 into him and said loudly so that everyone could hear, "I'm fine, how are you? Look what the teacher tried to do to you. You didn't deserve it. How much pain are you in?"

Most of the students watching wouldn't look at rank 3 directly. They were all focused on rank 1001 and some were now being even more careful. They didn't want to annoy rank 3 with a gaze he didn't like. After all, given the behaviour of other and previous top ranks, lower ranks weren't safe outside of the classroom. They wouldn't die, but they could always fall victim to being 'bumped into' leading to a painful consequence.

"Do I have to fight in the tournament?" rank 3 said disdainfully.

"Don't make jokes. This isn't the time for that. Because there is no way the student who fought uninjured against the intruder and rescued his fellow students wouldn't compete. A person like that would not leave the lower ranks to fight on their own. A person like that wouldn't abandon those weaker than himself, especially when that person is the only top twenty rank able to fight. And you're the team captain, team captains can't quit."

"I'll participate. But I won't be joining today's training, I'm taking rank 1001 away from here. You already know my skills. You can measure the others today and tomorrow we can do some team training. That's my view as the team captain."

"Very well, you're allowed to do that. That is as long as no one else objects."

The other students remained silent. Even if they opposed, from what they witnessed of rank 3's combat skills before, they couldn't be certain that they would stand a chance against him.

"No objections. That's fine too. All right, everyone, line up. I'll judge you one at a time and you two get out before I lose my patience."

"Yes, we will see all of you tomorrow."

"Ha, see," blurted out one of the other students while stifling a laugh.

Rank 3 clenched his fist. He was more than annoyed right now. The only reason he hadn't snapped was because rank 1001 was tentatively holding his other hand.

"What did you...?"

Before rank 3 could snap, rank 1001 flashed his screen at rank 3 once again. "Just leave them be, I want to go home. Please take me home."

"Yes, I'm sorry, I got distracted. Let's go."

Rank 3 gripped rank 1001's hand tight and made

the two of them exit the room quickly. Leaving behind all of his frustrations rank 3 sighed a sigh of relief. After they exited the building, rank 3 turned to rank 1001 and tentatively apologised.

"I'm sorry about that. I wasn't careful enough." Rank 3 gave a heartfelt apology to rank 1001.

"What is going on here? Rank 3, explain."

"Huh?" Rank 3 was completely surprised by the appearance and outburst of another student during the combat teaching period.

"Don't huh me?"

Rank 300 had come out of nowhere and rank 3 felt like he had been ambushed. He quickly became on guard for rank 1001's sake. Even if he thought he could trust rank 300, he wouldn't take the risk.

"Do you need something? I have something important to do." Rank 3 spoke dismissively.

"Fine don't be happy to see me. But you owe me an explanation." Rank 300's tone was enough for rank 3 to understand she was annoyed about something.

"Explanation? Explaining about what exactly?" rank 3 said confused; he didn't understand why she was here and what she wanted.

"My sister has left for now; she's pursuing outside interests. She might come back but it won't be as disruptive as last time. So aren't you going to ask me for help?"

"We'll be all right but thank you for offering."

"That's not what I meant. I couldn't care less about

that person. I'm talking about the tournament. When should we meet to go through your prep? You're the most valuable member of our team right now. I can't let you lose. I won't allow it."

"Oh that. Let's arrange that tomorrow. We have to go now." Rank 3 tried to end the conversation as fast as possible so he and rank 1001 could leave. As he tried to leave rank 300 glared viciously at rank 1001 and rank 3 noticed immediately.

"Heh, what happened to him? What annoying thing did he do this time?" Rank 300 spoke cruelly about rank 1001.

"Rank 1001 as always did nothing wrong. He was a victim of cruelty," rank 3 responded rebuffing rank 300's tone.

"So what!" rank 300 exclaimed loudly. "Why should you care about him? He's a nobody now and he'll be a nobody for the rest of his pointless life. You on the other hand are different. You have a good future; I only want to help you succeed." Rank 300 spoke as if she genuinely cared for rank 3's future.

"Yes and that's very nice of you but if you can't be nice to rank 1001, then I'll refuse to recognise you. I don't care what your sister says. If you hurt my rank 1001, then I'll hurt you, it's as simple as that." Rank 3 at the moment wasn't conforming with what rank 300 wanted, nor what her aims were.

Rank 300 didn't respond but stormed off angrily. She was annoyed at both rank 3 and her sister; her sister had obviously said something outrageous. That didn't change the fact that rank 3 had just threatened her over such a small insignificant matter.

'What did he mean by my rank 1001?' rank 300 thought angrily. Rank 3 was performing acts that rank 300 couldn't rationalise.

Rank 300 would have to carefully consider her options to make a calculated next move. She still wanted an easy time after graduating, after all that was the ultimate goal. Unlike those with powerful and influential backgrounds, she would have to work hard to not be expendable.

Rank 3 was even more annoyed than before. He was unhappy about feeling ambushed and what made him feel even worse, was rank 300's attitude toward rank 1001. Rank 3 thought that at most rank 300 would be indifferent, but instead it seemed she shared similar feelings to everyone else.

Rank 3 knew he had to just brush off this encounter. He started to relax and resumed his and rank 1001's journey back to rank 1001's home. They left the academy and when they did rank 3 finally felt at ease. It seemed that he was starting to no longer see the academy as a place of comfort.

They walked at a gentle pace back to rank 1001's home; rank 3 didn't feel like they had to rush and decided to enjoy their walk home together. After a while they finally reached their destination, rank 1001 opened the front door, and they went inside.

Immediately rank 3 pulled rank 1001 into him and hugged him tightly. "I'm really sorry about before, I should have done something." Rank 3 spoke with a tear in his eye.

Rank 1001 pulled back slightly. It was just enough for him to rip off his mask and bandages revealing his face. "There wasn't anything you could have done, don't be so hard on yourself. Anyway, don't you owe me something?" Rank 1001 blushed slightly as he spoke.

"Oh you're right. But you are sure you're OK?" Rank 3 was surprised when he realised what rank 1001 was most focused on.

Rank 1001 didn't reply to rank 3. Instead, rank 1001 put his arms around rank 3's waist, pulled rank 3 closer and kissed him. After the first kiss he stopped and then went back for a second. The second lasted much longer than the first and rank 3 was certain that rank 1001 was conveying his feelings, telling rank 3 that everything really was all right.

After a while, rank 1001 paused and took a step back. "That was nice, I enjoyed that. Are you staying for a while? Should I order food?" rank 1001 spoke and looked expectant.

"I'd like to stay for a while, but I have food back at the dorm. I don't want to put you out." Rank 3 still didn't like putting others out for his sake.

"It's no big deal, food is surprisingly cheap. Should I order the same as last time?"

"Yes please. But maybe only half this time." Rank 3 tried to find a middle ground for his conscience.

"Only half? So you do dislike certain foods. I'm sorry I hope you didn't feel like you had to eat any last time," rank 1001 spoke apologetically.

"No, it's not that, it's just there was too much for one person to eat, although how much did you eat after?"

"I don't eat much. I'll order everything just in case." Rank 1001 ran off after he finished.

Rank 3 didn't chase him but waited patiently for him to come back. Rank 1001 returned shortly with a smile on his face. "It will arrive in around two hours, so what should we do? I've got a few custom orders but as a rule, I tell customers they take as long as they take, so I can delay them a little."

"Oh, I don't want to pull you away from your work."

"It's not a big deal, I like spending time with you." Rank 1001 smiled happily and kindly at rank 3.

Hearing rank 1001's angelic voice say something so pure made rank 3's heart skip a beat. It wasn't the first time, but every time it happened felt like the first. Rank 3 was convinced he really did like being with rank 1001.

"I'll do anything you want to do."

"Well, that won't work. I don't do anything interesting: I train and exercise; I design and craft items; I perform programming and maintenance and a bunch of other boring stuff. None of which would entertain you."

"You train and exercise?"

"Oh, I know what we could do." A light flashed behind rank 1001's eyes.

"You do?" rank 3 responded with excitement and nerves.

"Yeah, take your clothes off, I want to take your measurements."

"My measurements?" rank 3 said embarrassed.

"That's right, I realised I should probably get started on designing you some clothing. I have the most durable fabric, it can be turned into flexible material, so you can wear it for combat and it should make training more risk free. The combat teacher wears an outfit made of high-quality material as well so it's not like she'll complain. I don't like her so I wouldn't accept her complaints, anyway. After all, I'm…"

"So you were upset with what happened?" Rank 3 interrupted rank 1001 as soon as the fear that rank 1001 was injured flooded his mind.

"Of course I was. The way she treats you isn't nice. She's the one who injured you before. How could I let anyone hurt my rank 3?"

"Hearing you say that makes me really happy, you know I care about you exactly the same. So where did you want to take measurements?" Rank 3 decided to give in and allow his measurements to be taken, even though it made him fell incredibly nervous.

"Normally I would do it in my personal craft work room or my bedroom, but it's still a mess down there and that would be on a printed mannequin. Normally I require measurements to be taken by the client prior to ordering. I only have a limited number of mechanical drones and they're busy at the moment, so I haven't even started repairing the testing rooms. Normally that would happen immediately. So I guess the third room on the left side. I'll go get my equipment and meet you in there."

"OK." Rank 3 was nervous but didn't hesitate when directed by rank 1001.

The two both went to their separate destinations, rank 3 slowly removed his uniform and the rest of his clothes. Rank 1001 raided his bedroom for the items that he needed. This was an abnormal situation, ever since their creation these items had never left his room.

Rank 1001 travelled back up in the elevator and made his way to the room that rank 3 had been directed to go in. Rank 3 was standing in the middle of the room, completely bright red and extremely embarrassed.

"Oh you can cover up any parts you feel embarrassed about; you don't need to keep anything on open display. When I need to take a measurement, I'll let you know."

Rank 3 felt that rank 1001 was choosing to completely ignore his current appearance. He at least thought and hoped that rank 1001 would look as embarrassed as he did when he viewed everything rank

1001 had to offer.

"Well I guess we're even now; you saw me in the same pose and now I've seen you. So you don't need to feel embarrassed about it." Rank 1001 spoke as he fully understood the situation. Rank 3 however didn't realise that rank 1001 had placed so much value and effort on the thought of what had happened before. Rank 3 assumed rank 1001 would want to forget that embarrassment from before, not take ownership of it. Right now rank 3 felt a new strange connection had formed between them.

Rank 1001 was carrying a large bag and placed it on the floor next to rank 3. He opened it and started retrieving all sorts of items that rank 3 had never seen before. Rank 3 recognised the measuring tape, but the other items were unknown to him.

"What is all that stuff? This isn't going to get more embarrassing, is it?"

"Relax, it shouldn't make you feel uncomfortable, although I wouldn't know. I usually don't take measurements myself and if I do, it's simple measurements on a machine printed mannequin. OK, I'll get started it shouldn't take too long, try not to move too much please."

Rank 1001 took rank 3's measurements and recorded other details with the various pieces of equipment that he had with him. "This measures body fat. This gives me an idea on your body's muscle thickness and your body's durability. Both will change in the future so I'll have to take your measurements again when that time comes."

All the tools used felt very invasive and rank 3 started to feel very uncomfortable. He would have protested or ran away if not for the trust he held for rank 1001.

"Will you be done soon? This is getting uncomfortable."

"Almost, just be patient please."

Rank 3 was forced to wait twenty minutes longer while rank 1001 examined his body. Almost every part was examined. When it was finished rank 3 felt incredibly exposed. Even if he was with the person he trusted the most, what was happening was pushing the limit of the benefit that provided.

"I'm finished, you can get dressed now. I do have some questions, but those can wait until you're finished." Rank 1001 spoke while pulling out a small notebook and pencil from the bag.

Rank 3 got dressed quickly and once he was, he was able to relax.

"What questions do you want to ask me?" rank 3 spoke softly and relaxed.

"How close are we? How much do I mean to you?" rank 1001 asked meekly and timidly.

"What do you mean?" Rank 3 was surprised to hear this question coming from rank 1001, especially as it was a question he himself wanted to ask.

"You accept me, right?" As rank 1001 asked this

question, he looked down at his own body.

"Of course I do. Why are you asking me that now? I wouldn't have spent so much time with you if I didn't like you." Rank 3 responded quickly and honestly, he wanted to reassure rank 1001.

"So you see me as someone that you like and accept or is it just like? I'm ready to understand if you don't accept my appearance." Every time rank 1001 mentioned his body he spoke with sadness in his eyes.

"Honestly, it's both but I don't want to make you feel pressured to return any feelings I have towards you. I'm happy how we are at the moment."

"So kissing doesn't mean what I researched it to mean?"

"What did you research it to mean?" rank 3 asked hesitantly. It was rank 1001's research that led him to pick rank 3 up in a compromising position when they had met properly for the first time.

"Kissing is a symbol of love, do you agree? It also means my body attracts you and not repels you, right?"

"I agree but I mean I don't."

"You don't. That's fine, I'll be finished with your outfit in a couple of days. I've got a lot of other orders so I won't be in the academy for a couple of days. Don't worry about it though. I have an allowance when it comes to work; it's an agreement with my company and the principal." Rank 1001 packed up his tailoring equipment and went to exit the room as he finished speaking.

"Wait!" rank 3 shouted desperately; he didn't want rank 1001 to leave.

Rank 1001 paused without turning around.

"I don't know, OK? I'm not sure yet but I definitely don't want to hurt you. I like kissing you and I enjoy every second we're together." Rank 3 blurted out everything he could think of, but even as he spoke he couldn't help but repress any feelings of love. The last person rank 3 loved, died.

"That's good enough for me. I'll have to hand stitch it so it will take two weeks and preparing the material will take roughly a week. That means it should it ready in roughly three weeks' time."

"Oh OK, thank you very much. Anyway I should get going. I need to start doing training outside of the combat classes if I want to survive the tournament," rank 3 said with a hint of frustration.

"You don't want to fight in the tournament?" Rank 1001 recognised instantly that rank 3 was upset.

"That's not important. I have to if I want to protect others. It's complicated. I don't want you to have to think too much about it. I know you're not interested in things like that, it would just bore you."

Rank 3 hugged rank 1001 and kissed him on the cheek, rank 3 then left without saying anything. He had accepted his attraction to rank 1001, but he had never considered the possibility of more. His emotions and his resolve had taken an unexpected hit and he would have to decide how he felt. Otherwise, he knew that he would only end up hurting rank 1001.

Rank 3 went to his dorm room, a place he was visiting less and less. It looked exactly the same it did a week ago. Today for the first time rank 3 entered the first any-use room; the room designed for training and exercising. There were many books and manuals as well as the numerous equipment. Along with the equipment was an open space with multiple training dummies.

Rank 3 carefully inspected the equipment. It was in perfect condition, and rank 3 noted that each piece of equipment had the same symbol on it, a shape like a brand mark. He had seen this mark before but hadn't given it any thought. He had seen it on both the state investigator and the combat teacher's combat items and clothing. Rank 3 had no idea what the brand mark represented, but he remembered that the combat teacher had mentioned a crafting company, so it could be possible that this brand mark belonged to them.

Choosing to stop thinking about something unrelated to his task, he set about reading the various manuals and started to build the foundation of his training routine. He planned to do a similar routine every day until the day of the tournament.

Chapter Eighteen
A second incident

Rank 3 woke up feeling refreshed. The afternoon and evening before had left him feeling exhausted. He trained and exercised as hard as he could. His goal would be for him to be much stronger by the time of the tournament. Luckily for rank 3, he had an ability that let him advance at a much faster rate than others: his regeneration. Wounds sustained in training healed while he slept. Even his muscles were able to grow in strength easily from being broken down and built back up again in a very short time.

Rank 3 got dressed and prepared himself for this new day. He felt confident now that he had experienced his first training results. Despite this, he was not in a good mood; he wasn't agitated but he was sad about knowing that he wouldn't see rank 1001 today.

Still, he knew he could manage to get through the day and rank 1001 would definitely be safe and wouldn't have to be on guard against everyone around him. This at least meant rank 3 didn't have to constantly worry.

The academic lesson went smoothly and rank 21 was absent once again, still healing from the wound he received from rank 3. The academic teacher was still in a bad mood despite both the absence of the state investigators and rank 1001, so the lesson was carried out in complete silence.

Rank 3 was cautious about how the combat lesson would go, especially as he would have to train with others that weren't the combat teacher or rank 21. Rank 3 was also nervous about the abilities of the others and if there was a chance that he would accidently injure them.

Rank 3 entered the combat building, passing the reopened arena. He travelled to the classroom at the back. He along with the other students entered the classroom and greeted their combat teacher.

"All right, today we're moving straight on to team drills. The last tournament match was a fake in more ways than you probably realise. Normally, the tournament is a whole day event with multiple matches, we've never started off with every student fighting. The usual way to do it, is to have multiple single matches, then doubles and after that is the five versus five. Usually a match involving ten students doesn't take place unless special approval is given. Today I'll be figuring out your pairings and later lessons I'll decide on who would make the best five-person team. For starters, everyone pair up with the person next to them. You now have five minutes to spar against each other and properly understand each other's abilities. After five minutes I'll arrange you into two vs two battle formats. We'll continue this type of training for the rest of the week. Any questions?"

"Will I be partnered with rank 21 when he is healed?" rank 3 asked, assuming no one else would want to partner with him.

"Hm? Yes that would make the most sense, but you have to get him to agree to it. He's been in a bit of a bad mood recently; it's funny he's a little jealous. Oh right, so rank 3 you can observe, as team captain you need to get to know your team." The combat teacher almost revealed something she was explicitly asked not to.

"Yes, it would be good to know the people who are also being forced to do this," rank 3 commented with disdain.

"You're wrong, we don't feel forced. We're all top forty ranked students, we have our pride and are willing to represent our academy. I thought you had the same pride when you jumped into the arena last time. I guess I was wrong," rank 22 remarked.

"Yes, why did you jump into the arena if you don't want to fight for the academy?" another student quipped All the students there doubted rank 3's integrity and intentions.

"I merely saw people in front of me that I could help, it was as simple as that. It wasn't anything complicated like academy pride." Rank 3 responded honestly and made no expressions to hide his distaste for the term 'academy pride'.

"Spoken like a true top ranker. You only care about

your own ideals," rank 33 said with a tone of disdain.

"I haven't done anything wrong," rank 3 said defensively.

"I know, it would just be nice if you weren't such a hypocrite," rank 22 spoke wryly.

"What did you just call me?" Rank 3 immediately became aggressive along with being defensive.

"We've all heard the rumours, and we saw it for ourselves yesterday. You would rather protect a student who has no love for academy 1 than the students who do." The other students were having their suspicions confirmed.

"That's not important. Don't talk about rank 1001 like that. He is a student just like you and me, that's the real truth."

"Of course it isn't, we are students who are going to fight on your team for you and the academy, but you would gladly beat us half to death for doing something rank 1 gave us permission to do. It is our right to treat rank 1001 however we feel like. It's been that way since the second day of rank 1001's first year. That's the truth. Rank 1001 doesn't belong here and is punished for acting otherwise. We are real academy 1 students, rank 1001 is not."

Rank 3 was becoming annoyed and not just annoyed he could feel a deep and intense anger swelling up inside him. "Shouldn't you be training already? It's not like you'll survive without it. I fought the intruder and I can already tell that you people are weak and worthless!" Rank 3 spoke with anger and disgust.

"If we're worthless, what does that make rank 1001? Even comparing him to dirt is too much," rank 22 asked with a wry smile.

"That's it I've had enough!" Rank 3 finally snapped.

"Boom! Crackle! Crash!"

Rank 3 lunged towards rank 22 with fury in his eyes. He punched rank 22 directly in his stomach, sending him flying across the room and crashing into the stone wall. But, just as rank 3 made contact, rank 22 electrocuted him burning his arm and hand.

Rank 22 was left lying on the floor in pain. He was lying in front of the hole in the wall made by his body. Rank 22 was easily the most injured out of the two and would need to go to the medical centre. Rank 22 was badly bruised and some of his ribs were broken, he was no longer fit for combat training.

"Teacher, I'll participate in the tournament but I won't work with any of these. I'll fight all the matches myself. And I don't need your training, I'm leaving." Rank 3 was angry and fed up with his current surroundings. His best course of action would be to leave before he angered or was angered by the combat teacher.

Rank 3 stormed out of the classroom and it was only as he neared his dorm room, did he realise what he had just said. He had said something outrageous. No matter how strong he planned on getting, that gave him little confidence that he could defeat the top five ranked academy 3 students all together in a battle. Academy 3 was only two below academy 1 and their students wouldn't be weak.

Rank 3 went to his room and started training. He knew he would have to give it his all if he stood any chance of winning. Any chance of surviving for that matter.

A few days passed and rank 3 had still not heard from or about rank 1001, causing distress. Rank 3 was even denied entry into rank 1001's home, Rank 1001 was nowhere to be found. Rank 3 assumed that rank 1001 was too focused on his work to answer. Rank 1001 had stated that he would hand stitch the outfit he was preparing and it was a long and complex process.

Rank 3 gave up after the second try as he didn't want to disturb rank 1001, especially if rank 1001 was working on his present for rank 3.

Rank 21 healed completely after a couple days of rest. He was back to his original shape and attended the combat lessons with the other students. Not doing so would have meant a scolding from his sister, a scolding he definitely wanted to avoid.

Rank 21 had yet to contact rank 3. He had heard about rank 3's disagreements with the other students but as he agreed with them, messaging rank 3 seemed pointless. Rank 21 had started to distance himself from rank 3, even his desire for them to be friends was diminishing.

Another week went by. Rank 3 was doing his normal training when his phone started ringing. He hoped it would be rank 1001 and eagerly rushed to his phone and answered it. "Hello," rank 3 said expectantly.

"Hi, rank 3, it's me rank 300. Why haven't you contacted me? We were supposed to come up with your preparations a week ago!" Rank 3 could tell instantly that rank 300 was annoyed with him.

"I'm sorry I forgot; I've been distracted," rank 3 replied honestly and was apologetic.

"You obviously have because you clearly haven't heard. Come to the arena, they're repeating the footage taken there," rank 300 ordered rank 3. Her tone was deadly serious.

"What footage?" Rank 3 was confused, he assumed rank 300 had only called about him not contacting her.

"Academy 3 were arriving early to avoid the masked person from before, but it's clear now that this person is an enemy with resources."

"What are you saying?" Rank 3 was shocked to hear mention of the masked person.

"Academy 3's students and teachers were attacked, and that's not all. Even a guardian was defeated. You really need to watch the footage; it's something that you have to see to believe. You won't be able to understand otherwise."

Rank 3 quickly got changed and made his way to the arena. Rank 300 was already inside along with the majority of the other students, even teachers and other

243

staff had come to see this nightmarish scenario for themselves.

"Rank 3, come over here," rank 300 called to rank 3 She had already managed to secure a booth.

"Rank 300, how serious is it? Did you see anything about it beforehand?" Rank 3 seeing the amount of people knew this incident must be serious.

"No, no one in my family did, it's unprecedented. Our nation has been at constant war for centuries but we have never received an attack on our soil. We've always been the invaders; this is payback for something we did. What other reason would there be?"

"But why would they target academies, why students?" Rank 3 was uneducated in the workings of states.

"That's easy, we're the next elite soldiers. We're the ones who win the battles and the wars. This must be the work of a powerful and dangerous group, I'm sure of it." Lights were flickering behind rank 300's eyes.

"Are you saying they all were killed?" Rank 3 was fearful he would have to witness someone die.

"No one died, which is the worst part."

"How is that bad?" Rank 3 was surprised to hear no casualties was a bad thing.

"A being who easily defeats teachers nearly all of which are expert war veterans and a being who defeated one of the three guardians, the warrior guardian no less. A being who does that and doesn't kill. Do you know how powerful someone would have to be to exercise that sort of control? There is a monster roaming around in our state, how can we feel safe now? Don't look at me like I'm exaggerating, watch the clip and you'll understand. Remember, I'm a brilliant analyst. I know a monster when I see one."

"I'll watch it, but I already think you're overreacting." Rank 3 was hesitant. As soon as he heard no casualties, he immediately thought the person responsible couldn't be that intimidating.

Rank 300 played the clip; the footage was taken halfway through the incursion. All the academy 3 students were either unconscious or hiding behind their teachers. There were ten teachers in total, over three times the amount that would normally be supervising the group. This time they weren't sent just to supervise but to guard as well and it had been proven that they were necessary.

The teachers unlike the students had permission to carry tools and weapons for combat. Each teacher had a combat focused ability and their tool complemented it. Most teachers had an ability related to controlling, creating, manipulating a force or element of some kind. One teacher could summon flames, another lightning and other elements could be seen clearly. Along with these teachers, the other teachers that didn't have an element related ability, either had a transformation or extrasensory ability, transformation abilities boosting physical attributes and extrasensory abilities boosting fighting ability and coordination.

Their abilities alone wouldn't have made them achieve the positions that they had secured. All of them also had a high base physical level. Their speed and power far above the average person, they could only be hurt by each other or someone on the same level.

Of course there were individuals that were above them in power and ability, but they would never have to fight them. Those people stood at the top of the state and were rarely seen in person; however, their level of power wasn't exclusive to themselves.

So when rank 3 saw their opponent his first impression would have been that their opponent would lose. They faced only one individual. Rank 3 recognised the individual due to the individual wearing the same mask as the one before. Even though a mask would not have been enough on its own, rank 3 knew it was the same person, their build was also exactly the same. They were around five feet with a small frame and along with their mask their body seemed expressionless.

Like last time the individual had a blade, this blade was longer than the one before but much thinner. Despite it looking somewhat fragile on the screen, it screamed of danger.

The fight between the teachers and this individual should have been overwhelmingly in favour of the teachers. Even if individually they were weaker, all of them together should have been more than enough. This was not the case.

The teachers didn't lose a hard uphill battle, simply

because they were not given time to. In a fluid motion like a deadly flowing wave, they were all cut down, each wound proved to be non-fatal, but that didn't stop the scene from looking horrific. Blood sprayed everywhere. The only good thing about the screen was that rank 3 watched the event in silence otherwise he would have heard terrifying screams. Screams borne of pain and fear.

Although those screams wouldn't last long, the masked individual after defeating the teachers and students swiftly knocked them unconscious. It was when the masked individual went to leave that the footage was most interesting and most relevant.

It was as if a comet had descended from the sky. The guardian seemingly appeared like an angel or perhaps a demon, due to his conflicting actions and appearance. He crashed into the earth creating a crater in which he walked out of completely unharmed. The warrior guardian was known for being impetuous. He was always the first to volunteer for missions only the guardians could complete. Despite being the oldest, he was considered the most reckless.

Rank 3 continued watching in the same manner, triggering rank 300 to step in.

Rank 300 paused the footage with the guardian's arrival. "I'm getting the impression you don't know about the state guardians also known as the state's most powerful soldiers."

"I've never heard of them," rank 3 said annoyed

that she had paused the footage. Rank 3 was becoming an avid fan of analysing footage.

"That explains why you don't understand the severity of the situation, you think this is something we'll all forget about in a few days."

"That's how it was last time. Also last time no one died as well. Why make a fuss when people get a few cuts and bruises?" Rank 3 felt pity for the victims but not sympathy in regard to whether it was unjust. Rank 3 no longer had any feelings about his beating; he had left it in the past, to him it didn't matter any more.

"The incident in the academy has been swept away by the senior staff and senior members of state. Even my sister had trouble investigating for as long as she did. Not that that will stop her though, she can be really stubborn."

"I don't care about what happened to our tournament team or academy 2's or academy 3's teams. As long as no one died, why should we care?" Rank 3 didn't believe the situation called for such a strong response.

"Were you living under a rock before you came here? When we graduate we all join the army and fight in the wars, not everyone comes back from that. The one thing we should be able to rely on is that we're keeping the fight over there. Innocent people could get hurt if a monster is left on the loose. You're starting to be really annoying." Rank 300's opinion of rank 3 had plummeted.

"I'm sorry, it's just I'm in a bad enough mood as it is. Please explain the guardians so I can understand the importance of what happened." Rank 3 finally gave in, even though he wanted to only think about rank 1001.

"We're all on edge, it's OK. There are three guardians, the warrior, the tower and the shield guardian. The most famous is the warrior. He's the only one whose face is known to the public the other two are mysterious. Now the main reason to understand the fear: the warrior is said to be at the peak of physical strength and power, speed and agility; his body itself is a weapon of mass destruction. Not only that, he is one of the few people to possess the rarest ability of all, he can regenerate."

"He can regenerate?" rank 3 said surprised. Rank 3 could also regenerate, and this gave him a sense of comfort when it came to being injured. However, he had never seen it as his greatest asset in a fight – it was still a slow process after all.

"Yes and not only that, it is said that his regeneration is level six, the highest in the state. One of the highest known in the whole world."

"Level six!" rank 3 blurted out. He had never heard of anyone having such a high level, the difference between each level was already like night and day.

"Yes level six, he can regrow limbs during a fight. Not only that, he can transform his body. He can harden his skin and even grow larger up to three times. Before this happened he was considered to be the only known monster. With his defeat our state is vulnerable, our neighbours will take advantage. Now do you understand?" Rank 300 spoke in a serious tone and rank 3 could sense the fear and danger in her voice.

"I think so, play the footage." Rank 3 was now fully motivated to watch the footage and would carefully examine everything that happened, although he didn't fully understand the ramifications of this incident.

Rank 300 resumed the footage. The warrior guardian was already a giant of a man before he transformed, standing at seven feet tall and being almost as wide, his body brimming with muscle.

"Here take this. You'll want to hear what he says." Rank 300 passed rank 3 a small black earpiece, the same one that rank 1001 used to help him use his screen. Rank 3 would use it to listen to words spoken by the guardian.

The warrior guardian walked slowly out of the crater that he had made from crashing into the ground. Despite his mammoth stature, his most noticeable feature was the look on his eyes; he had the face and gaze of a vicious beast.

"Can I take it that you did all of this by yourself?" The warrior guardian looked extremely happy despite his wild ferociousness.

The masked individual turned to face the guardian. He didn't say anything nor did he make any motions, he just stood there cold and expressionless.

"Don't want to say anything. That's fine by me. I've been looking forward to finding a worthy challenge. I haven't fought anyone seriously for almost two hundred years now."

"Two hundred years?" rank 3 blurted out suddenly.

"Shh! Keep listening," rank 300 scolded.

Rank 3 was shocked by the revelation that someone could live that long. He was even more taken aback by the prospect that it was due to regeneration. If that was the case, just how long would he live for?

"OK, let's get started, if you have any fancy abilities now would be the time to use them. I don't want you to disappoint me," the warrior guardian goaded and was excited for what would come next.

It was the warrior guardian that made the first move. He moved fast, faster than anything that rank 3 had ever seen before. It was almost a miracle that the recording was able to capture his movements. However, when the warrior guardian reached the masked individual, the masked individual cut off the guardian's hand.

The attack was too fast for the recording to accurately detail, all that could be seen was a flashing image, a blur. One moment the guardian was landing a heavy blow and the next, the masked individual appeared to pass through him and the guardian's severed hand was on the floor.

"Nice moves, I'm getting really excited now," the guardian said excitedly.

The warrior guardian was unfazed by the loss of his hand; it was clear though that his injury wouldn't last long as his hand had already started to grow back. It would only take a couple of minutes for it to return to its former state.

"Now I'm going to get a bit serious." The guardian's eyes turned red as he spoke.

The warrior guardian's body changed dramatically. It looked as if it was covered in scales and sharp jagged rocks, as if the ground itself had been layered upon him. Not only that, he had grown to be almost ten feet tall. The warrior guardian breathed a sigh of relief, as if a heavy burden had been lifted.

"Try that again and see what happens now." The guardian's tone changed to be more serious.

The warrior guardian moving at an even greater speed than before, resulting in him becoming nothing more than a large blur on the screen, attacked the masked individual once more.

Rank 3 was expecting to see some sort of difference. Perhaps the masked individual would be hurt or unable to damage the guardian's body. But, no. The result was the same as before: the guardian had now lost both his hands.

"Argh!" The guardian screamed in pain, being transformed made his body more sensitive to the pain of an injury, the payment for increased durability. "Hah, guess I'll have to go all out. You were fun to fight." The guardian's tone became very serious, and it was clear that he was suppressing the pain with anger.

The warrior guardian grew several feet taller and

his body took a form looking closer to that of a giant jagged diamond. His hands were still regenerating, it would still take another minute for the first one to return. However, the guardian was unfazed by this fact.

"Before I kill you. Will you tell me your name?" the warrior asked both from curiosity and his warrior spirit but also to buy himself time to heal.

The masked individual ignored the warrior guardian and instead chose to take a fighting stance. It was the first time that he had done this. Rank 3 wondered if it was due to the masked individual recognising the warrior guardian's strength.

"Yes, that's it, give me everything you've got. I want you to die knowing you had nothing else left to give! Those who do that receive my highest praise." The guardian spoke proudly but his anger could still be felt in the air; he had still been forced to feel pain.

Ting! Snap!

The masked individual had moved at a speed much faster than before; he had struck intending to remove the guardian's arm but had failed. The top of his blade had snapped off instead of slicing through the warrior guardian's flesh.

The masked individual felt the end of his sword and shook his head at it. He was obviously displeased with its performance. The weapon he had used to injure his opponent had become useless.

"What will you do now? You can't hurt me in this form. Do you have anything left?" The guardian felt more relaxed feeling his abilities would easily overcome this opponent, even if this opponent was much faster than him.

The masked individual responded to the warrior guardian for the first time. He didn't say anything but simply nodded yes.

"That's good, because when I start attacking it will all be over. Huh?"

The masked individual motioned to the warrior guardian to attack him, a fatal mistake in the warrior guardian's mind.

"Very well, I'll give you want you want. There is no way I can lose now!" Both of his hands had healed, and he was in his most powerful form; he was the embodiment of confidence.

The warrior guardian took a deep breath and pushed down deep into the earth. His movement happened in an instant. The warrior vanished. Rank 3 was completely surprised and shocked by it. He wasn't sure how fast, but for the recorder to be unable to capture it, it must have been faster than anything he'd ever seen. This battle had transcended anything rank 3 had experienced, witnessed or even imagined.

The warrior guardian used a straightforward direct attack. He intended to blow his opponent away with a single strike aimed directly at the head. This attack had caused instant death to all who had received it before.

The recording managed to record the moment of impact. It didn't clearly show what happened, but it was obvious that it was the guardian that was slammed into the ground. The masked individual held the warrior guardian's wrist in his hand. The warrior guardian had a singular expression on his face, complete shock and it was slowly turning to fear.

On the screen, a small slender five-foot masked person was now towering over an almost fifteen-foot giant. A completely unexpected outcome for all who witnessed the footage.

The most interesting part of the recording was also one of the parts that couldn't be viewed or heard clearly. It wasn't a hundred percent clear, but it looked like the masked individual moved close to the warrior guardian to whisper something in his ear. It was a short exchange, but it was enough to cause instant and true fear. Tingling and trembling feelings covered the warrior guardian's entire body, and they penetrated deep into his spirit.

It was now that the nightmarish scene would begin.

Even if his spirit was weakened or broken, the warrior guardian's body would be healed shortly, after that all he needed to do would be to lose himself to rage to escape his hell.

It was too late though, rank 3 could only look on in horror as this nightmarish scene played out in front of him. The warrior guardian was trying desperately to focus.

The masked individual ignored the warrior guardian's actions completely. Crunch! The masked individual dug his fingers into the warrior guardian's diamond like flesh; the warrior guardian cried out in pain, his screams were blood curdling.

In one swift move that made rank 3 want to stop watching and run away from the screen, the masked individual ripped the warrior guardian's arm from his body. The warrior guardian passed out from the pain. Despite his impressive regeneration, a serious wound in his transformed state was too painful to handle. Fear and hopelessness swarmed his mind, and it collapsed from the pressure.

The warrior may have been able to endure an injury like this, but this was the first time he had received this kind of severe wound, this severe wound and the extreme pain meant that he had lost this fight. The physical and mental, in both parts he had been crushed. It might not have been so if he was properly prepared. It couldn't be said his abilities were overwhelmed, but he was crushed completely. It was the only outcome and everyone had to accept it.

The warrior guardian's transformation was undone, his body returned to its original size and his flesh became soft. In an act that could only be described as one of extreme cruelty, using the remainder of his broken blade, the masked individual removed the rest of the warrior guardian's limbs. The masked individual finished his onslaught by impaling the warrior guardian into the ground, striking though his stomach. The masked individual left his broken blade behind and walked off calmly.

Seeing the end of this footage would make the observer think that the masked individual was just a passer-by, without a care in the world. The footage ended shortly after the masked individual's departure.

Rank 3 was in a state of shock. He had never imagined or truly understood just how powerful people could become in the world. Even though this was shocking information, rank 3 couldn't help but feel worried about rank 1001. Rank 1001 was now always at the centre of rank 3's worries. Whenever rank 3 imagined or saw someone get hurt, he immediately thought about what was most precious to him.

"Do you understand now?" rank 300 said softly. She could tell rank 3 had been shaken like all those who had watched the footage before him.

"I have to go," rank 3 said. As he passed by rank 300, his face was turning pale and he was starting to panic.

"What are you talking about? What's more important than being here?" Rank 300 was shocked and confused by rank 3's sudden exit.

Rank 3 ran out of the academy without saying a word.

Chapter Nineteen
Figuring out confused feelings

Rank 3 went immediately to rank 1001's home. It was the only place he wanted to be right now. All he could think about was rank 1001 and how much he wanted to see him.

As rank 3 reached rank 1001's home, by sheer coincidence he saw rank 1001 travelling from the opposite direction. Rank 1001 was dressed differently. He still had a mask on, along with his gloves, but he wore smart shoes and a suit. In his hands he held his red and white walking stick along with a briefcase.

At first rank 3 doubted that it was in fact rank 1001, but that doubt didn't matter when he saw the state of the suit. It was cut up and ripped in many places; there were even some blood stains.

Rank 3 ran as fast as he could to meet up with rank 1001. He grabbed rank 1001's hands, causing rank 1001 to shiver and tremble in fear. Rank 3 forgot about rank 1001's natural disposition outside of his home, and he immediately released rank 1001.

Even though he knew it would be wrong, it was the quickest route to get to his goal. Without rank 1001's permission, rank 3 quickly and gently removed part of the mask covering one of rank 1001's eyes.

When rank 1001 saw rank 3, he felt a mix of emotions; he felt a mix of fear and anger but most of all a sense of comfort and another warm feeling emotion. Rank 1001 grabbed rank 3's hand and led him into his home.

When they arrived inside, rank 1001 removed his mask and the bandages covering his face. "Why didn't you announce yourself before you grabbed me?" Rank 1001 asked with a hint of annoyance and something that rank 3 felt to be like regret.

"I'm sorry, I saw the state of your suit and panicked," rank 3 answered honestly. He wouldn't deny that he was overcome by his emotions.

"There's something on my suit?" Rank 1001 looked down and his expression changed. "Oh there is. I didn't realise."

"You didn't realise? What happened to you?" rank 3 asked. The panic in his tone was obvious.

"Some people attacked me because of my mask. It was fine though, once they found out who I was they left me alone," rank 1001 responded and gave the impression it had happened before and that he was now used to it.

"Someone attacked you? Where were you? Why are you dressed like that? None of this makes sense, and I just found out that that masked intruder attacked another group of people. You need to tell me these things so I know that you're safe." Rank 3's face had paled. He was giving in to panic and made it clear that he was deeply affected by rank 1001's disappearance.

"It's sweet of you to care, but I go on business trips all the time, I'm used to this sort of thing." Rank 1001 didn't understand why rank 3 was acting the way he was.

"A business trip?" Rank 3 had received an answer, but it was one he didn't expect.

"Yeah, I had some business in city 2 and I stopped over in city 3 before I came back. The best part though, is that the material for your outfit should definitely be ready. Isn't that exciting?" rank 1001 said happily and eagerly.

"Weren't you scared?" Rank 3 didn't want to believe that rank 1001 had to endure such a hardship; especially alone.

"No, I'm used to it. Besides, there is no point of being scared unless you know you're going to die. That's why I don't understand the fear surrounding this masked person. No one has died." Rank 1001 sounded oddly interested in current events.

"What about the warrior guardian?"

"Have you come here just to ask me questions about a masked person and some academy 3 representatives? If that is why you're here then I can't help you." Rank 1001 dismissed rank 3's question and tried to find out what exactly rank 3 was after. They had made no plans to meet today.

"No. It's embarrassing."

"Oh?" Rank 1001's eyes lit up with sparks. "I see. You came for a kiss," rank 1001 stated happily. To him that would be a sweet surprise, one that he would readily accept. "Come here then." He opened his arms wide, inviting rank 3 to embrace him.

"That would be nice but, well I mean, I want to I do, but that's not why I'm here. It's because I got scared when I watched the footage of the masked attacker. I couldn't help but feel powerless and I couldn't stop thinking what would happen if someone like that attacked you. If that happened I..." Rank 3 became flustered and started to panic.

"Calm down, I'm not going to die. No one hates me enough to try to kill me. So now that you're here, are you hungry, I can order you something to eat? Or a drink perhaps, I did receive something from one of my largest customers. It's rare tea leaves; you can't grow them in this state. They're pretty tasty."

"That sounds nice," Rank 3 said tearfully. He couldn't control his reaction to someone who says they hadn't died because someone didn't hate them enough.

"Don't cry." Rank 1001 wiped the tear off rank 3's cheek. "I'll let you know everything next time. We're both fine so let's enjoy each other's company. OK?" Rank 1001 smiled brightly at rank 3 and kissed his cheek.

"OK," rank 3 said while wiping his eyes. He stopped tearing up and followed rank 1001 down the corridor.

"Turning this room into a guest room is becoming even more useful, you can't have tea without a kettle and glasses," rank 1001 said while feeling proud of his previous decision.

The two of them entered the guest room and rank 1001 sat rank 3 down on the side of the bed. Afterwards he walked over to the kitchen area, filled the kettle with water and placed it on the oven to boil. He then collected two glasses.

Rank 1001 removed the tea leaves from his briefcase, closing it quickly afterward to conceal its contents. Once the water was boiled, rank 1001 used it to make tea by mixing in the tea leaves. He then poured it into the glasses and brought it over to rank 3.

"Here you go, a cup of tea courtesy of me."

"Thank you, rank 1001, that's very kind of you. I've calmed down a bit now. So what was your trip like, apart from those impolite people?" Rank 3 had calmed down and was eager to know more about what rank 1001 had been up to.

"It was good, I got what I wanted. All the general orders are organised through servers, situated all around the place. I only travel to greet new clients, or if I'm delivering a particularly discrete or fragile custom order. This journey was the latter. I can't tell you the details, but it went well. I even got a souvenir, and I enjoyed myself. So it was definitely a trip worth the effort. How are you feeling? I know you might be shaken by that footage, but aren't you glad you won't have to fight a tournament match? Both academies will now agree to postpone and hopefully the state will prohibit tournament matches for the time being. Getting rid of something unnecessary sure sounds satisfying, but we'll have to wait and see. It would be unfortunate if the state acted recklessly."

Rank 3 didn't listen to every word that rank 1001 said. Despite what he said he was still shaken and struggling to focus.

"Mmm. This tea tastes really nice, you should try some." Rank 1001 took a drink from his glass and looked expectantly at rank 3.

"I'll try some in a minute. Thank you for this, I just got overwhelmed. I guess you're probably right I won't have to fight in the tournament, that means I benefitted from that horror. What a cruel joke."

Rank 3 downed his glass of tea and laid down on his back on the bed. "I'm starting to regret coming down here. I liked knowing nothing." Rank 3 spoke, filled with regret.

"We wouldn't have met if you didn't enrol at the academy. That means something. We even promised to look after one another."

"That's just it. By the time I'm strong enough to protect you, you'll probably have died of old age. It doesn't seem likely I'll be able to give you a happy or safe life. I just found out that the warrior guardian is well over two hundred years old. 'Sigh'. I wonder what I'll be like when I reach that age." Rank 3 couldn't help to worry about the future, especially concerning rank 1001 and himself.

"Why are you worrying about something pointless? Just enjoy here and now. I'll make you another glass of tea. You don't have to worry about training for a few days, so why not relax?" Rank 1001 was completely indifferent to rank 3's talk of ageing.

"Can I stay here tonight?" rank 3 asked, sounding desperate.

"Of course you can. I enjoy your company." Rank 1001 was slowly accepting someone completely into his life.

"I can't help thinking about the outcome if a monster like that attacked you, and even if I was there, I wouldn't be able to protect you or myself. I can't help thinking you would be better off without me; I've only caused you more pain than anything else." Rank 3 was thinking negatively and could only focus on negative memories.

"Hmmm?" Rank 1001 sighed a deep sigh full of complicated emotions. Rank 1001 then joined rank 3, the both of them lying on the bed together. "I don't regret any of our time spent together. If I had even a hint of doubt I wouldn't have agreed to make your outfit. Just think about it, would someone who feels that you cause them pain do this?"

Rank 1001 rolled on his side to face rank 3. He wrapped his hand around rank 3's face and kissed his cheek. Rank 3 instantly started to blush.

"I guess not. You're right, I'm sorry, I got shocked and scared and I couldn't control my imagination. Thank you for caring so much," rank 3 replied and kissed rank 1001. "I'm feeling better now, but you're right I can relax for a few days. Can I stay here with you for that time? I don't want to be away from you at the moment. I'm sorry I'm not exactly sure why."

"Of course you can. I'd really appreciate the company but you can't watch me work, that's too private."

"That's fine, we can still have some secrets from each other. Shamefully I have some of my own." Rank 3's gaze shifted from rank 1001's eyes.

"Let's make another promise then."

"Promise to do what?"

"When we reach a point where we are so close that we can have no secrets, we promise to have no secrets and no secrets from that moment onwards. For now we're allowed one or two, that sounds good, right?"

"Yeah, that sounds good, but are you certain you don't mind me keeping things from you? You know I'll answer any question you ask me honestly." Rank 3 shifted his gaze back to rank 1001's eyes, almost getting lost in their golden beauty.

"That's why I won't ask you to tell me."

Rank 3 went to respond but was unable as rank 1001 kissed him directly on his lips, their lips entwined and both became very relaxed.

"All right, I'm going to start working. I'll be back

in a few hours. Please make use of all the facilities."

Rank 1001 went to get off the bed when rank 3 grabbed his hand. "Wait! Please." Rank 3, giving in to his feelings, couldn't bear to be parted from rank 1001.

Rank 1001 paused. He could see from rank 3's pained expression and knew that rank 3 was feeling uneasy.

"What is it? Are you still not feeling well?" rank 1001 responded, concerned.

"Can you stay here with me for a little while?" rank 3 asked, surprisingly shyly.

"I can do that, but it will delay your gift. I refuse to use inferior quality material for your outfit," rank 1001 said proudly and compassionately.

"That's fine, being here with you is more than enough right now," rank 3 said softly and blushing. Being so direct with his requests was something that he wasn't used to.

"All right then," rank 1001 replied happily. He knew the gift would be greatly delayed, but he enjoyed rank 3's company too much to refuse his request.

Rank 1001 dragged rank 3 into the middle the bed. "What are you doing?" rank 3 asked, becoming even more embarrassed.

"When I'm with you I'm able to sleep without my normal aid and usual method. Sleep is also considered a good form of healing, especially when it's next to someone you're close with. That's what I've heard, anyway."

'Gulp.' Rank 3 was unsure what to expect was about to happen.

"Lie down next to me, I'll wrap in you my arms and you wrap me in your energy, that really helped me sleep last time."

"OK." Rank 3 responded to rank 1001's plan nervously.

Rank 1001 wrapped his arms around rank 3. Rank 3 in turn summoned his energy in the form of thin red threads and wrapped rank 1001 in them. Rank 1001's face and arms were left exposed but the rest of his body was completely covered.

"Doesn't this feel nice. I've never felt this close to someone before," Rank 1001 said gently and quietly. Even though it was just the two of them in the entire house, whispering made it much more intimate.

"Yeah it does, this feels really nice. I've never been in a situation like this before. No one has hugged me this comfortingly since my mother died. That was eight years ago," rank 3 said with a mix of happiness and sadness.

Rank 1001 pulled rank 3 even closer, tightening their hugging embrace. They were firmly connected to one another. Rank 1001 then kissed rank 3 on the cheek, and after their eyes locked, they both nodded and they kissed each other's lips.

Rank 3 couldn't remember how long they kissed for, but it was more than enough for him to become completely relaxed. And at some point, with both locked in each other's embrace, they had fallen into a deep sleep. Rank 3 didn't know much about rank 1001's usual sleep habits, but rank 3 himself felt like even his spirit had rested and recovered; rank 3 was now unsure how long it had been damaged for. Realising his soul had been put back together was both a joyful and frightening thought.

BEEP! BEEP! RING! RING!

Rank 3 opened his eyes suddenly; alarm sounds were ringing throughout the whole building. Rank 3 rose slightly causing rank 1001 to grunt his frustrations but rank 1001 was reluctant to open his eyes, trying his best to ignore the situation.

Rank 3 retracted his energy and rank 1001's body was forced to slowly awaken. Rank 1001 opened his eyes and glared frustrated in the direction of the front door and then angrily looked up and shouted, "Babe, shut it off! I'm not in the mood for this!"

Rank 3 was expecting something or someone to respond, but no response came. Surprisingly a moment later the alarm stopped ringing.

"Thanks, babe! Rank 3 can you lay back down, I can still sleep or," Rank 1001 blushed a bright red mixed with spots of pink, "we could kiss again." Rank 1001 was perfectly comfortable kissing but openly asking for it still felt embarrassing.

"First, who is this babe person?" rank 3 asked with a hint of accusation.

"Babe is my personal house assistant; I built and

programmed it myself, it's not that advanced I'm not very good with complex electronics. Anyway, come here." Rank 1001 tried to pull rank 3 closer to him.

Rank 3 decided to gloss over the fact he was unsure what personal house assistant meant. He knew there were people like that in his sky island home. They were all dressed smartly and were forced to do a variety of jobs, all of which his family members were too lazy or too proud to do themselves.

Rank 3 laid back down and started to relax. Rank 3 and rank 1001 put their hands on each other's faces and drew each other closer. Just as they were about to start kissing, a loud banging noise came from the front door.

"Babe!" Rank 1001 shouted angrily. It was the first time rank 3 had heard him speak this way. Rank 3 wasn't sure if babe was someone that rank 1001 would hurt but rank 3 would make it so that was unnecessary.

"I'll go see who it is," rank 3 said while stroking rank 1001's cheek and preparing to get up and out of the bed.

"Fine, I'll go get a mask from downstairs. Can you keep the both of them occupied until then, please?"

"Of course I can, don't worry I won't let anyone hurt you or interrupt your life here."

"Thank you, I'll be back up shortly. I'm not happy about this at all. I was very happy until they interrupted us."

Rank 1001 jumped out of the bed and stormed off into the corridor angrily mumbling about having to be conscious of those around him.

Rank 3 was unsure about what was happening. The speed in which rank 1001 had left the room was confusing, almost as if he was running away from rank 3. Rank 3 took a deep breath and left the room. He turned up the corridor and walked to the front door. He was still wearing his academy uniform, so if needed he would use that connection, to protect him and rank 1001.

Rank 3 pressed the button to open the door, and to his surprise he was greeted by a familiar face. "Rank 3 from academy 1? What are you doing here? You better not be breaking any rules that can get rank 300 into trouble." The state investigator immediately scolded rank 3. It came off as a natural response to seeing rank 3.

"State investigators! What are you doing here?" Rank 3 responded to their appearance surprised and spoke distrustful towards them.

In front of rank 3 were two state investigators. They were the same two as before but this time the male investigator was also present. Rank 3 could feel the male investigator's piercing gaze but did his best to ignore it as he attempted to keep them away from rank 1001.

"Rank 3, do you even know where here is?" the state investigator asked patronisingly.

"I'm reluctant to say it out loud, in case you're prying into somewhere you shouldn't," rank 3 said proudly. The identity of this place was a secret he would keep.

"Haha, it's funny when to us you look like a trespasser. This is one of the crafting company's complexes. It's the closest to city 1 and that's why we're visiting this one first. Now that we're here, let's start with the questions shall we. What are you doing here? How did you find this place?"

"Crafting company? I have no idea what you're talking about. I was invited here by the person that lives here."

"That's helpful. Are they an employee of the crafting company or someone connected to an employee or the company itself?"

"I don't know anything about that."

"Well you better go find them because…" The state investigator dropped two blades on the floor, rank 3 recognised them instantly. The undamaged blade belonged to the intruder that he fought against and the broken blade was the same one from the footage with the warrior guardian. "We are led to believe that both of these are products of the crafting company and are here to investigate because of that. If you don't know anything, get out of the way and let us in." The state investigator took two steps forward, moving closer to rank 3.

"I can't do that." Rank 3 stretched his arms out to block the entrance.

"You're just a student you don't get a say. What?"

271

The investigator changed from being hostile to shuddering.

The female state investigator immediately took a step back and looked up into the corner of the doorway. "What is it?" the male investigator asked. He had been with her long enough to know that her precognition was never wrong.

"This building is heavily guarded, I'm going to need you to destroy both of the corner areas, they're both concealing weaponry."

"Is that absolutely necessary? I'd rather not show my ability."

"You didn't have any problem with using it before. What's different? Just because there is a brat here you can't do it?"

"Hmm!" The male investigator sighed a sigh filled with his frustration. He didn't want to get into trouble.

"Wait!" the female investigator commanded.

"Make up your mind!" The male investigator voiced his annoyance.

"Someone else is coming idiot, can't you sense these things."

Rank 3 upon hearing those words turned around and to his delight he saw rank 1001. Rank 1001 was wearing his normal outfit for entertaining others, others except for rank 3. Rank 1001 was wearing his mask and bandages were covering his head. Gloves and slippers completely covered his hands and feet, and his robe covered the entirety of the rest of his body.

Rank 1001 paced quickly towards rank 3 and the front door. As soon as he got there he put his arm in front of rank 3: a statement blocking the state investigators from directing their attention towards rank 3. Rank 1001 in his other hand held his small screen with words written in it. He held it up for the investigators to read.

"Who is this? Another brat to deal with?" the female investigator asked rank 3.

Rank 3 didn't know how to respond until rank 1001 handed him the screen.

"Read it," the female investigator commanded while taking a guarded stance.

Rank 3 started reading. "This is my home and you have no right to be here nor do you have any authority to say otherwise. Please leave now."

"Ha, judging by your size you must be younger or the same age as rank 3. Are your parents here, odd looking child?" The state investigator acted very patronising to rank 1001, mocking him for his appearance.

Crunch. Rank 3 in anger crushed the small screen in his hand and his face was filled with anger. Rank 3 couldn't help but leak his red vibrant energy.

The male state investigator put his hand on the female investigator's shoulder and whispered something in her ear. As he did rank 1001 attempted to punch him. Rank 3 grabbed rank 1001 in time and luckily the state investigators didn't notice his small outburst.

"Very well, we'll leave it for today but we'll be back and we'll have the proper paperwork showing our authority. Goodbye, rank 3, enjoy it while it lasts." The female investigator picked up the blades and left.

Rank 3 held on tightly to rank 1001 while he waited for the state investigators to leave. Rank 3 promptly closed the front door and released a very angry rank 1001. Rank 1001 ripped his mask off and ripped parts of his other clothing in anger, and for a second rank 3 thought he saw a rainbow but it vanished.

"Babe, next time you see them outside, immediately call customer 11 and relay all the details involving their visit."

"Confirmed."

"So it does reply."

"If it's a delayed order, it will confirm. Forgetting that for a moment, I won't ask you where you would go but I want you to promise to never leave or be parted from me. Promise me right now." Rank 1001 was visibly shaken by their visit and his voice and body trembled.

"What's brought this on? Those state investigators really affected you, didn't they? Do you need something, anything?" Rank 3 pressed his hand on rank 1001's cheek and stared at him with caring eyes.

"I need your promise." Rank 1001 spoke almost sounding desperate.

"I promise but that doesn't include things like

attending the academy. We have to be apart briefly for some things, is that good enough?"

"I hope so," rank 1001 said solemnly. Rank 3 felt like rank 1001 was keeping a secret from him. "I'm going to start working now. There is a way to salvage the material, it's annoying, but I'd do it for you. I would work until it is finished but I'll come back in twelve hours and we can spend some time together, and then we can sleep next to each other again. Does that sound OK?"

"Can you stay with me instead? It's just so much is happening."

"I can, but it will mean the material will become unusable. It will delay your gift."

"That's fine, I just don't want to be apart from you right now."

"I'm very happy to hear that. So what should we do today? We can do anything. I can order you food if you're hungry. I don't care what it is or how much it costs, if we're spending time together then nothing else matters. But, I promise to complete your gift, no matter how long it takes."

"What do you do when you're not working? I want to know what things you're interested in. I want to do those things with you." Rank 3 realised it not too long ago, that he wanted to know everything about rank 1001.

"I don't do much. I go to the academy. I handle custom orders. I research materials and components. I come up with new designs for a variety of products, and I exercise. I also program babe when it's required and craft special items like your gift and the equipment used for your first visit. All that keeps me occupied." Rank 1001 gave a slightly more detailed answer than last time.

"Don't you do anything to relax? Aren't you pushing yourself too hard?" Rank 3 was worried that rank 1001 didn't know how to relax properly.

"I don't think so. I have a dream and I will achieve it. How I achieve it may change, but what I'm doing right now is important to me."

"What is your dream? It must be big." Rank 3 was eager to hear the dream of the person closest to him.

"It's still a secret, I'm afraid." Rank 1001 was hesitant to give a proper answer but also felt bad about keeping it a secret from rank 3.

"Oh that's fine. But in your dream am I there?" rank 3 asked nervously. If rank 1001 said no, rank 3 knew his soul would shatter right here and now.

"That's up to you," rank 1001 responded with a hint of sadness.

"I want to be. OK. Today we'll spend time relaxing, you can't do any work today. I'm going to teach you how to relax. Place your trust in me."

"I'll do whatever you want me to. Babe handles the day-to-day stuff, anyway."

"Great, thanks for letting me spend this time with you." Rank 3 gave rank 1001 a kiss on his cheek.

Rank 3 was happy and excited to spend time with rank 1001. However, he also was unsure how to relax properly. On the sky island he was always alone and did everything by himself. He didn't have to do any chores such as cleaning or cooking, but he didn't interact with the ones who did either. His main activities were reading, playing by himself and sleeping. He had a minimal and lonely lifestyle.

"So what do you want to do with me?" rank 1001 asked with a hint of excitement. He very rarely had no control over his planned activities.

"We could have a meal together, with both of us sitting down and eating."

"Oh, like a date."

"Date?" Rank 3 blurted out, surprised. They had never used that term between them. "Yeah, I guess we could do that, but you know what that means?"

"What does that mean?" Rank 1001 expecting an immediate answer.

"It means we're properly accepting each other, we're a couple now. Right?" rank 3 said slowly and quietly. He was afraid rank 1001 would reject him.

"Haha." Rank 1001 laughed at those words.

"What's so funny? I'm being serious."

"I know it's just, isn't it a bit late for you to be realising that? As soon as babe finished researching, I knew this is where we would end up. Everything we do at the moment is something couples do. We've been a couple for a while now."

"You're right, I've been stupid."

"Don't say that, you were just nervous right? I always get nervous when you're around. I was constantly worried when I thought you would have to fight in the tournament against academy 3." Rank 1001 finally expressed his true concern for rank 3.

"I love that you care about me so much, I care about you too. I know what we can do today." Rank 3's eyes shone brightly with ideas and caring for rank 1001.

"What can we do?"

"Well first." Rank 3 kissed rank 1001. "Let's just relax by each other's side. What else we do doesn't matter too much, but I definitely want to keep kissing you."

"That's great. I like kissing you too. It's the only time I can have physical contact with someone without, well without certain problems." Rank 1001 spoke while staring deep into rank 3's eyes.

"I hope that's the case, I want to be only one you care about. You shouldn't be thinking about other people, you belong to me now." As soon as rank 3 finished his sentence, he became very embarrassed. He meant it but saying it out loud was a bit too much for him to hear.

"It almost sounds as if you love me. Do you love me?" Rank 1001 spoke softly and hesitantly; he wanted an answer but was afraid of what the consequence might be.

"Well I, I'm not sure, I think so but I can't tell. I

don't remember what that feels like."

"That's good enough for me. I feel similar except I've never loved anyone before. Please wait here, I'll be back in a minute. It's a surprise so don't follow me."

Rank 1001 ran out of the room. He ran down the corridor and entered the elevator. Rank 3 waited patiently for his return, not wanting to spoil the surprise. Rank 3 also thought about what rank 1001's previous years without him must have been like. Rank 3 was resolved to make their future a happy one.

Rank 1001 didn't return for ten minutes; each minute seemed to pass longer than the last. Rank 3 was getting impatient.

After another ten minutes rank 3 was just about to run after rank 1001 when to his surprise and relief rank 1001 appeared holding two small objects.

"What are you holding?" rank 3 asked, excited and curious.

"Hold out your hands," rank 1001 said as he walked over to rank 3.

"OK." Rank 3 put his hands out in front of him. Rank 1001 stopped in front of rank 3 and placed the small object in rank 3's hand. He looked down at it and a smile immediately appeared on his face.

"How did you make this?"

"I used a machine to make them. I'll make new ones myself, but for now this was something I wanted to do. I made one of each of us, so we can look at each other whenever we want. They are our own personal and private reminder of our promises. Sorry to do this again, but wait for me here while I get dressed, I want to take you some place. It's somewhere I consider very special."

"Where?" Rank 3 was instantly interested in a place that rank 1001 considered special.

"It's another surprise." Rank 1001 gave rank 3 a quick kiss and ran back down the corridor and into the elevator.

Rank 1001 had been gone for five minutes when rank 3 heard a loud noise. Beep! Beep! Beep!

It was the doorbell, but unlike last time rank 3 was not eager to answer it and was perfectly happy to wait for rank 1001. Ignoring the noise, he instead gazed with care and longing at the golden statue of rank 1001.

The doorbell only sounded a few times. Afterwards rank 3 heard a loud banging on the thick metal door. Bang! Bang! Bang! And then silence.

There was no more noise for another minute until rank 3 realised he could sense a large amount of energy building outside.

BOOM! CRASH! The metal door that was over two metres thick had a large hole in it and the debris had filled the corridor.

Rank 3 could see part of it landed outside of the guest room and immediately went to investigate.

"Alert. Unauthorised person or persons in home. Removing them now," babe sounded throughout the corridor.

"Not this thing again," the only wounded member of the party complained. He was the human shield that dealt with the outside defences. Despite his appearance not being too bad, he was in a very poor condition.

"Who are you?" rank 3 shouted down the corridor at the unknown intruders.

"Alert. Unable to activate countermeasures due to risk to guest or friend."

"Looks like you've finally got a use. The patriarch's son seems to have grown up a bit, you certainly have found your voice." A cold and wry voice accompanied the group that entered rank 1001's home.

"You are…?" Rank 3 focused on their internal energy and it was similar to his own. They were members of his family.

There were five intruders in total and the one that was injured stood at the back, three stood in front of him and the fifth stood at the front. The fifth was now the only one talking. Each wore a combat outfit that rank 3 had seen in the past. They were red similar to their energy and covered their entire bodies, they also wore red capes and red helmets. The fifth member removed his helmet so that his words would not be misheard.

"Son of the patriarch, acting on the patriarch's orders, we have been sent to retrieve you and take you back to our family's home. We have already collected your belongings from the academy. If you have any in whatever this place is, collect them immediately and we'll be on our way." The fifth spoke respectfully when mentioning the patriarch, but his expression showed his clear disdain and disgust for rank 3.

"Don't lie to me," rank 3 said softly but angrily. "Father and I have an agreement for me to stay here. You're just here for your own personal enjoyment." Rank 3 was very apprehensive and took a step back.

"It's true that it is enjoyable to watch the patriarch's son squirm, but we wouldn't be allowed to come down here and do that. We are here regardless of your protests and denials; we are acting on the patriarch's orders. The patriarch demands that you return this instant. The ground has become far too dangerous for a weak brat like you."

"Prove it, prove my father sent you!" Rank 3 refused to believe them; they had never given him any reason to trust them. His past experiences with them only made him believe the complete opposite.

"Grab him. I'm not explaining any further," the fifth member said coldly.

One of the three members behind the fifth in a flash like movement hurtled towards rank 3. Rank 3 tried to make himself ready in time. He was unsure how to respond though, the gap in their abilities was sure to be incredibly large and it was possible he wouldn't be able to overcome it.

Just as he reached rank 3, one of the three was struck completely off guard; he was struck by a panel of the wall, connected to a large piston. As he landed still conscious, he was able avoid the second attack: darts filled with potent sedatives.

Even though he avoided the darts, his left arm and ribs on the left side were broken. He crawled back behind the fifth. Trembling in pain he stood next to the other injured one at the back. Now two of them had suffered injuries.

The fifth member launched a bolt of red energy at the device used to injure his family member. He destroyed it in an instant. After the dust settled, he saw another figure approach. "Oh? And you are?"

Chapter Twenty
Unmasked angel

A few minutes before the arrival of rank 3's family members, rank 1001 had hurriedly arrived in his room, and he rushed around looking for clothes and bandages. The hardest choice he would have to make though would be what mask he would wear. While he juggled these thoughts, he also wondered if he should have a quick bath.

"Babe, do I need a bath?" rank 1001 asked feeling self-conscious of his now completely exposed body.

"No, you don't, my lovely."

"Aw, thanks babe."

"Do you need any services, my lovely?"

"I'm thinking about my outfit. What should I wear?"

"Outfit a is for the academy, b is for business travels, c is for home attire and d is for guests. Please select an option, my lovely."

"What should I wear for a date?"

"No programmed response. Do you wish to add a response now?"

"Yes. Response is as follows: whatever you feel most comfortable in, my lovely."

"Response confirmed."

"Babe, what should I wear for a date?" rank 1001 asked impatiently.

"Whatever you feel most comfortable in, my lovely."

"You're right, babe, thank you for your advice. I think I know exactly what to wear. I'm going for a mix of b and d. I'll wear c underneath instead of bandages."

"Confirmed. Gathering items for your selection."

"Thanks, babe, also where is my... wait who is that?" Rank 1001 spoke surprised. Something that shouldn't be happening had just begun.

Beep! Beep! Beep!

"Babe! Outfit d and prepare and activate all methods and tools for removal of intruders. Also where is my... argh this isn't fair I thought we would have more time! I'm not in the mood for five more interruptions! Today was supposed to be relaxing." Rank 1001 was panicking; the day that had the best start to it was only getting worse and worse.

"Gathering materials for outfit d only."

"Babe, protect rank 3!"

"Confirmed."

Rank 1001 with assistance quickly rushed around the room getting his attire ready. The only downside to rank 1001's outfits apart from outfit c, was that they all took several minutes to prepare and put on. Rank 1001 was starting to become very stressed. He wanted to cheat and run to rank 3 as he was but he knew that would go against his most basic rules.

As rank 1001 was getting dressed the large explosion took place up above only increasing his anger and frustration. He had to trust in the home that he had built to protect rank 3 for the time being. It wasn't that hiding his flesh was more important than rank 3, it was just something that rank 1001 saw as a primary survival measure.

"Alert. Unauthorised person or persons trying to enter home. Removing them now."

Rank 1001 was finally finished preparing. He picked up his mask; this one was completely white except for a small flower pattern. The flower pattern could only be seen if you were close to the mask. Rank 1001 also picked up one other item and ran to the elevator.

"Alert. Unable to activate countermeasures due to risk to guest or friend."

Rank 1001 was feeling incredibly stressed and was starting to believe that he had built the world's slowest elevator. Rank 1001 had put an earpiece in his ear and a small microphone in his mouth so he was in contact with babe at all times.

"Babe, please report the current home status."

"Two intruders injured, front defences compromised, one corridor defence damaged, guest or friend in possible danger. Other defences remain active."

"Babe, admin request. Change current guest/friend

to date and grant advanced privileges and protections."

"Confirmed."

"Thanks, babe."

Rank 1001 sprinted out of the elevator and appeared behind rank 3.

"Who are you?" the fifth member asked menacingly.

Rank 1001 ignored his intruders and instead made his way to rank 3.

"Babe, guide me to date," rank 1001 ordered, feeling desperate to locate the person important to him.

"Confirmed."

With babe's assistance rank 1001 located rank 3 with ease and put his arms around him claiming rank 3 as his own. Rank 3 hugged rank 1001 back and glared violently at the family members that had come to collect him.

"Are you all right, rank 1001? I'll explain everything, just don't move away from me." Rank 3's main concern was and would always be rank 1001's health.

"Babe, put me through to the speakers."

"Confirmed."

"How dare you people disrupt our date? You should know you're being very rude and I am not happy about it!" Rank 1001's voice rung out through the corridor; everyone could clearly hear him speak.

Rank 3 found it odd to hear such an angelic voice talk so angrily. Rank 3 was certain that rank 1001 was getting angry for his sake and that made rank 3 extremely happy, even if he was also terrified for rank 1001's safety.

"Our family will gladly pay for repairs to your home and property. We are only here to collect our errant family member." The fifth spoke more amicably to the unknown masked individual than he did to his own family member.

"Why did you damage my property instead of pressing the doorbell or knocking politely? It couldn't have been easy for you to break down my door. I wonder if any of you have the energy left to take something of mine." Rank 1001 was starting to speak arrogantly, as if he was a spider and they were flies caught in his web.

"We do whatever we want. You are just lowly ground trash. I tried to be amicable because of the patriarch but accidents happen. As you well know, don't you, rank 1001 of academy 1?" The fifth member's tone returned to being hostile.

"How do you know that?" rank 3 asked shocked and surprised. He also started to feel nerves that not even rank 1001's embrace could calm.

"I know that if I were to associate myself with a person like this, I would die of embarrassment. The patriarch will not be impressed; it is obvious to me that he didn't realise just what you've been associating yourself with." The fifth member's voice was filled with disgust and malice.

"Father is the one that made it so, without Father's help I never would have found this place. Our being together is important to me. Return to my father and tell him that." Rank 3 hoped that as long as he was on the ground there was a chance; if he could contact his father from here, maybe he could convince him to let him stay.

"Just because you came down here does not mean I will treat you any differently. Don't act tough because there is someone else here. Have you forgotten your childhood? Should I remind you why you don't mix with or go against us?"

"I never knew my parents, neither one," rank 1001 said softly and slowly. "Even knowing one parent is a blessing, don't you agree?" Rank 1001 aimed his question directly at the five intruders.

"I don't care about the opinions of ground trash. Son of the patriarch get over here or I'll make it so rank 1001 will have to crawl on the floor for the rest of his life." The fifth member dismissed rank 1001's words despite their relevance to his and his other family members' lives. The fifth member had chosen to get angry and act cruelly to the person in front of him. Words meant very little to someone of his disposition.

Rank 3's heart skipped a beat. In his earlier years he had suffered a fate like that, it was because of that, that he was able to endure the painful loss of his hands and feet due to rank 4's cruel attack. When he was younger, a group of his family members broke his legs and spine. They threw him out of a tower and for good measure they themselves broke his pelvis. They wouldn't have done it if they weren't a hundred percent sure that he would heal. They enjoyed seeing rank 3 writhe in pain. The cruellest part was the reason for it was because of something incredibly petty.

"You wouldn't dare. If you touch him, I'll punish you," rank 3 responded angrily. His family members had never seen him act this way.

"Ooh! Looks like someone has developed a temper. What happened to the quiet boy who never uttered a word even when his bones were broken?"

"He's now stronger and very angry," rank 3 said coldly.

"You can't win. Don't even try." This voice belonged to a new individual, a sixth member of his family. Rank 3 recognised this member; this member was even well known on the ground.

"Why are you here?" both the fifth member and rank 3 asked in sync. They were both shocked by his appearance.

Rank 1001 immediately placed rank 3 behind him.

"You're running late." The sixth person scolded the five members.

"Yes, well there is a reason for that, it took us far longer at the academy than we had planned, it was just a small delay." The menacing fifth member turned into a frightened child fearful of a scolding.

"Save your excuses for the patriarch. Son of the patriarch, please come with me, your humble servant."

The sixth member walked past the fifth and knelt down.

"I don't want to," rank 3 said shakily. His resolve to protest was wavering.

"Your father is worried about you. There is a dangerous person running around down here targeting academies, you're in danger. You will take and earn your place as the patriarch's heir, now come along. Leave the ground behind and return to the sky." The sixth member was respectful and sounded almost caring.

Rank 1001 dragged rank 3 several more steps away from the sixth member.

"Don't run away, little one. I'm only here to collect the son of the patriarch."

Rank 1001 took several more steps backwards. The sixth member stood up, followed them and stopped. Another metal panel was launched towards the sixth member. Unlike the other member, this sixth member stuck out his hand and stopped it with ease. He snapped it off of the wall. The darts shot out at him but he blocked them effortlessly using his own energy. His energy was bright yellow it was because of this he was labelled, the wrathful servant of the sun.

"Don't use little tricks on me. Son of the patriarch, please say goodbye. If you do so I will leave only with you. I will not be forced to take action against this would be kidnapper." The respectful voiced sixth member started to talk wryly with an odd sparkle in his eye.

"Kidnapper?" rank 3 responded shocked. It was

obvious that rank 1001 was in danger.

"Yes and kidnappers deserve to be punished." From the tips of his fingers, the sixth member shot out five bright yellow beams of energy, each of them impacting on rank 1001's body. They scorched away parts of his robe, leaving only the bandages in sight.

"What did you do?" rank 3 shouted angrily. The weight of his words could be felt by all those around him; they were heavy and violent.

"It was just a warning, son of the patriarch. Young master, please let me take you home. Leave this other one behind and go back to where you belong."

"No, all of you get out!" Rank 1001's voice came from all directions and assaulted everyone's ears. "Rank 3 would gladly give up the heir to the patriarch's position so someone else can take it and he can stay here. Isn't that right?"

Rank 3 didn't know how to respond. This course of action sounded like an answer to their current dilemma, but that didn't mean it would be a permanent solution. Rank 3 had to think deep and fast.

Rank 3 pulled rank 1001's head close to his.

"I need to ask a favour; I need to change one of our promises. I have to leave to keep you safe but I promise I'll find you again. I'm not leaving forever, as I said before, we have to be parted sometimes right? You just got hurt because of me. I'm too weak to protect you on my own."

Rank 3 had long thought about using the patriarch's

position to protect his precious rank 1001.

Rank 1001 was shocked; he didn't want to believe he had just heard what he just had. Did that mean everything was a lie? Rank 1001 realised that having hope for the first time was something that he didn't want to experience again. Having his hope shattered was turning out to be incredibly painful.

Rank 1001's expression sunk and he looked hopeless; he was starting to panic. His mask hid his expression and when he squeezed rank 3 it didn't feel as warm as it did before.

"It will be all right. You're in danger if I stay, I'll go to my father and I'll sort this out. I'll come back for you." Rank 3 couldn't help but talk with a hint of hopelessness.

Rank 1001 still didn't respond. However, unknown to everyone around him, he was crying.

"Please respond. You know I do love you. You see, I know it for sure now. I love you." Rank 3 said these words for the first time and meant them from the depths of his soul. "Please try to understand. I have to do this."

Rank 1001 ripped off of his mask and bandages covering his head, revealing his hair and face. Rank 3 took no notice of rank 1001's appearance and focused solely on his tears.

"Haha, what happened to him?" The fifth member was pointing and laughing at rank 1001.

"Is this some sort of joke?" the sixth member asked. Rank 1001's appearance was not normal.

Rank 3 wiped a tear off rank 1001's cheek.

"Don't cry, this isn't what I want but we don't have a choice."

"We have a choice; we can choose each other and choose to keep our promises. We just have to trust each other. Trust me, please. I can keep us together." Rank 1001 spoke sadly, and he was crying through every word.

"Ha, I wouldn't trust anything someone that looks like that says. It seems a piece of trash can actually look worse than trash." The fifth member smirked but to his surprise he felt a sharp pain, a red whip sliced him across his face. "Ow! That hurt, brat." The fifth member raised his hand and his own orange energy flowed from it.

"Put your energy away, we are servants of the patriarch and we cannot harm his son nor will I tolerate you getting in my way." The sixth member only glanced at the other five, but that was enough for them to understand their situation.

"Hmph!" The fifth member responded with a frustrated sigh. He slowly retracted his energy and glared at the sixth member sulking about his situation.

"Son of the patriarch, please don't lash out, that other one's appearance is just unusual, I've seen many things in the world. His appearance is just weird, the others just aren't used to seeing something like this, that's all. Although I can't help but chuckle either. Everyone is entitled to have to an opinion no matter how ridiculous they look. Every person bleeds the same."

Rank 3 glared violently at the sixth member. He turned back to rank 1001 who was still crying and he put his hand on rank 1001's cheek. It was in this moment that rank 3 realised that rank 1001's appearance had changed. "Which one of you did this?" rank 3 asked shouting. He glared viciously and violently at his family members.

"Did what?" The fifth answered indifferent to any action he or one of the others may have committed.

"Who hurt my beloved?" Rank 3 was distraught by the feeling that something he couldn't stop had damaged his precious rank 1001.

"Young master, we haven't done anything. I hit him a few times, but I didn't touch his face," the sixth member answered respectfully.

"You said I looked normal." Rank 1001 spoke sadly.

"You did. Now you look different. I'll handle it." Rank 3 tried to dispel rank 1001's worries.

"Bad different?" Rank 1001 quietly and tearfully asked.

"It's... different." Rank 3 didn't know how to describe rank 1001's appearance. It most certainly wasn't his angelic form.

"What does that mean? Are you not sure the person you say you love and the person who loves you looks good enough? Is my appearance repulsive to you now?" Rank 1001 ended up making his first confession in the middle of an accusation. It was not what he had intended, and it caused immense heartache.

"It's not that, it's just I don't know what to say. Why do you look like that? It's not how you normally look." Rank 3 was worried that rank 1001 had been hurt and he worried he would be unable to help.

"This is how I look!" Rank 1001 started ripping off his clothes. He removed his gloves revealing his hands which looked the same as his face along with his feet after removing his slippers.

Rank 3 was confused. He had seen rank 1001's bare flesh before and he didn't look anything similar to this; the colour of his skin was wrong.

Rank 1001 ripped off nearly all of his clothes and bandages all except for the bandages around his waist and the top of his thighs.

"This is how I look, you said I looked normal. I showed you everything before. Do the colours really mean that much to you?" Rank 1001 started crying even more.

"Ha, no way he said that. If he did, he was lying," smirked the fifth member.

"Let's just get you dressed again, then we can deal with this." Rank 3 spoke while putting his own jacket over rank 1001's shoulders.

"Did you lie?" Rank 1001's tone was now a mix of sadness and self-hatred caused by his growing distrust of the only person he had dared to care about.

"Why are you asking me that for?" rank 3

responded softly and calmly, while he continued to wrap up rank 1001 in his jacket.

"Are you breaking your promise? Are you admitting you lied? Are you going to leave today? Are you repulsed by me? Can you even look at me without wanting to back away or wrap me up?" Rank 1001 unleashed a torrent of questions, but even as he tried to find the truth, his mind and heart were breaking.

"It's not any of those things, it's just if something has happened to you I want to fix it."

"And if nothing has happened to me? What if my appearance is a side effect of my ability? What then?" Rank 1001 had finally revealed a single detail about his ability.

"That can't be the case, abilities don't have side effects like this. Almost all side effects are useful, they don't do this," the sixth member said smugly. He thought he had seen enough of the world to be an expert on it.

Rank 1001 started crying even more than before, like a tap turned on full. Tears streamed down his face. He hadn't been made to feel this way for a very long time.

"All of you just leave." Rank 1001 spoke through his tears. He had finally had enough. "This is my house, no one else belongs here. I'm happiest when I'm alone. I've always been alone, that's how it should be!" Rank 1001 struggled to speak through the tears. If he wasn't angry as well as upset, he would have crumbled into a crying mess lying on the floor.

"We go wherever we need to, even if we didn't have business with you today if we had it another day you couldn't refuse us," the fifth member said proudly.

"The vanity of someone who's afraid of falling really is something. If I had that choice, I would have pushed you off instead. Or at least had the decency to jump off myself!" Rank 1001 spoke coldly, a tone rank 3 had never heard him speak in before. Rank 3 was certain that his family were hurting and making rank 1001 feel unsafe. If this continued rank 3 was afraid he wouldn't be able to recognise his rank 1001.

"What did you just say?" the fifth member said softly, trying to contain his anger. If it was true what he heard, a private and personal matter from his past would come to light. "I'll wait outside, please don't take too much longer, sun's wrathful servant. I'll be sure to see you again, rainbow freak." The fifth member glared violently at rank 1001 and turned around.

"Get out before I kick you out," rank 1001 shouted angrily. Rank 3 could see and feel that rank 1001 was getting overwhelmed by the situation.

The fifth member, dragging the other four members with him, left the house and went outside. He was furious but wouldn't act out in front of the others.

"Please calm down, rank 1001. Your condition is getting worse." Rank 3 tried to calm down rank 1001. The colours on his body facing the front door were changing at a much faster pace.

"It's a condition now is it? You're saying such hurtful words. I've heard them all. You look like a walking rainbow, a freak. Why does it change colour, can't you at least control it? Does it cover your whole body? Even the parts we can't see? If you look in the mirror do you frighten yourself? Just go and hide yourself away, stop troubling everyone else. Your existence is unnecessary and inconvenient to others. Why do you exist at all? Why are you the one forcing me to feel these things?" Rank 1001 finally revealed one of his deepest secrets.

Rank 3 didn't know what to say, rank 3 had had a pain filled childhood but at least it wasn't based on his appearance. As soon as he left his family, no one had held any immediate disgust for him or made any harsh snap judgements.

"Rank 3, you are different and you don't cause it to trigger or respond, but that shouldn't be the reason you want to spend all your time with me. At first it was what made me fascinated with you, but it was getting to know you that made me want you to be mine alone. So please just get out, I can see that my body is the only one I can love. I was wrong to hope otherwise. We're just not compatible." Rank 1001's angelic voice was broken, he now sounded like a weak tortured lonely child.

Rank 3 looked rank 1001 up and down, rank 1001's entire visible body including his normally golden hair and eyes was now a mix of colours. Some parts did indeed resemble a rainbow. There was an almost infinite amount of colours and the colours seemed to pulse and change like a living painting. Every part of his body could be one colour one second and another the next, even his hair was split into a multitude of colours. Rank 1001's eyes weren't as divided, but they still contained at least five colours all meshing, pulsating and changing together.

To rank 3, his angel now looked like a freaky living painting. It was as if rank 1001 was wrapped up in a tortured rainbow. And it was obvious that rank 1001 felt as such.

Rank 3 pulled rank 1001's head into his chest and whispered, "I'm actually from a family in the sky. I'm not sure where it is located but please wait for me, my love. No matter what you look like you'll always be my angel. I will come back down for you. I promise I won't let this get in the way of our future. I'll overcome and save you from the cause of all your pain." Rank 3 kissed rank 1001's cheek and gently pushed him away from himself.

Rank 1001 stumbled backwards, the promises they had made were being shattered by those around them. The worst part was that rank 3 had already given in to their promise breaking demands and rank 3 made another promise on top. Rank 1001 felt like rank 3 had refused to fight for them. Rank 1001 couldn't understand why he wasn't worth enough.

Rank 1001 couldn't help but assume it was because of his appearance, and he thought anything he did from this moment onwards would not stop rank 3 leaving. So, rank 1001 stood still doing nothing but crying and being in pain.

"Fine, let's go. Take me to my father." Rank 3 walked confidently and proudly. He was completely resolved to sort out his situation and return to what was precious to him.

Rank 3 walked past the sixth member and the sixth member followed him outside. As they crossed through the large hole rank 3 shouted back, "I promise I won't be too long. I'll see you soon!" rank 3 said with a tear streaming down his face. He wanted to break down and cry forever, but he knew he had to be strong for the both of them.

Rank 3 left with the others. The fifth member knew he would have to wait for another opportunity to return here.

"Now that you've left, everything is broken," rank 1001 said sadly as every promise they both had made was shattered on the floor surrounding him.

Rank 1001 fell to the floor embracing their broken promises and the cold hard surface. As the group left, his appearance changed, the multitude of colours vanished. His skin turned a healthy pale shade of pink, his eyes and hair both returned to a beautiful golden colour. He laid down and curled up into a ball, tears constantly streaming from his face.

An abandoned angel without its mask is a fragile being indeed.